Evinall

(ee-vuh n awl)

"There will forever be some Eve in all of us."

By Adam Witkowski

Dedication

I first would like to dedicate this novel to all the strong, wonderful women in my family, especially my mother, who raised me to be a self-respecting and courteous gentleman. Secondly, and with a very heavy heart, I dedicate this book to all my fallen brethren who battled addiction and lost, or who were a victim in some way of drugs and alcohol, and the other young lives that tragically ended too soon listed below. Most are just from the small, upper-middle class, average, "All American" town of Franklin, MA that I grew up in. You are ALL missed but NEVER FORGOTTEN! I love you all.

<3 Russell C.

<3 Robert L.

<3 Jack C.

<3 David P.

<3 Brandon M.

<3 Johnathan F.

<3 Michael M.

<3 Christopher M.

<3 Aaron G.

<3 Amy C.

<3 Craig C.

<3 Paul M.

<3 Michael C.

<3 Greg G.

<3 Michael W. J.R.

<3 Stephen A.

<3 William B.

<3 Jeremy A.

<3 Brian C.

<3 Corey S.

<3 Michael D.

<3 and any others I regretfully missed

Part 1

Chapter 1

Evinall was destined to be my swan song. I can't explain why, but I always felt it was my duty to provide the world a miracle it needed to restore hope and deter mankind from eating each other alive. I apologize if I sound arrogant, but what a wonderful drug I created that might be doing just that. When taken properly, Evinall eliminates all the body's addictive dependencies making addiction a curable ailment of the past. Now, the name my parents cursed me with at birth, that I spent most of my life despising, Nerotius Karlin, is mentioned in conversations with the likes of Edward Jenner, the pioneer of vaccines, and Alexander Flemming, with his creation of penicillin, regarding the greatest contributors to medicine.

I was awarded numerous prestigious accolades for my achievements as well as the "lucky" number seven position on the Forbes "Top Ten Wealthiest People in America" list (a title I feel should be renamed, "Most Corrupt and Untouchable Criminals Society Loves and Loathes" excluding yours truly of course).

To put it loosely, money will never be a concern for any Karlin for the rest of time, unless they run out of trees to print it on. I made a joke once in an interview, shortly after Evinall's release, that I was interested in buying my own private planet to retire on if the property taxes were reasonable. KarlTech Ingenuities Inc., the medical research corporation I founded earlier on in my career, has also made countless numbers of "Most Powerful Corporations" and "Best Places to Work" lists as well.

So, what's the catch? Let me start by clarifying that Evinall is, ironically, a very powerful but non-habit-forming stimulant that safely energizes the brain, so sleep is no longer required, ever. That's right, the burden of fatigue is eradicated, and Evinall's recipients add an average of four waking months to their lives annually, if taken properly. On the flip side, a lifespan is reduced anywhere from twelve months to twenty years, based on how long my magnificent elixir is taken. Enter the million-dollar question: would you rather live a shorter, yet more productive, addiction-free life of the highest quality, never wasting a single minute of your prime years unconscious, or do you continue tossing and turning, counting sheep and praying to get those vital eight hours that still don't seem like enough? Feeling groggy and exhausted, you consume enough coffee each day to drown a thousand tweaked-out Colombian cocoa farmers and spend around one-third of your prime years asleep and dead to the world each night.

Our species has an extensive history of substance abuse that has plagued us for as far back as records suggest. Consuming toxic substances like alcohol, smoking cigarettes, guzzling energy drinks, even experimenting with recreational drugs to get a little stamina boost during the day or to help us unwind a little at night...and all for what? What is the grand prize we get to take home when the whole charade is finally over? Being able to proudly declare we lived our lives to the fullest extent?

It seems the price of living a "full life" is a costly one. As our health fails, we start to lose the ability to do the things that make life so grand in the first place, like making love, creating art, and driving a convertible with the top down on our way to the beach. We lose our looks, hearing, memory, and even bowel controls. It is hard to believe our "golden years" accompany hip replacements, shingles, or worse, Alzheimer's Disease; wielding the capability of leaving a formerly healthy, sharp-minded and prideful adult puzzled by the mystery of "Who keeps shitting their pants?"

As the creator of Evinall I've wondered; what is the appeal of reaching the senior years of life? Do people crave the adrenaline rush they'll get after successfully walking down a few stairs because they managed to avoid another potentially fatal slip and fall? Is it the intoxicating gratification only a yard sale bargain of epic proportions provides that will have them desperately clinging to life? No, it's because most people are terrified of death since nobody knows what happens after we pass away. My philosophy and the motto of Evinall is: "A lesser life of more is greater than the longest life with less."

In the years before Evinall's release, the pharmaceutical

6

industry was a massive, over-fed cash cow that grazed through money flourishing pastures, only slowing down to drop an occasional golden nugget of shit that served as the precious fertilizer fueling America's corporate greed. Seizing the opportunity, I reached out with prickly fingers and, with tight gripping fists, I latched onto and yanked those big slippery teats, and I continued to tug until they finally erupted, spilling a sea of riches that would flood the bank accounts of every KarlTech employee. Together we basked in the glorious fortune, sharing fairytale plans of our early retirements. KarlTech Ingenuities Inc. became the Mt. Olympus of medicine, and there I proudly sat upon Zeus's throne.

Hosted over the course of a beautiful, sunny June weekend on Boston Common, we at KarlTech ceremoniously introduced Evinall to the public. Along with free food, music, and gifts, we provided outdoor seminars with detailed information about how our new drug was going to create a healthier, happier world.

One of the most positive affects Evinall had was it gradually improved our society as a whole. An increase of 33% in professional productivity was the average for users after only one year on the market. Recipients earned more than they could keep track of, so much that feel-good stories of people donating time and money to the needy became somewhat of a competition, and six and seven-figure donations became the norm. The number of college graduates increased by 35% in the first four years, a time during which drug-related arrests went down by 27%.

As a gesture to thank the reinvigorated citizens of our country for their overwhelming acceptance and support, I decided to make Evinall free to all American military, law enforcement, first responders, and teachers, if prescribed. We witnessed our economy become the strongest it had ever been, and The Nobel Prize in Medicine would eventually be my thanks for creating "a smarter and safer world for all to enjoy."

Secretly, I knew it would be a short-lived reign, however, since my early retirement plans had already been set in motion. Later that year, Evinall had only been on the market for six months when I announced my retirement to the public, for which I was brutally criticized once again.

What a bunch of rude, unappreciative, indecisive assholes! Earlier on in my professional career, the ass kissing I received from the media was impressive, as they sang praises of my genius for inventing the Automated Diagnostic Machine (ADM), which I will explain momentarily. Two years later, in an interview with Braddock Nix from ThePatriotPress.com, I shared with him my vision to develop a cure for addiction, and he could barely refrain from laughing in my face! His article inspired others to question my work, and soon I would be the laughingstock of the medical world. Six years later, the press was back on its knees with a mouthful of my ass in lieu of Evinall's release.

My early resignation boomeranged them back around full circle, as I was ruthlessly dissected under the public's microscope once more. Paparazzi bartered and sold my photos to the highest bidder, and my face was back on newsstand shelves and websites in no time. My career, my actions, and motives were put on trial and again, subjected to scrutiny. Theories about what my future held after my retirement ranged from a bid at the presidency to suicide, as I remained media fodder for months until a juicier, fresher story finally took mine's place. It was during that period I fully understood and empathized greatly for the similar lives the Red Sox players endured!

I'm often questioned about how I developed my paramount panacea and what is the secret behind Evinall, to which most are surprised when I modestly reply, "table salt." Allow me to elaborate; somewhere around two hundred thousand years ago, our species began to evolve on the supercontinent of Pangea, on what is now known as Africa. Throughout the evolutionary process, from microorganisms all the way up to homo sapiens, the cells we are comprised of developed a natural craving for sodium chloride. Mankind also adopted other behaviors, which helped us endure the struggles of daily life and survive the trials of time, but it was the original desire for salt that made sure we acquired the necessary amount needed for the cells in our bodies to function properly. Without it, they would break down and fail and eventually our bodies would die. Over the course of time, all our other addictions stemmed from that one original, seemingly harmless, desire for table salt.

The idea came to me when I was running late for my lunch break. As I stressed over my notes, I found myself craving a big bag of salty potato chips. I went to the cafeteria at KarlTech and fed my hunger with the exact answer to the problem I had been aggressively searching for. I must have sat there for an hour, staring at that one chip between my fingertips, as I pondered the notion of an answer so readily available and blatantly apparent, costing a mere two dollars despite the millions that had already been spent trying to discover it. If they hadn't known about my quirky tendencies beforehand, my surrounding employees might have thought I was in a state of hypnosis or simply just crazy. From then on, my task was to develop a way to eradicate that craving, and let me tell you, re-writing hundreds of thousands of years of evolutionary instinct at a molecular level was no easy feat, nor cheap. What began as a ridiculed, often laughed at theory scratched up and strewn throughout many spiral-bound notebooks in my college dorm room, eventually metamorphosed into what the American Medical Association has hailed as the "life-changing, life-saving wonder drug of the twenty-first century." It is currently available in extended-release tablets, fruit-flavored dissolving strips, or by visiting an ADM location.

My dream finally came to fruition; Evinall was completed and added to the medicine banks inside every one of my self-designed Automated Diagnostic Machines, with new locations opening up across the globe daily. Starting at USD 100, a patient can step into any one of state of the art, sterilized, handicap accessible, private booths, and within minutes receive a full medical diagnosis for whatever ails them. There is a self-adjusting sleeve most people place their arm into, though it is able to accommodate paraplegics by maneuvering down for a leg to be placed inside, that checks vitals such as blood pressure and pulse rates. Once an extremity is in position, patients place their hand (or foot if using the leg) on a sterilized pad, scanners acquire multiple readings such as body temperature, blood sugar, cholesterol levels, and many others. There is an opening just below the high-definition display screen where a transparent face mask emerges and conducts a retinal scan and "viral survey" as the patient blows into a mouthpiece. Next, the marvels of KarlTech Ingenuities go to work, and in less than two minutes a physical is complete. It can accurately take blood readings without drawing a single drop. Vitals, along with the blood diagnosis, appear on the touchscreen while the voice of the supercomputer informatively explains the results, in whichever one of the three hundred languages the patient chose during the initial introduction. Multiple options for treatment are then offered by what has proven to be one of my most successful inventions, the "Robopharmacist."

The Robopharmacist is essentially a robotic pharmacologist that utilizes the massive supply of different pharmaceutical and herbal ingredients contained inside an indestructible medicine bank, to concoct an impressive 92% of prescriptions on the market, as well as a number exclusive to KarlTech including Evinall. Their projected percentages of success are displayed on the screen. Vaccines can also be administered intravenously through an opening in the extremity sleeve or prescriptions can be put together on the spot to take home. Finally, an amazingly accurate prognosis is given complete with follow-up instructions, recovery times, health tips and the option for doctor's notes for work or school. A bottle of vitamin-enriched water dispenses on your way out along with a printed, updated copy of your medical records, which are also emailed to the patient. KarlTech has gradually taken on the role of America's most trusted primary care physician, which allowed us to tap into a well of riches that still seems to have no end.

As the whole nation continued to become healthier and happier as a result of my marvelous medical contributions, a growing number of heart-warming and inspirational recovery stories flooded the press daily. The media outlets were too busy covering positive news and missed the discovery of the headless body of a level-three, high-risk sex offender named Stephen Shangraw. He went unreported the week he appeared sitting upright on a park bench holding his head in his lap.

The newspaper featuring the story of his acquittal was folded and tucked under his right arm. There also wasn't any coverage of the murder of Norman Chauncey, another level-three sex offender who had been recently paroled after spending five years in prison for sexually abusing children. He too was deemed a high risk for repeat offenses, but before he had the chance to hurt anyone else, his body was found sitting on the front step to his house, also holding his head in his lap. Now, if you count last month's decapitation of Eduardo Diaz, an unpredictable and extremely violent bookie who operated the area's largest dog fighting circuit, you have three very similar homicides, suggesting the first serial killer in almost seventy years has decided to make Boston his hunting ground.

At one time or another, we have pondered a variation of the following question; If I were to obtain an endless supply of money and, hypothetically, could do anything I wanted, what would I do? This is where I "bid adieu" and part ways with the sane members of society because nobody else ever responds "by dismembering scumbags with a machete," like I do. Resembling the marvelous product of millions of years of evolutionary fine-tuning, I am the great white who relentlessly hunts this ocean, as the rest of the world unsuspectingly treads the waters above. I stalk from beneath the shadows, calculating with immaculate proficiency the absolute perfect moment to strike. Then, without even knowing what hit them, my victims fall prey to the one remaining addiction holding me hostage. It is a secret no pill nor therapy can cure, one I must carry back into the shadows and, eventually, with me to my grave: my unquenchable thirst for murder.

Chapter 2

I thoroughly enjoy imagining all those who once ridiculed my idea now impatiently waiting for their turn to get dosed at the nearest ADM. Now let me clarify something, I did not create Evinall with hopes of having any of the ridiculous, press-cuddly titles they gave me afterward, nor did I create it to fatten my bank account. I did it because the person I loved more than anything in the universe asked me, on her deathbed, to promise never to give up. To promise to finish the fathomless work I obsessed over year after year, teetering on the brink of insanity and almost costing me my marriage... to promised I would finish it for her. And I couldn't push the words out past my trembling lips fast enough. "I promise Baby, I promise."

And I did. I did the unimaginable, and I named it, in her honor, so there would forever be some Eve in all of us.

Eve had only been inside a hospital on two prior occasions before she collapsed while we shopped at Captain Parker's fish market. It was three days before our tenth wedding anniversary, and we decided to start celebrating a little early. So, we were out buying all the items for me to make her favorite dish: grilled teriyaki salmon steaks served with lemon zest spinach and mashed cauliflower. As we headed to check out, she looked at me strangely and said, "I feel light-headed..."

But before she finished her sentence, her legs went out from under her, and she toppled over landing on a display of bottled spring water. I grabbed her quickly with one arm, and with the other, I struggled to dig my cell phone out from my pocket as I yelled frantically for help. She was out cold and would only regain consciousness briefly during the ambulance ride to Thornbury Hospital, and again for a short moment after when she was in the hospital bed.

I recalled the story she told me of her first visit to an emergency room, which was the day she was born and that happened to be just around midnight on December 24th. She, however, did not arrive in the manner most newborns do; as life-altering, precious, little bundle of joy welcomed by two adoring new parents. No, she arrived with the style and grace a flaming bag of dog shit would; dumped off and forgotten at the Emergency Room entrance of Thornbury by one of the countless, decaying, junky souls who had been plaguing the surrounding city for as long as any of its residents could recall. Her mother was never identified, but most of the hospital staff believed her to be a young, drug-addicted, abused runaway who had recently been admitted for bruises and lacerations on her face, no doubt the work of the low-life pimp who enslaved her. She was probably forced against her will to give up her baby and decided the hospital was a safe enough place to leave her, given the gruesome and unthinkable alternative her despicable employer most likely offered.

A triage nurse discovered her wrapped tightly in an old, worn out, men's pullover hooded sweatshirt and with a cigarette-smelling wool mitten pulled over her head like a fuzzy little rooster. And whoever dropped her off also decided an empty beer case would be a suitable crib. So that was how she spent her first moments of life; clothed in grimy, second-hand stinky clothes, as her little round face, with her big green eyes and rosy red cheeks, peeked out from a soggy cardboard container searching for the mother she would never find.

Her cries grew louder and louder and finally caught a nurse's attention. After a couple of hours, an intensive examination, a warm bottle of vitamin-packed formula, and a change into a fresh baby onesie, the doctor declared she was not only in miraculously good health, she also had no dependencies to any substances! Since there was no parent or legal guardian to name the precious little holiday miracle, the doctor allowed the nurse who discovered her to do the honors, to which she appropriately named her Eve. Eve was eventually adopted but spent most of her early life bouncing around from foster home to foster home.

The second, and only other previous time Eve had ever stepped foot inside a hospital was six years ago, the day we lost the only child she would ever bear. Seven months of the most joy-filled anticipation was abruptly followed by seven hours of the most terrifying, tumultuous labor. Eve slipped and fell on a patch of black ice and landed face down with great force on the pavement, just outside our home in the suburbs. The impact caused internal bleeding which then caused multiple other problems, as well as prematurely triggering her to go into labor. I rushed her, as quickly as I could, to the same hospital where she proved miracles do come true twenty-eight years earlier. We hoped and prayed she had one more in her. Unfortunately, that was not the case. It was the hardest and most emotionally taxing experience of our lives.

So there I sat once again, terrified as the ambulance raced us back to Thornbury Hospital. The entire ride I did my best to hide my fear, though all I could not help but think was, "this must be bad," and I was right. Eve never got sick, and I mean never. Up until she had collapsed in the market, I had learned to accept her remarkable health as another one of the countless mysteries that surrounded her, made her so enchanting, and I had fallen in love with as quickly as they were revealed to me. A runny nose I had seen maybe once, but in 36 years never actually sick. And in typical Eve fashion, she didn't believe anything was curious or spectacular about that.

"I just have good genes," she would say or credit it to the various organic fruits she grew in our garden and enjoyed each morning with her breakfast and tea.

But I always knew she was something so divine words cannot do her justice, like the first family of doctors and nurses who declared her "a living, breathing miracle," maybe even something more.

I recall talking to her in the ambulance, and I told her every time I heard the siren of a fire engine, it made me think of when we first met. I gripped her hand tightly, but not too tight. I did not want to hurt her, but my anxiety was at its max. I talked about that first night when we were both attending university, and how she pulled the fire alarm in her friend's college dormitory because she saw me on two prior occasions but did not know who I was. She only knew I lived in the same building and that was her way of arranging our first meeting. She saw me and wanted to meet me, and I would soon learn whatever Eve wanted, Eve got. She approached me and smiled.

"Shitty night for a fire drill," she said as she offered me a can of beer.

"Yeah, though I'm not seeing any smoke or people running out in flames. I'm starting to wonder why I bothered getting out of bed for this," I remarked.

"Some punk probably just on a fraternity dare or something like that. Do you mind if I ask? Is Barbie aware that you raided her wardrobe?" she said as she plucked at my friend's pink sweatshirt I had abruptly thrown on as we were evacuated from the building.

I felt my face flush with embarrassment, but before I could fire back with a witty reply, she said, "I'm Eve, Eve Brooks" proudly with a wink. "And if you make one Adam reference, I'm taking that beer back."

She walked in a circle around me and looked me up and down apparently sizing me up! When she finally stopped, she smiled and stared at me with her radiant, emerald-green eyes, as if she was subliminally commanding my mesmerized soul to let go and let her in. I was speechless and temporarily paralyzed. She had me from that moment on and for the rest of our lives together. She still has me and forever will, so long as the rhythmic thumping can be heard echoing outward from my chest, as if calling to her from the broken heart I bear inside me, that she had claimed as her own what seemes like lifetimes ago. She will always have me.

I recalled the poor nurses who had to deal with me as I ran about asking questions and shouting answers to the doctors and staff. How could this happen? Eve had a stroke. Didn't they know who I was? There was no way the wife of the great Dr. Nerotius Karlin could be sick. It made no sense to me, she was too precious, too irreplaceable for that to happen. Yet there she lay, gently holding my hand as the I.V.s and monitors dripped and beeped. I ran my fingers through her hair from her forehead down to the top of her neck the way she loved, watching the skin on her arms, but she didn't get goosebumps like she normally did. Another bad sign. When her eyes finally opened for the last time, I was right at her side staring at her, and she at last spoke. She told me I was her miracle and I had given her all a woman could ask for and more. She weakly squeezed my hand back and asked me to recite a poem I wrote about her, earlier on in our relationship. It was about my battle with addiction and how I cleaned up for her, using our love as my "higher power." So, I did. I cleared my throat and recited:

They've barricaded my sweet charade
with their homemade remedies, I fear
Bearing my breakables, I stagger

A chill has intertwined my spine
sweating sins that broke the paradigm
Riddles written in the dark
were all I had to pass the time

Hold tight my dear, I'll take you away from here

Listen for your weary wanderer
and his ancient song, sung out of tune
This desperate lover rescinds his resignation

They churn a dagger in my blistered back
but I'm formulating my attack
And as I surface, I slowly breathe
Should I plant the seed I wonder?

One more chance to breathe
Take a breath, my dear

Millions of brilliant comets are
braiding light kaleidoscopically
And succumbing to my stellar deity

Hold tight my dear
I'll take your breath from here

She smiled and fought to keep her eyes open and locked onto mine. "You'll always be my stellar deity," I said, brushing some rogue strands of hair back behind her ear.

One more hour and the aneurysm would claim her. How did our life together go from picking out choice cut salmon steaks to me alone, with her dreadfully cold hand in mine? The doctors said they would let me stay for as long as I wanted, but I could only bear being there lost and alone for a few moments after she passed. How many times had I been in that hospital and seen other people in my shoes? Too many to count. Thornbury is an excellent hospital for head trauma and neurology, the best maybe in the entire country, but there was nothing they could do for my poor sweet Eve.

In a fog, I staggered across the hall, past the nurse's station and over to a window that was cracked open. Pushing up the screen, I vomited and sobbed into the rhododendrons that had just started blooming in a bed of mulch below. I never knew such pain existed.

Chapter 3

Besides creating Evinall to fulfill my promise to my dearly departed Eve, I had originally set out to cure addiction during the better part of my mid to late twenties, ever since I struggled as a recovering addict myself. Both of my parents were university professors, but for two highly respected, highly intelligent people, they sure had no idea about the disease nor how to treat it. Both were psychology professors, not addiction counselors.

I first showed warning signs of my disease during my sophomore year of college. Boston University Medical was where I attended and, against my parents' wishes, I lived in the campus dorms. Mom and Dad argued it would be safer and cheaper for me to continue living with them and I should commute to school from the only place I had ever known as home, where we lived in Franklin, Massachusetts. They also expressed concern about being exposed to underage drinking and partying in general. Neither ever took a sip of alcohol in front of me, and controlled substances were the work of the devil to them. I was also raised Catholic and made it all the way through my confirmation, despite my protests of all religions. In the end, I did everything to appease them and get them off my back. I did it because I knew I would be counting on them to help pay for my college in the years ahead.

My first year at BU Medical was one of my best as I maintained a 3.9 GPA and made the Dean's List. It wasn't until my sophomore year that I began drinking, and it was only because that was what the pretty girls did and I wanted to meet and socialize with them. I had my eyes on this one young lady, Katherine Kennedy, who was in my Organic Chemistry and Critical Thinking classes. Come to find out though, she didn't have her eyes on me. I wanted to talk to her, but I couldn't muster up the nerve. We had friends in common, but I was never included in any of the gossip talk in class about the previous weekend's parties. Finally, I asked my roommate to take me with him one night to a social gathering he was heading off to and, much

18

to his surprise at my request, he agreed. I'll never forget that night because it was the first time I tried any kind of alcohol. The warm sensation it gave me inside my belly could not be accompanied quickly enough by another, and then another, and low and behold, a full-blown addiction was born.

As my partying increased, my grades began to steadily decrease. Never before in my life had I received a grade lower than a "C." The closest I got was once, in high school, in an advanced Latin class during my junior year, though, I was able to do some extra credit work and squeaked by with a rare B-. As I drank more and more frequently, suddenly the best grade I had was a "C," and I almost lost my scholarship. An acquaintance suggested at a party one night, when I was bitching about my declining GPA, I use a bit of cocaine to help me through long study sessions. In my drunken stupor, I agreed to try some and instantly fell in love.

Kathy Kennedy was at an off-campus party one night and looked more beautiful than ever. Boy, she really knew how to turn it on and catch the attention of all the young men nearby. I remember distinctly how I approached her that evening and introduced myself. Coming from a bathroom packed with six other coke sniffing clowns, I waltzed over to her with my false sense of confidence and walked right in between her and some other guy, who was trying his best to impress her. She looked surprised by the level of confidence I had demonstrated as I approached her and said, "Would you please take my hand, so I can tell my friends I've been touched by an angel?"

She giggled and turned to her girlfriend, whispering in her ear. Then, to my horror, her friend made a gesture wiping the tip of her nose with her finger, and the two of them laughed and walked away. I ran into the bathroom, where there were people still sniffing lines, and checked the mirror. There was a spot of blood crusted on my nose and my nostril looked like the rim of a margarita glass! I hadn't checked before leaving the bathroom, and she busted me. That would be the first and last time I ever spoke to Miss. Kennedy.

I eventually brought my grades back up and all seemed well on the educational front. That is until I could no longer afford my increasingly growing cocaine habit. I was too dependent to give it up cold turkey, so I did as most addicts do: lied, hustled, and stole to support my drinking and drug habits. How I was able to pull off juggling two addictions while keeping up my GPA is still a mystery to this day that I cannot offer any explanation for.

During my junior year was when I met the love of my life and the woman I would eventually marry, Eve Brooks. She and I connected on a level I never experienced with anyone else before or since. After about a month of harmless flirting, we began to talk daily and hung out as often as we could since we both could not seem to get enough of each other. She didn't have any issues with drugs and only drank when she was out socializing with friends. Somehow, I managed to keep my drug use a secret from her, at least in the beginning. As I moved from my junior to senior year, I also moved on from cocaine to crystal meth because it was so much cheaper and lasted longer than the coke. It seemed a no-brainer to me. Somehow, I managed to graduate with honors, but my drug use was growing out of control and people were starting to take notice.

Over the following four years, I took a boatload of courses and eventually received my doctorates in Genomics and Pharmacology from Tufts University. Eve and I seriously dated the entire time, and we were both madly in love. My parents started to question my unpredictable mood swings as well as my thin physique and the dark circles under my sunken eyes. It became a hassle for me to talk my way out of their interrogations, so I stopped going home to visit. Eve received a desperate email from my parents inquiring about my recent change in appearance and questioned if I was, in fact, abusing drugs. In a performance that would have won me an Oscar, I acted so outraged by the accusation and declared they both must be senile. Then I promised I wouldn't speak to them until they apologize first. It would be years before we spoke again.

During my post-grad studies, I landed a job at a company called Rommel Research where I studied under a man who would become my mentor, Dr. Camden "Chip" Browne. He taught me how to run a company from the ground up. Chip's methods were questionable at times, but he didn't care. He knew he produced more than anyone else and did things however he wanted. The old pirate took a liking to me, stating he saw a lot of himself in me when he first started out. When we originally met, he was sixty-one-years-old. When he left the company, due to his colon cancer discovery, he was sixty-five. I had the privilege of working as his apprentice for just under four years, and I was devastated when he finally passed at the premature age of sixty-six. Chip was responsible for building my solid work ethic and "never give up" attitude that shaped me into the extremely successful and equally as a fortunate businessman and doctor I am today. He was also the first person to accurately identify my own disease: addiction.

During the second year working beside Chip, we were crafting an advanced, more efficient prototype of a machine called a dermatome: a device used to create new skin grafts for burn victims. One day, when we took a break from work, I pulled out my rough designs of what evolved into the ADM machine. I was moving and thinking at lightning speed. Typically, I worked at a fast pace, but that day I was electrified. Chip must have noticed me jumping from one topic to another and my attention going from one task to another, with little or no pause in between my sentences.

At lunchtime, I opted out of eating with him and instead, went to my car where I snorted a few lines of Percocet. Mixing opiates with speed was my way of taking the edge off. After lunch, when we returned to the lab, I was noticeably sedated compared to how I acted throughout the first half of the day. Chip stopped me in the middle of a sentence and put his hand up in front of my mouth, silencing me. He then grabbed me by my elbow, like a misbehaving child escorted out of a store, and walked me over to the sink. He pointed at my reflection and arched his eyebrows.

"What is it?" I asked honestly.

"Who is that?" he answered.

I was perplexed. Was this one of his little learning games? It must be, I thought.

"Why that's the world-renowned Dr. Karlin and his almost equally handsome mentor Dr. Browne," I said smugly.

"Seriously, don't joke around. Take a good look and describe to me who it is that you see. Who is looking back at you?" He made his point.

I looked and saw a deteriorating, sickly version of the happy, healthy man I used to be. Again, he asked me who we were looking at, but I couldn't answer. I knew what he was getting at, I just wasn't sure how much he knew or understood.

"What is it, Nero? Painkillers? That seems to be the growing fad these days."

I shamefully bowed my head and said not a word.

"Does anybody else know about this? Your parents? Eve?" he asked.

"My parents questioned me, but I denied it and Eve doesn't know. I don't know how she doesn't, I must be doing a good job at hiding it from her at least. You, not so much. Are you going to tell anyone? They'll terminate me for sure." I asked in my most innocent sounding voice.

He agreed not to inform management if I promised to get treatment. Treatment?! I wasn't a drug addict! What was he thinking?! I would simply stop using, at least before and during work, and life would carry on as usual. But what really happened was I didn't last another day.

My first three attempts at quitting were unsuccessful. I managed to stop using cocaine and meth, but the opiates had sunk their hooks deep inside me. Never before had I experienced "dope sickness" and it was worse than the most terrifying description I had ever heard. I wouldn't wish that kind of pain and discomfort on my worst enemy. Well, maybe I would... As soon as I began to feel the butterflies churning in my stomach or started to get the cold sweats on my back, torso, and head, I dialed my dealer and was high within the hour. In the months following Chip outing me, I didn't get better, I got worse. It was almost as if the secret was out and so why hide it? He knew it took time, patience, and a lot of effort to kick an opiate habit. If he ever called me out again, I planned on feeding him some horseshit about falling off the wagon, but I did well up until that point. He saw right through my lies. The only person I fooled was myself.

Eve was the next person to confront me about my addiction. She told me she had a very intense, very emotional heart-to-heart talk with Dr. Browne that made her extremely concerned. What an asshole, I thought. How dare he drag her into this and upset her! That's how mixed up my thought process was. I thought HE was at fault for causing her worry, not me. What did they know after all about the hardships of kicking an addiction, besides what they read in textbooks? They couldn't possibly comprehend what it did to my body and how it warped my mind. Looking back on how I behaved, I acted exactly like the struggling addicts in denial that I myself had read about. I thought I had the world figured out and nobody could tell me what to do nor change my mind. At least not until Eve threatened to leave me.

I'll never forget that day because it rocked my whole world. Eve and I attended a friend's wedding where I went off the deep end. At the reception, I attempted to be inconspicuous as I took full advantage of the open bar. I waited for the moments Eve was engaged in conversation with others, or for when she would be dancing to sneak off to the bathroom to sniff lines of Oxycontin. The 80mg pills were all my dealer had, and I wasn't going to go the entire night without something, so I bought ten of them at a discounted price. Typically, I was used to the 30mg Percocet, sniffing two at once. I made sure I took enough during my first trip into the men's room in case I didn't get another opportunity for a while to return and do more. Crushing up two 80's, I blasted them and made my appearance again in the reception hall.

Throughout the evening I managed to make five more trips to the bathroom, doing all ten pills by the halfway point of the reception. I was a mess. My pupils were so tiny they were almost gone entirely. I couldn't manage to keep myself from rambling on and on about who knows what nonsense to anybody nearby. Cottonmouth made my lips stick to my gums, and my tongue was pasty and swollen. I was drinking lemon-lime soda up until that point, and Eve knew it because at one point she sipped it to make sure it wasn't alcohol. After that, I was in the clear. When the dry mouth got to an unbearable point, I switched to gin and tonic. From that point on, I only remember ordering the next drink before I blacked out.

Eve woke me the next day and I discovered I was in a hotel

room. A nice one judging by the bed I was in. She told me, with a disappointed look I had never seen before, that I embarrassed her and she didn't deserve that. I agreed. She also said I was an asshole for losing complete control of myself. Again, I agreed. She didn't go off telling me what I needed to do to get my life back in check, all she said was if I wasn't in a treatment center or hospital by the end of that day, she was leaving me. I wholeheartedly agreed, then I cried.

We arrived at the detox lodge around dinnertime that day. I had a bag packed that was thoroughly searched before I was instructed to strip down and then I was searched. Never would I have imagined my life to take me there, not as a child, not as a teenager, not as a know-it-all postgraduate student studying at one of the best colleges in the country. It was such a humbling time for me, but I toughed it out. Of course, I had a staff of nurses and doctors watching over me, supplying me with more medications than I abused on the streets. For the most part of my week-long detox, they kept me nice and zombified until I was ready to go to a more stable unit. Another three weeks and I was ready for the next step: moving back home and attending a methadone clinic to receive a daily dose.

I rented my own apartment close to campus at the start of my first semester at B.U. It was in a nice area surrounded by even nicer, more expensive boroughs of the city, none of which had a methadone clinic. The closest one was a twenty-minute drive from my front door, and it was in a rough section of Boston. Eve and I discussed and decided it would be best if she stayed with me for at least the beginning of my outpatient treatment. I did not object and loved the fact I could see her gorgeous face every day.

Eve was sweet and nurturing. Every day without exception, she woke up with me at 6:00am, and we went to the methadone clinic. Most of the time she stayed in the car while I went in, but every now and then she accompanied me and had a quick chat with the nurses, to let them know how well I was doing. The better I behaved and complied with the clinic's policies, the better chances I had of getting my doses to take home to administer on my own, dwindling daily drives to the clinic down to as little as two a week.

She was so wonderful to me throughout the recovery process.

Eve knew what a blow to my ego admitting my disease was because, for a while, I looked at it as a weakness, not a disease. It wasn't until I met the second most important person in my life that I would learn the difference. My sponsor turned out to be another mentor and became a best friend of mine, though he claims: "I'm not your friend, I'm your sponsor."

We're best buds all right, I don't care what he says!

Eventually, I received take-home doses, earning one at a time over the course of a year. Two and a half years almost to the exact day I first entered the clinic, I completed the program, weaning down to one milligram of methadone and then nothing. Receiving a letter of completion, I felt a greater pride completing that program than when I graduated from school, probably because it was harder for me to kick drugs and alcohol than graduate magna cum laude. Eve was proud of me, and it felt wonderful to see her in such good spirits. It was a very positive time for both of us; she had also graduated with honors with a Master of Science in Biomedical Sciences, and I was offered a promotion at my job. Everything was going perfectly when Chip died.

His battle with cancer was finally over, and the poor combatant could finally rest at ease. I was upset but weary because I knew sudden tragic incidents like that could spark a relapse, so I did what I did best and buried myself in my work. When I finished my regular work, I worked on my own ideas and the rough sketches of the ADM machine I only shared with Eve and Chip.

Chip watched me as I excitedly explained my ideas to him and he made comments about how I was destined for greatness, and to never stop dreaming because I saw things others could not. His final gift of encouragement came when I was notified by his attorney that I had been named in his last will and testament, much to my surprise. I never gave it a thought before then, but he wasn't married and had no children. When I thought about it, I was probably the closest thing he had to a best friend.

Chip worked for thirty years at Rommel and saved most of his earnings, while he also made wise and lucrative investments during his life. Nothing could have prepared me when I learned about what he left me in his will. There I was, a recently clean doctor, fresh out of school, with not more than a pot to piss in and a heap of college loans to my name, sitting across the mahogany desk in some swank attorney's office discussing the last wishes and demands of my dearly departed friend. It was surreal. I felt as though I was watching the scene unravel from up above, like a spectator seated on the ceiling. The lawyer read while I sat and listened.

Chip had a significant amount of money saved up. After his diagnosis with cancer, he pulled out of all investments, cashed in all his bonds, and sold the shares of stock he had, pooling all of it into his savings account. There was a total of seven and a half million dollars in his account, and he decided to leave most of it to me! The half million he donated to a charity he supported during his life fed the homeless people of America. An envelope revealed the shocking news to me. It read as follows:

Nero,

My dear friend, you have brought me great joy throughout these latter years, and I will forever be grateful and cherish our friendship. To show you how much you mean to me, I have decided to leave you with seven million dollars on two conditions. One: you marry that wonderful woman Eve. I have lived a long life and NEVER met two people more in love than you two. You'll never find another like she and I know it is the right move. Two: you keep dreaming and aiming for the stars. You remind me so much of myself except I never had the means, when I was younger, to bring my visions to life. With the money I'm leaving you, you create the ADM machine. If Rommel doesn't want to back your ideas, leave and start up your own company. You should do that anyway, why let them earn all the profits? Speak to my lawyer about getting started, he will help you to get going. If you ever need anything, don't hesitate to ask him. I have trusted that man with my most private and pricey belongings, and he has always made good on his word.

Keep up the amazing work and always follow what your gut tells you. I wish you a very long, successful, and happy life, my good friend. Enjoy the money and spend it wisely, you have the whole world ahead of you. Remember; the mightiest oak in the forest was once a little nut.

I'll be keeping a watch out over you,

Dr. Camden Browne

It was unbelievable, but it was all very true. There folded up in the envelope behind the letter was another smaller piece of paper. I removed and unfolded it, revealing the first drawing of the ADM machine I showed Chip. I drew it on the back of a paper napkin from the cafeteria at Rommel. We were sharing lunch when I first let him in on my secret idea, and he told me to draw it out so he could better picture it. I thought he just wanted to get a good laugh at my artistic abilities, or lack thereof. I did my best to draw it, and he seemed impressed as well as enthusiastic. Chip fed off my energy and loved it when I came to him with new ideas. That little piece of paper I had drawn out years before proved how much he believed in me, and from that moment on, I was determined to make him proud, no matter from where he watched over.

I eventually used the money to start KarlTech Ingenuities Inc. and hired Eve as the first official employee. Our mission was to continuously search for new and improved ways to better the quality of life for people who have medical issues. The first ADM machine opened to the public six months after KarlTech started its operations, and I can honestly say I believe I did my late mentor proudly. If there is a heaven somewhere, Chip is sitting there with that big contagious smile of his, looking down proudly at all I have accomplished. I can only hope my extracurricular activities occur when he's preoccupied with beautiful women. I'm sure he isn't a big fan of the murders.

Chapter 4

Like most recovering addicts, it is imperative for me to keep myself preoccupied with numerous mentally and physically strenuous activities to maintain my sobriety. The most dangerous time for me is any and all downtime (when I feel idle) and the most dangerous company for me is, in fact, my own. For when the curtain falls, and the crowd leaves for home, this protagonist curls up into a fetal ball, head tucked in, and eyes clenched shut in my dark and desolate little corner of the world. Trembling, I pray for some higher power to protect me from my inner demon, forcing it to retract its venomous fangs and loosen its tightly coiled grip.

Why does, of all people, the creator of the wonder-drug whose sole purpose is to slay such a dreadful nemesis, fear any potential relapse? Because the most shocking of all the skeletons that reside in my closet, may not be my moonlighting activities as the "Butcher of Beantown," -- as referred to by Braddock Nix of the PatriotPress.com. My biggest secret is I have never personally taken a single dose of Evinall. That was my gift to the world that I offered up as a way of saying thank you to whatever forces brought my precious Eve into existence and graced me with the honor of spending those irreplaceable years together, despite the abrupt and unwarranted ending. No, I need to fight this battle on my own for my fallen brothers and sisters, whose names were sadly forgotten, along with the rest of the casualties who fought this war before us, so that I will never forget. The pain and temptations that could unexpectedly rain upon me serve as a warning that my defenses should always be on high alert. They provide a constant reminder of the potentially devastating storm brewing inside of me that I need to avoid unleashing at any given cost.

Eve passed away on Friday the 13th in October, a month we both greatly anticipated each year, as we festively tried to out-spook each other with childish Halloween pranks. That year though, the decorations she tediously set out, which were no doubt the best in our hometown of Franklin, remained as she left them well after the turn of the new year. Sitting in my over-sized black leather recliner, I swiveled slowly from side to side, I could almost hear her humming the theme to The Phantom of The Opera, as she typically did while she turned our massive home into a ghoulish wonderland, until the very last cotton cobweb was meticulously placed, and the fake candles were centered in each window. She knew how I childishly loved Halloween and she did her best to make each year as remarkable and memorable as the previous. It became somewhat of a tradition for us to spend Labor Day weekend, racing around town, searching store after store for any and all decorations we hadn't already owned, to add to our collection. The thought of having to take it down after she worked so hard was enough to bring me to tears, and it did.

I pulled myself together when a news alert made my cell phone vibrate in my pocket. Keeping up with the latest scoop became an obsession of mine. It started years ago when my name first made the headlines due to our achievements at KarlTech. The news alert was something out of a movie. Apparently, a zookeeper from the San Diego area was arrested for animal cruelty. Not a big deal, I'm sure that happens more than the general public is aware of. The story at first was only covered by southern California's local news channels, but then, in a shocking turn of events, it received nationwide attention. Evidence that the suspect was involved in some type of terrorist plot had surfaced. It appeared unexplainable chaos was capable of popping its obnoxious head up at random, like those annoying whack-a-mole carnival games.

The incident was too much for me to bear, so I deleted the alert from my phone and tried to focus on something more pleasant, like the winning streak the Patriots were on. It was no use though. I kept thinking about the reasoning behind life's tragic events. I mean if there truly exists a higher power, where is she to deliver justice to the guilty and protect the innocent? What is the reason for allowing millions to suffer from disease, abuse, torture, and pain for no apparent reason? I weighed the pros and cons of adopting the discrete and subtle life of a vigilante. Never missing the opportunity to slay the metaphorical two birds with one stone, I formulated a plan to bring my own personal brand of justice to as many criminals who were not incarcerated and managed to hide among the law-abiding contributors to society: the same unsuspecting people who the criminals would eventually prey upon. Guided by an ironic set of ethics, I officially swore myself in as Boston's new morally-inspired garbageman.

When I said I followed a set of ethics, it is more of simple, yet essential, set of rules which help me target the deserving criminals while avoiding capture. As I do with any task, I set out to achieve, the first thing I did was to compile a thorough list. On it were the names of the crooked and corrupt men and women I knew from the years I spent in the limelight, many I knew on a personal level. These people were the ones who I deemed corrupt beyond repair and therefore expendable. If I was labeled a pompous prick or vainglorious villain, I felt it was a noble title.

It became clear to me I must seek out these members of society, who were undoubtedly unavailing parasites the world would never miss and wipe them out of existence. Murderers, rapists, sex offenders, and even big money extortionists were the vile human beings whose names found their way onto my list. There was no need to lug around this dead weight, it was too costly, but no one seemed to have time or patience to address the issue, except for me. I thought it was like trimming the excess fat off society. Most people feel they could benefit from shedding a few pounds, I am discretely providing the service of narrowing our waistlines.

It seemed fitting the "Deuce Juice" would pop my homicidal hymen given our history together. His face was burnt into my memory years ago when I was in my mid-twenties and attended the methadone clinic. As I made my way down the dingy side-street the clinic was located on, I suddenly heard a scream like none I heard before, from man nor animal. That piece of shit lowlife was only about twenty feet from the entrance of the clinic. With his left hand, he dragged one of his working girls by her hair, screaming obscenities at her, and brought her over to the back of a parked car. He lifted her up with ease and slammed her face on the top of the trunk. She reflexively covered her face with both hands and curled into a fetal position, as she rolled off the vehicle and landed on the icy sidewalk.

The Deuce was a large man. He stood at about six feet tall and weighed around two hundred pounds. But I had a good three inches on him, and easily thirty pounds. Before realized it, I sprinted over and kicked the back of his right leg hard with my heavy snow boot. He let out a pain induced roar, which greatly satisfied me. Acting quickly to prevent a counter-attack, I cocked my fist back and unleashed one devastating right hook, that landed squarely on his jaw and knocked him out cold. By then, the clinic's front door security guard made his way over and surveyed the scene briefly before helping the young working girl to her wobbly feet. She looked at me with bruised eyes and probably a bruised ego and thanked me for my heroics. It was at that precise moment when I witnessed the alarming look of fear and shame in her eyes, I promised myself I would somehow, someday, do something about this problem of modern-day slavery. Now, I do just that wielding a 24" razor-sharp, black, steel machete, as the Deuce would find out firsthand about twelve years later.

James Champa was the Deuce's real name, and he was your stereotypical, loud-mouthed African-American pimp, who always had a sweaty forehead and wore a purple pressed suit, gold chains, and matching rings. I watched him for four weeks until I finally decided it was time to make my move. Sitting in my black pickup truck, I observed his every move while I gripped the steering wheel tightly and clenched my teeth with equal force. That was it, the final stalking as my time to strike had arrived. He was the same worthless waste of life he was years ago at our first encounter. It baffled me he was able to squeak through the cracks of our justice system and avoid any substantial jail time.

I watched him step out of his antique Cadillac while barking angrily into his cell phone as he entered a Seven Eleven. Boy did he have a temper. If one of his girls shorted him money, the fines were tough. They would actually consider themselves lucky if all they received was a slap across the face with his extremely long fingers, decked out with chunky bling rings. Sometimes, he grabbed a fistful of their hair and jerked them from side to side, as he explained how much their extensions cost him. There were also times when he

31

hocked up a big one and spit on them. Then, to top it all off, as if their self-esteem was not low enough, coming from whatever dysfunctional backgrounds, they were routinely subjected to him raping them.

It took every last ounce of resistance in me to not shift into drive and floor it, smashing all 6,000 pounds of Detroit's finest machinery into his chest and, hopefully, pinning him to the graffiti-decorated brick wall on the side of the Seven-Eleven he stood in front of. I had no doubts I wanted him. He would make a wonderful candidate for my first victim. The "Deuce Juice" they called him, more like "Deuce Douche."

When he finally exited the store, he stood under the awning and smiled at two teenage girls walking in, showing off his scummy gold teeth. He stood for a moment, packing his menthol cigarettes on his wrist, right next to his gaudy gold watch. The Deuce's disgusting smile sealed the deal for me. After he entered his powder blue pimpmobile, he began his nightly routine of slowly cruising up and down the dark city streets searching for the prostitutes he enslaved. The rain set the gloomy scene of my birth as a murderer.

After thirty minutes and four stops, where he collected the earnings from a half-dozen working girls, he slowed and pulled alongside the curb outside his sleazy triple-decker apartment building. This was the part of his ritual I observed on many prior occasions, the precise moment I waited for. He went inside to drop off his blood money, smoked some crack from a dirty glass pipe, and returned a little later to resume his street cruising.

That was it, there was no turning back from that moment, no mulling or do-overs. My life forever changed as I transformed from the world-renowned pharmacologist and humanitarian, who was adored by most of the public, into a newly born, ruthless headhunter. Wearing a shadow for a face, I wielded a magnificent, terrifying, and unforgiving blade that would slice through a human head like a samurai sword through a plump, sun-ripened tomato.

My personal criminal record detailed one, twenty-year-old public intoxication charge I rightly earned after I was over-served at a post-season Red Sox game. My patience was tested more than I could manage, by three visiting Yankee's fans, and my efforts to teach them a lesson on how to take a loss like a champ might have been more successful if my legs weren't so unstable. Moving forward, I couldn't afford the slightest error if I planned to continue enjoying the pleasures of a life not confined by bars and razor-wire-topped fences. Even the tiniest miscalculation could snowball into a disastrous outcome, jeopardizing my identity and thus my freedom.

My headlights were already off as I stopped one block away and killed the engine in my truck. Forty yards ahead of me he sat, under a flickering streetlight that would soon be off for good, thanks to a well-placed shot from my pellet rifle. I took aim from the passenger window next to me and snuffed out the only source of light. The Deuce didn't notice the faint *pop* sound it made before the shattered glass rained down softly. The blanketing precipitation provided good enough cover to drown out the sound. His windows were up anyway, as he lit his usual late night blunt, turned the music up in his car, and lounged back into his white leather seat without a care in the world it seemed. Who said pimping wasn't easy?! I watched as the interior filled with smoke and thought, "Wow, his last breath of life will be filled with a mixture of shitty skunk weed, menthol cigarette smoke, and pine tree air freshener?" How pathetic.

Checking all directions, I made certain the coast was clear. Deuce lived in the last building of a dead-end street in a decrepit part of South Boston, an area where those who prowled the streets after dark were not the type to call the police if a crime occurred. The moment of truth arrived. Did I hesitate? Nope.

I wore a not-so-original black ski mask and matching black sweat suit that evening, paid for in cash at a thrift shop I passed every day for almost two decades on my way to work, yet never before entered. I bought three pairs of sweatpants (two black, one navy blue), two black zip-up hooded sweatshirts, and a couple pairs of running sneakers to give the impression I was an avid runner gearing up for intense training. This didn't raise suspicion nor stand out from any other sale. The annual Boston Marathon was an event the runners trained for year-round, even in the less appealing areas of the city.

The enormous blade I would soon christen was black from

handle to razor-sharp tip. I purchased it years ago from a Home Headquarters Warehouse and used it originally to clear away thorns and other brush from the shoreline along the far edges of my backyard lake property. It was exactly two feet in length with a slight curve and had a serrated back for sawing through thicker vines. Its sheath was a black durable canvas material which I had sewn a nylon loop to, about three-quarters of the way up its side, to strap it across my back. The handle I wrapped in black duct tape to give extra grip. I wore rubber coated gardening gloves that were tucked into my sleeves and I duct-taped them around my wrists. My sweatpants were tucked into my black combat boots and, again, duct tape was used to secure them in place. I also wrapped tape around both boots to cover any identifiable boot prints.

Every item was cleaned with diluted bleach then checked three and four times, I made sure nothing was loose nor unnecessarily exposed or susceptible to breaking. What good would it do to get one tantalizing taste of the blood-rich justice I so desperately desired if only to have it taken away with the slamming of a disgusted judge's gavel, and then of a steel prison cell door? No mistakes.

A rush of adrenaline hit me as I continued to squeeze the steering wheel so tightly my knuckles popped. A few hours earlier, I removed the dome light, so my cover would not be blown while exiting and entering my truck. After slowly stepping out and gently closing the door behind me, I waited for The Deuce to open his car door, and quietly began my pursuit. As he vacated his sleazy pimpmobile, I heard Jimi Hendrix screaming "I'm a voodoo child," as The Deuce stood tall and stretched, yawning loudly with a cigarette stuck dangling loosely from his lower lip. I made every effort to remain silent after exiting my vehicle, as I switched gears from a steady, crouched walk into a swift jog. Crumbled pieces of asphalt rimmed the potholes and freckled the desolate street like muddy little landmines. I avoided the black rubble that popped and crunched beneath my feet as I closed in on my prey, but years of the city's neglect proved it an almost impossible feat. No matter, the sound was inaudible over Hendrix's masterful guitar playing. "Man, what a song!" I thought to myself.

At last, when I was about eight feet away, I hissed, "psst, hey

Douche!" as I brought my machete up and into a precise swinging position that would have made my little league coach proud. His double chins rolled as he glanced over his right shoulder and then suddenly, his eyes widened in terror at the sight of the enormous blade I held above my head. With one powerful swoop, I landed a perfectly placed blow that glided smoothly into the left side of his neck and then straight through and out the right. It was easier than I had anticipated and the sound of his head plopping on the street resembled one of the diced jack-o-lanterns I had practiced on for this special night.

I didn't lose stride as I circled around to return to my getaway vehicle, but I had to look in admiration at my work before I vanished from the scene. Deuce's body fell to its knees, but the blood did not spurt out as I had anticipated. It bubbled out for a few seconds and then flowed steadily, before it lurched and came to its final resting place; on its side, in the gutter of a dirty, shitty street where it belonged. To my amazement, a little cloud of smoke slowly crept out past his purple, chapped lips once his head came rolling to a stop next to the pathetic carcass. A look of absolute horror was still set in his eyes as they peered in lifeless astonishment, straight up and into the cloudy night sky. What a finale! I burst into laughter as I jumped into my getaway truck and started it up. Driving past the deceased Juice, I rolled down my window, held my head out, and howled, "Now that's some voodoo shit, Jimi!"

Chapter 5

Eve had a mood ring she loved dearly and never took off, ever since she was a little girl. She used to say it predicted my mood moments before I came home from work! She was always right with her predictions. Eve cherished the ring, and I cherished her, so I put it on a chain and wore it around my neck after she passed. It strangely turned a gray-white color I never saw before and has since remained that way. The chain was a bit longer than others I've worn in the past, but I wanted it that way so when I moved, it tapped on my heart, reminding me she was always with me.

The fourth of July was Eve's favorite holiday, we decided to get married around that time. July 2nd was our anniversary date, and we usually celebrated it on the Cape together. I drove down to our summer house in Orleans, as we did each year, to celebrate. I tried to forget that night because I relapsed before I realized it. In an instant, I let my guard down, and I lifted the glass up. It was terrible, I was a complete disaster. The first six beers went down smoothly as I sat by my infinity pool. I tried to enjoy the last moments of a tangerine sun majestically retreating behind the shimmering blue Atlantic, unaware of my inner darkness impatiently waiting to emerge and take hold of the night.

I found it easier to cowardly hide my drinking bouts behind the shadows, and so, for most of my active time, I consumed alone throughout the twilight hours. The final rays of light sank below the ocean on the distant horizon along with any remaining shred of willpower I clung to that evening. One last peaceful moment of clarity came over me, provided by the sound of the waves as they lapped the shoreline just beyond the flourishing rose hedge.

As the hours passed, the self-respecting Nero known to most, transformed into the self-loathing creature I made countless promises to do my best to restrain. Every time I shamefully returned to the refrigerator to grab another cold one, I noticed a picture, held up by little plastic fruit magnets, of Eve and I embracing a handsome, rebel maniac. It was taken during the first year we were together at a Strawdogs concert in Australia when she and I jumped on stage and sang along with the lead singer, Chris "Ox Cock" Oswald. Each time, I paused in front of the refrigerator to look at her radiant little face, with her rosy, red cheeks, adorable little button nose, and of course those dazzling emerald eyes that captivated all who were blessed with the privilege to gaze into them. They cast a hypnotic trance as mysterious as she was. Guilt and disgust eventually consumed me, and in my drunken stupor, it seemed to destroy all evidence of Eve's existence was the only way would get past her death once and for all. And so, I made a fire.

Luckily, our Cape property is on a little peninsula and completely isolated from neighbors because eventually, my fire pit resembled what I imagine the launch pads at N.A.S.A. look like after the shuttles take off for space. It started with the picture on the refrigerator, along with a few others that were scattered around the first floor of our luxurious summer dwelling. It took me two hours and roughly 168 ounces of summer ale to finally throw the first photo into the crackling fire. There I sat, alone on the beautiful bluestone patio of our beach house; drinking, laughing, sobbing, and yelling...relapsing alone.

When at last the well ran dry, I spiked my heavy glass beer mug into the blaze and roared. I spun around in a circle pointing like the greatest tight end the NFL ever produced, Rob Gronkowski used to do in the end zone for the Patriots. Except nobody was cheering for me. I had no one running up, slapping me on the ass and headbutting me for another amazing performance. This did not please me at all. Where were all my screaming, adoring fans?

I then decided the Adirondack patio chairs should join the inferno, followed by the rest of the furniture and potted plants that decorated our meticulously landscaped pool area. In the outdoor bar, I grabbed a couple of bottles of liquor from the top-shelf and chugged them down. When I smashed one that was half-full into the growing inferno, it made a big blue *POOF!* as it exploded. Grabbing with both hands at my collar, I made my best Incredible Hulk impression and tore the over-priced Black Lab t-shirt off my sweaty body. When I caught a glimpse of my reflection, as I strutted by the glass sliding door leading into the dining room, I briefly admired my chiseled physique that rivaled my childhood idol Gronk.

From the kitchen, I gathered bottles of olive oil, liquor, and cooking sprays and placed them in a wicker basket. There wasn't much else on the first floor I felt like setting ablaze, so I headed through the foyer and upstairs toward the master bedroom. Eve's closet was, in her typical modest fashion, only a quarter full of summer clothes. I removed them and threw them into a pile on top of our king-size sleigh bed along with her shoes, a jewelry box, more framed pictures, and her perfumes. Looking like an over-stuffed hobo's bag, I tied up the four corners of the comforter and dragged my cumbersome collection back down the curving staircase and grabbed the wicker basket filled with flammables before returning outside to the fire pit. It only took seconds, after tossing in the massive ball of Eve's memorabilia, for the flames to grow higher than my six feet three-inch frame. "Boo-yeah!" I shouted as the last aerosol can exploded and took off like a rocket.

The intensity of a roaring fire is no match for that of my disease and its constant demand for more. More alcohol, more chaos, more of whatever is in sight it desires. There are no "off limits." There is no stopping my plague until it is granted its wishes, or until I slip into unconsciousness.

My pathetic, infantile tantrum took a turn for the worst. When I couldn't manage to light the grill in my drunken stupor, I punched the stainless-steel lid and pushed it completely over. The propane tank clanked as it hit the stone patio. Of course! Why hadn't I thought of that before? I disconnected the tank and placed it a safe distance from the fire as prepared for its detonation.

I walked quickly to the pool shed but found the door closed. "GARG-A-FUCKING-MEL-GIBSON," I shouted for some reason, as I smashed and tore through the screen door, landing flat on my face.

My ankle responded with a pop, a minor injury, the booze helped suppress the pain. What the hell had just happened? Wait, booby traps! Of course, these jungles were littered with them. I had to be more careful from then on to successfully carry out my mission.

Pulling myself up to my feet, I determined that my ankle was toast. This was not the time to be a pussy though, Charlie was hot on my tail, and I had to get the fuck back to the L.Z. Grabbing every last pool float and toy, I emptied the entire contents of the shed into the elegant infinity pool.

I then stood beside the diving board and removed the last of my clothes. It was time to set off the payload. Just before jumping into the deep end, I hurled the propane tank into the center of the raging fire. I took cover in the center of the pool and radioed in for air support because Charlie was closing in. I was not sure how much more gunfire my rubber zebra could take, but my air support would have to get there soon if I was to hold off this onslaught.

RECON, RECON what's your location? Do you copy?" I shouted into one end of an orange noodle.

No answer.

"I'm pinned down and out of ammo. I need reinforcements, do you copy?"

Silence.

"BRAVO? ECHO? TANGO? CASH? ICEMAN? GOOSE... DOES ANYBODY FUCKING COPY?!"

They were all dead.

Goddamn it! We never should have underestimated the Viet Cong. You never, under any circumstances, underestimate your opponent. That was our greatest mistake. Well, that, and not buying thirty-six beers as opposed to twenty-four.

KABOOOOOOM!!!

The gas tank exploded with devastating force, much to my liking. Bits and pieces of glass and glowing embers erupted out in all directions in a sweltering heat wave. Luckily, I was protected behind the many pool floats and somehow managed not to suffer a single injury. The payload had been successfully delivered, and the battle was won. I abandoned my post in the water and walked over to survey ground zero. Suddenly I felt short of breath, I put my hands on my knees and held my head down.

"Breathe, nice deep breaths, breathe." I felt Eve's ring swaying and tapping against my sweaty chest as I cinched my eyes shut. The flames were now taller than the first-floor windows, and my skin began to swelter.

"Goodbye Baby," I said as I snapped the ring from the necklace and tossed it into the blaze.

That is what she would have wanted, right? For me to move on. Probably, but not like that. Not by drinking again and letting my emotions get the better of me. We both knew how that always ended.

What the fuck had I done?! That was her sacred little ring, and I just threw it away because I felt sorry for myself?! I dropped to my knees before the roaring, crackling, popping fire, and skimmed the embers until I saw where the ring landed.

My last memory of that night was shutting my eyes and saying to myself, "Nero, this is going to hurt, you dumb drunk fuck."

That was the second most painful experience of my life.

Chapter 6

"Smoke, the Queer, wake up."

Russ. Of course, he was my emergency contact, my best friend, my rock.

"Hey, your little girlfriend, Braddock Dicks, is outside and she wants a statement. Do you want me to tell her you're fine and not to cancel your vacation plans to Provincetown next weekend?"

He was referring to Braddock Nix, of course, the pain in the ass reporter from ThePatriotPress.com., who has made a career out of ridiculing mine. I despise him, and Russ loves it. He never misses an opportunity to remind me of what an enormous thorn in my side Mr. Nix really is and finds it humorous to pretend the two of us are secret lovers.

"Wake up! Your little acorn dick is showing, and there are nurses around, hot ones. Wake up!"

Only his boisterous voice could bring a smile to my face after spending a night in hell.

SNAP *SNAP*

What the hell was that? Prying my crusty eyes open, I said, "cheese," as Russ leaned down beside my face and snapped a couple of selfies. This couldn't be happening. What a prick!

"Oh, this is going viral brother! Instant internet fame and fodder for the media leeches, they're gonna love it. You've had a fun weekend, huh? Why didn't you invite me to your little pool party?"

Thanks for coming," I babbled.

"Well, you're lucky you're handsome. Are you feeling okay?" Russ asked.

"I feel like, I mean I can't feel..."

"Relax, you're going to be just fine. I mean your hands look

41

awful but then again, hands are overrated, right? You're at Thornbury, so just try to take it easy. They have enough state-of-the-art shit here to get you patched up in no time. Christ, half of it they probably bought from you! The doctor will be here in a few minutes with the details."

"How did I...What happened?" I managed to whimper.

"The fire chief said you might have overdone it this time with the fire pit. He said most of the damage to your house was from the water used to put out the blaze and informed me that the insurance adjusters have already been out to assess the carnage. The bottom line is, you're alive and never allowed to play with matches again my little pyro princess."

He brushed my short, brown hair to the side of my forehead, so he could look into my eyes, though I could barely keep them open.

"No more close calls, okay?" he said.

I wondered how long I had been unconscious. A couple of days? A couple of weeks? I felt groggy as though someone was slowly pushing my head down into my shoulder. My eyes were crusty, my mouth was pasty, and all I could taste was the metallic flavor of whatever medicines they had pumped in me.

"Let me see those big brown eyes, Nero. Okay?"

My memory was foggy and the details I would recall in due time, but I was already embarrassed by the actions that had landed me there. I was well known and respected in the medical field that by then, rumors of my drunken tirade had undoubtedly spread throughout the entire building.

Thornbury Hospital is located in Brighton, Ma a hectic town bordering Boston's city limits, and it was one of the best hospitals in the country. I knew the majority of doctors and nurses who worked there, and most of them knew me, at least by reputation. I was one of the most successful recovering addicts in the world and a role model to countless others, both sober and those struggling to stay clean. My relapse was more damaging than I like to admit.

"I said no more close calls, right?" Russ repeated.

I hate letting him down. He has been there to carry me through the toughest times of my life, and the only thing he asked for in return was for me to keep on fighting, no matter how rough the road ahead got.

"I said, OKAY Nero? Where's the damn doctor? I'm going to order an emergency enema to help wake you up."

"Christ, OKAY!" I moaned and opened my eyes as wide as possible.

"Awe, there he is! Just making sure we're on the same page here, Buddy. Next time you feel like turning your beach house into a volcano, you better call me first, okay?"

"YES! OKAYAY! You're a real pain in the ass, you know that Russ?" I grumbled and tried to maneuver myself into a more comfortable position.

"Yes, I do...I love you, Nero," he replied.

"I love you too, dick."

He leaned down, put his thick forearm behind my neck, and then pressed his forehead against mine. "Just because your name is Nero, it does not give you the right to try to burn down Rome," he said with a grin.

We both laughed. I would not be as successful and fortunate as I was if not for Russ Cornelison. I sure as heck wouldn't have made it through Eve's passing without his support. We met during the first month I attended the methadone program years ago. I walked into the clinic one morning to receive my daily dose, with my head down trying to hide, and there he was sitting on a chair by the nurse's window with a plastic tab sticking out of his mouth; he was getting a drug test. I too had to take one of the many, random drug screens I received over the course of my treatment at the clinic. Standing awkwardly beside his chair, he looked over at me.

"These things taste like Satan's taint," he groaned.

The thoroughly tattooed barbarian sitting next to me had long, black, wavy hair that came down to his scraggly goatee. He was wearing a black muscle undershirt that tightly covered his brawn frame, with black faded jeans, black leather combat boots, and a pair of, also black, fingertip-less, leather gloves. His voice echoed, resembling what I imagine a grizzly bear would sound like if one could speak.

Russ smiled and introduced himself. Surprisingly, he stood up and offered me his seat, which I willingly accepted, fearing for my life. His forearms were like a gorilla's, only maybe bigger and the ink on them portrayed scenes of demons and gargoyles battling with Jesus.

"Strawdogs huh? Here I thought I was the only one, those sluts," he said, referring to the shirt I bought at their concert in Australia the previous year with Eve.

Music was always a good conversation starter and possibly a way to show I am a good person, not deserving to die or engage in a confrontation with this terrifying individual.

"Check out the blonde at the nurse's window," he said motioning with his head. "I would carve that ass into the side of a mountain and then fly a plane into it."

I burst into laughter, spitting my plastic saliva tab across the floor, almost hitting the young blonde woman's foot. From that moment on, I would never be prepared for anything that came out of my new friend's outrageously entertaining mouth. Russ is without a doubt the most intimidating creature I've ever come in contact with, yet with the manners of a five-star restaurant's waiter. He never misses an opportunity to hold a door open for someone or carry a hefty bundle of groceries to an elderly woman's vehicle. He is a prime example of why we cannot judge books by their covers. Russ is the only person who is always 100% honest with me, regardless of my feelings. His compassion and integrity run deep, solid no matter what. That's why he is my rock.

"Can we get a nurse over here, please? This man has had an accident," he shouted, waving his big paw out into the hallway, motioning for one of the nurses to come in.

"What are you talking about Russ? What accident?" I asked.

"Keep your voice down, wait until you see the "Woodeye"

coming in to change you," he answered. He pointed down to my crotch, which was wet for some reason.

A "Woodeye" is what Russ refers to as a sexy woman, a term he evolved from the phrase, "oh boy, would I!"

"It's not real piss, it's just apple juice. I grabbed it from your lunch tray and sprinkled you a little. You can thank me later after she's done wiping off your balls."

Russ has picked me up and dusted me off more times than I can count, and I have done the same for him too. He wouldn't flinch to step in front of a moving vehicle or a stray bullet to save my life, and I grew to feel the same for him as well. The fact I became one of the most successful men in America provides him with endless opportunities to try to embarrass me and bring me back down to Earth or, "Pull my head out of my ass," as he refers to it.

A well-groomed, handsome, Irish-looking male in his mid-fifties, with short strawberry blonde hair neatly combed to the side, drew back the curtain and poked his head in, smiling at us.

"Hi Nero, I am Dr. Howard Chase. How are you feeling this morning?"

He looked more like an accountant than a doctor. His voice was straightforward and to the point. He would make a good interrogator, I thought to myself. I waved my paddle-like bandaged hands back and forth and said, "Very good sir, come in, tell me what's the damage?"

"We'll start with the worst of it. I regret to inform you that your hands and lower forearms have been severely burned and you will require multiple skin graft treatments to make them appear as they once were. For third degree burns such as yours, it is not uncommon to require at least eight to twelve separate skin grafting sessions.

"Electroshock treatment is also required to stimulate the nerves. We did everything we could to try to save them, but unfortunately, the burns were too deep. Next is the issue of your ankle. You have a second-degree inversion ankle sprain, which should heal completely in two to three months. We have everything we need here to do the grafting, but I understand that you are in the very fortunate position

45

to have an abundance of medical resources at your disposal. The decision is yours; you can receive the standardized treatments that we provide here, or you can utilize your own means for treatment elsewhere."

I remembered hearing feedback from patients who were benefiting from KarlTech's dermatomes, about how painful skin grafts were.

"I will receive treatment at KarlTech but thank you, Doctor Chase, for all that you have done. I really appreciate your time and efforts."

He explained to me, in more detail, what I could expect as far as recovery time. His prediction for my hands and arms was six to eight months, and they should appear close to what they once did. Apparently, rummaging through the orange-red embers in the fire pit in search of Eve's ring cost me greatly, and I wasn't even sure what had happened to it! That was until Russ pulled it out of his pocket once Dr. Chase left, and I was surprised and pleased to see he put it on a new chain.

He dangled it in front of me. "This little fucker is what you torched your claws up for? I'm assuming it's Eve's. I'm not going to lecture you, not right now anyway, but you will promise me that we will work on your recovery once you get settled in a little. Do we understand?" he asked me like an angry parent lecturing his bratty little son.

"I understand and agree. That was a one-time incident, won't happen again, I swear."

Russ understood better than anyone just how little weight the promise of an addict held, especially one who had relapsed. All promises of new, better, worry-free times ahead. Yup, nothing but smooth sailing into the sunset. He was part of the game for too long to invest in any of my half-hearted promises which were why he ran the show HIS way.

We took the necessary steps to get me back up on my horse and learn to ride again at HIS pace. Russ was my sponsor, and I took an oath to listen to and adopt his teachings and guidance. It worked in

46

the past, and I was confident it would work again. I'm not claiming it was easy but having my best friend as my spiritual mentor and sponsor sure was an added bonus. I loved Russ like a brother, the rest of the bullshit would eventually work itself out.

The necessary procedures I required I arranged to have administered with KarlTech equipment at my home-based laboratory, in the basement of my Franklin home. The registered nurse with the blonde hair, Russ' Woodeye, had me sign my release papers, holding the pen in my mouth, and my release from Thornbury's care was official. The whole situation was surreal to me. Had I really caused all that chaos in just one evening? The burning of Eve's personal belongings, the insanely huge fire, blowing up a propane tank, injuring my ankle, and burning off a large portion of my hands and arms... Did that all really take place or was I just dreaming?

I was wheeled out of the emergency room in a wheelchair into the scorching sun. I looked up at Russ and said, "This is going to suck huh?"

In the reassuring yet mocking tone my good friend had perfected into an art form, he reassured me by replying, "Just take it easy, Paddy Cakes, you're going to be alright. It will suck a little here and there but what are you going to do? Sometimes shit sucks. Don't be a pussy. We deal with it, that's what we do. You're in good hands now," he said it with a wink, as we both stepped into his SUV.

"You'll have plenty of time to gather all of your toys and concoct a new pair of mitts once your health improves a little. I am not letting you out of my sight. We have a lot of work to do, so reach deep and pull out a pair; it's going to be a rough ride." He was not joking.

Chapter 7

"Paddy cakes" is where I got the idea to create removable skin gloves that can copy the hand and fingerprints of others. I had a 3D bioprinter shipped to my home from KarlTech that I used to construct my own skin grafts. The machines are typically used to create new living tissue, but I had modified that one, so it generated large sections of skin and even entire organs.

During the process, I discovered a way to easily forge the identities of others by making skin gloves with a soft, impressionable top layer, that will imprint whoever squeezes it. I can wear a blank pair of gloves in plain sight without raising suspicion since they blend in perfectly with my normal skin tone. Once an impression is made, I'll slip them off and scan them back into the bioprinter. The machine makes a duplicate copy I can wear to strategically place the prints wherever I desire. Talk about identity theft! I am able to frame criminals who have previously eluded capture and prosecution due to a lack of evidence. All I have to do is shake hands with them, and they are incarcerated in no time.

Already knowing my thoughts and intentions from numerous discussions, Russ was well aware of what I wanted to do. He always said that he would stick with me through thick and thin. So, we eventually began compiling a list of people who qualified for my "services" during the few months following my hospital release. We separated the candidates into groups based on the severity of their crimes, the potential to commit future crimes, and my accessibility to them. One name that stuck out was Richard Reed.

Russ was the one who suggested Richard because he was a high risk of causing more problems, despite being on probation and the police in his town "keeping a close eye on him." Richard Reed liked to play with fire and had a long rap sheet that increasingly grew in severity over the past few years. The prior winter, a senior living center in Quincy, Ma was burnt to the ground, and it happened to be one of the places Richard delivered groceries to as part of his job. No evidence could link him to the crime, but an employee claimed he saw Reed on the premises not long before the fire started. His testimony was dismissed, eventually, because he was behind the building smoking a joint at the time, he had witnessed the crime. They tossed his statement out claiming his perception was impaired and therefore unreliable. It was a shame because the blaze claimed three lives: two elderly residents and one staff member, who got cornered inside a third-floor room by the fire and jumped out the window to his death trying to escape the flames. Three innocent dead and he got away with it, which only boosted his confidence and made him more of a threat.

Russ and I agreed Reed was a prime target, so we began working on a plan of attack. I could have followed him around, learned his schedule and daily routine, and removed his head from his body using my favorite piece of sharpened steel, but that was too easy. I want certain people to suffer for their sins and rot away in a smelly, cramped cell, where they can brood over their crimes or just simply waste away. Either way is fine by me. Reed was one of those people.

Besides working in a fancy, expensive restaurant, Russ also volunteered at a couple of soup kitchens around Boston, where he made quite a few friends. The people of less fortune, who go there for warm meals, appreciate the fact that a chef of his caliber making a good living for himself is generous enough to lend his talents to the city's shelters. The other volunteers and staff claim the number of people coming in off the streets searching for food had risen quite a bit since word got out that a real gourmet chef sometimes cooks the meals.

Once mealtime is over, Russ comes out from the kitchen, walks around, asks if everything is fine with the food, and introduces himself to any and all new faces. He sits and talks about sports, current events, and the weather to show them they are his equal, despite their current disadvantaged living situation. So, Russ became sort of a rock star to the homeless, and they love seeing him, not just because they know they are in for a tasty treat, but because he makes them feel better. Street people flock to where Russ is cooking and line up to meet their royalty. That is why he's my hero: "King of the

Cooks" and a great friend to the people who need one the most, as well as yours truly.

After we decided on Reed, Russ asked around to see if anyone had seen him or knew where he was living. Sure enough, someone informed him they knew Reed's sister and that he had been staying at her apartment near Andrews Square in South Boston. The informant said Reed took the commuter train (nicknamed the "T" by Boston natives) down a few stops to an ADM and received an Evinall injection there on a monthly basis. From what Russ was told, Reed was a recovering heroin addict but still drank in excess, which is strongly recommended NOT to do while taking Evinall. A drink here and there is harmless, but continuous consumption of alcohol mixed with the medicine can potentially cause and accelerate liver damage.

That didn't seem to bother Reed, who wanted to set the city ablaze. I knew exactly which ADM he frequented because I know where everyone is located around the city since I referred people and patients to them for years. It is the one on Talbot Ave. in Dorchester: a very large, VERY dangerous, urban section of the city that neighbors South Boston. There are more AMD machines in lower income areas since that is where drug abuse is statistically most prevalent.

Russ had a rough idea what day his informant saw Reed on the T, and according to him, it was during the middle of the month and at nighttime, approximately 8:00pm. This made sense because we found out he worked 11:00am- 7:00pm. Reed most likely went back to his sister's apartment either to change or eat or both then headed out for his dose. All I had to do was narrow it down to the exact day, and I would know when he would be returning there for his next injection.

The basement of my home is nothing short of a fully-functioning research laboratory and office. My computers are linked to the primary server of KarlTech Inc., and I have access to every piece of information running in and out of there. This includes the security footage of each ADM location. There are two cameras outside and two cameras inside every branch to protect the abundance of medications and multi-million-dollar medical computers and equipment inside. I obtained access to the one on Talbot Ave. and went through the footage, waiting for Reed to make an appearance. It took a bit of time, but eventually, there he was.

When a person uses an AMD, they enter their personal information, and it's kept classified as detailed in state and federal laws. So, everything from a person's weight to their blood's oxygen level is recorded and saved. Richard Reed was a Caucasian male who stood five foot eight inches tall and weighed one hundred and seventy-three pounds. He had a blood pressure of 120/75 and tested positive for hepatitis C and H.I.V. when he last visited the location on the 17th of the previous month. Helpful information if one had planned on beheading him and spilling his blood. But I was not doing that. I was going to meet him there in five days, on the 17th at 8:00pm and introduce myself to the man I would later frame for attempted arson.

The bioprinter crafted a perfect pair of baby-soft skin gloves I gently pulled over my hands. They ended just past my wrists, and even though it matched my skin color beautifully, I made sure to apply a little foundation makeup to blend them in perfectly with my real skin. I wore a pair of leather gloves over them because the surface of the skin gloves are heat sensitive. That's how, when another warm hand presses into the smooth skin, an impression is made.

I planned to protect my precious palms by putting the leather gloves back on until I returned to my lab. Later, in the lab, Russ would carefully remove the skin for me while he wore latex gloves. Then, we would place the skin in the bioprinter where they were scanned and duplicated into a new pair of gloves, creating a new identity for me to wear.

When the 17th arrived, I was ready. I wore dress pants and a button up white collared shirt that had KarlTech Inc. embroidered on the right breast and the name "Kurtis" embroidered on the left. Russ and I drove to the ADM location, and I went inside, taking with me a metal briefcase containing tools that are used to perform diagnostic tests, to make sure the machines function properly. I waited inside while pretending to do routine updates to the computer system. I had to turn a patient away, stating the machine was temporarily out of service.

It was about 8:30pm when Reed finally arrived. He was scruffy looking, with scraggly, unkempt blonde hair, a five o'clock shadow, and jeans and a t-shirt that seemed as though they hadn't been washed in the past decade. That guy delivered food people ate?! I pulled off my leather gloves and stuffed them in my pockets.

"Is this thing working?" he asked as I stepped outside to greet him.

"Yeah, I was just giving it a tune-up, should be all set now," I responded.

"Were you re-filling the thing or something?" he said, glancing down at my silver briefcase.

I bet he was wondering if I came to replenish the medications inside, which a pair of armed guards do as needed. I imagined he was staring at my silver case thinking about what might possibly be inside and probably trying to calculate its street value. If there had actually been medications to refill the machine in it, that value could range anywhere from $50,000 up to $600,000 or more.

"Nah, I'm just the computer tech. If everything isn't running at 100%, I get a call to go see what the deal is. This one is fine, I just finished updating and backing up all the software," I explained, as his attention began to wander. "Hey, you look familiar. Don't I know you?"

Reed looked at me for a moment and said, "I don't think so pal, you must have me confused with some other guy."

"No really, I think I know your sister," I said.

That got his attention. "Tammy? How do you know her?" he asked.

"We used to party over by Andrews Square," I said, making a gesture like I was smoking a joint.

"Yeah, that's probably her. You're not one of her baby daddies are you?"

Wow. What a nice family!

"No, unfortunately, she never had eyes for me." I lied, though he seemed not to notice.

"She still lives there. What'd ya say your name was?" Reed asked me with a lisp most likely caused by his lack of several teeth.

"Kurt, Kurt Kummer" I responded, pointing to the name on my shirt with my left hand and sticking out my right one to shake his. He looked at me for a second and then gave me a firm handshake with his greasy hep C hand. Thank goodness I designed the skin gloves to be impenetrable to most bacteria and viruses!

"Oh yeah, I think I remember you. What's up Kurt?" Apparently, I wasn't the only liar in attendance.

"Not much. Same old shit, bigger pile, still no shovel to speak of. How about you? How have you been? You still partying?" I asked with a fake smile, giving him a wink.

He shook his head and then motioned toward the ADM behind us. "Nah, I stopped about a year ago. That's what I'm doing here, getting my new fix." was his response. Man, his teeth were gross. After examining the chips and brownish-yellow stains, I imagined his breath smelled like a shit that a Sasquatch took after eating a few rancid onions and maybe a dead walrus fetus. Whooooo!!!

"Ah, I see. How does that Evinall shit work for ya?" I inquired.

"It's great. Keeps me straight and it even helps me with my work. I've been holding down two jobs now because of that Evinall shit," he said, somewhat mocking the way I said it and sounding a little annoyed.

"I don't have the time or money to fuck around with junk or any other crap like that anymore. And I really don't have much time right now to chit chat either. I gotta run, but I'll see ya around if you're lucky." he said returning a wink. His mockery was obvious and started to make me reconsider beheading him. That piece of shit had no idea how close to the devil he stood. "Good seeing you Kurt Kummer. Hey, keep on coming," he said with a garbled, phlegm-choked chuckle, giving me a thumbs up. What an asshole! That might have just cost him his fucked up, filthy, troll-like head that no mother could love, even with help from all the crack and crystal meth in the world, I thought. Keep on coming. I'll be coming for you alright Richie, just you wait...

"You too, keep up the good work," I uttered as I walked away, holding my breath so I wouldn't have to smell Bigfoot's dead walrus shit.

I wondered what the second job he referred to was. The only other job I was aware of, besides delivering food, was burning properties to the ground that didn't belong to him, along with anyone unfortunate enough to be trapped inside. He probably didn't include that on his resume though. Even he wasn't THAT stupid. Or was he?

I put my leather gloves back on and carried my case under my arm to the parking lot across the street where Russ was intently watching.

"Everything cool?" he asked in his Papa Bear voice once I opened the door and got into my truck, which he was driving.

"It's all gravy, my friend. Let's go back and make some arsonist mitts."

"Roger that, Kurt Kumstain. You pulled that off nice and easy. You're really becoming a pro at the art of deception huh? He appeared to be a bigger piece of shit than I had imagined. I bet he smelled like Alcatraz on a rainy day."

I laughed. "Yeah, the guy was pretty ripe. Imagine what he smelled like when he was using? Probably went weeks without showering. Russ, I wish you could have seen his chompers. Oh boy does he have a nice case of methmouth! But he'll have all the time in the world to work on his personal hygiene after I see to it that they lock his ass up. This is going to be a lot fun buddy," I replied.

"So, you're not cutting the scumbag's dome off?" he asked sounding slightly disappointed.

"Nah, I think this one I'll send upstate. With any luck he'll bump into a relative of someone he left in a pile of soot and justice will be served that way, ya know a lock-in-a-sock?" I said with my notorious devilish smirk. "Trust me, I'd love nothing more than to fillet the prick on the sweltering-hot asphalt or give him a nudge as he peered over the edge of the Hancock building's roof, making a nice red stain all over St. James Ave., but I'm not going to." As Russ heard my reply, he suddenly got a silly look on his face that I knew all too well. I knew what was coming.

"Hey, that reminds me of a joke." Of course, it did, I thought. He continued, "So two EMT's arrive where a suicide jumper landed and splatted all over the sidewalk next to a skyscraper. One of them looks at the other, after removing the dead man's wallet from his pants and reading a card he had removed, pointing to the bloody mush all around them, and says, 'Hey, get a broom and start sweeping up this mess! This guy is a blood donor."

I was laughing before he even finished the joke. Russ was full of similar, tasteless jokes that he shared with me all of the time. Most of them he actually made up himself. He went on telling me another.

"What did the leper say to the hooker?" I was laughing too hard to ask for the punchline. "Keep the tip!" he answered.

This is how the ride back to my house went. Two men, conspiring to commit multiple felonies, who had just finished stalking and stealing fingerprints from their intended victim, not concerned in the least bit. No, instead we were telling horribly offensive jokes and laughing, without a care in the world shared between the two of us. But this is what usually goes on when I am in the company of the best friend, besides Eve, that I have ever had. We shared the same sick sense of humor that would offend most hardened criminals, that was a mixture of sarcasm, ball-busting, and wisecracks that the blue-collared citizens of Boston shared, men and women alike! Hardened folks like this living in my beloved Massachusetts would tear you to shreds with rapid-fire, witty remarks one minute, but then beat the shit out of any outsider who mistreated you the next! We worked hard, lived harder, but respected and loved each other the most. The way residents pulled and bonded together in the aftermath of the horrible Boston Marathon Bombings back on April 15, 2013, is proof of what I am stating. One of my uncles told me a story that took place in the following days of the tragedy. He was a few streets down from where the event occurred, helping a friend pick up a couch bought from an online ad. While the two of them were driving away with the couch tied to the roof, another car ran a red light and turned down the street they were on, almost hitting them. My uncle, who was driving, rolled his window down, sticking his middle finger out at the other driver, and shouted, "HEY!!! You almost hit me you fucking asshole!"

He went on saying the operator of the other vehicle slammed on his brakes, coming to a complete stop right next to my uncle's car, and yelled back, with his head hanging out his window, "Yeah?! Go fuck yourself ya fagot!" My uncle, never being a man to take lip from anyone, shot back saying, "You want to get out and come say that to my face you pussy?!"

This went on a few moments longer before the man who almost caused the accident finally said, "Hey, you know something? You're a REAAAAL fucking asshole. But I love you. I'm sorry man." My uncle told me, without even hesitating, he replied, "I love you too dickhead. Boston strong!" and he drove away.

That's just how it can be around Boston. Unfortunately, there's still racism, and the city is one of the most segregated in the country, despite being founded by red white and blue-blooded, patriotic, Yankees. The Red Sox were one of the very last Major League Baseball teams to sign an African- American player to their roster and former team president and owner, Tom Yawkey, was a known racist. One of the streets that Fenway Park is located on used to be famously named "Yawkey Way" until it was changed back to its former name, Jersey Street after Massachusetts residents protested that it be changed. And there is no shortage of organized crime history that we try not to think or talk about. From the Italian mobsters in the North End to the ruthless Latino gangs in East Boston to the nightly shootings and murders in Dorchester and Roxbury, and then the Irish crime organizations in Southie. The infamous Winter Hill Gang that was once run by that piece of shit Whitey Bulger was responsible for countless unspeakable crimes and ordered killings including Albert DeSalvo prison stabbing in Cedar Junction in 1973. You might know him better as The Boston Strangler. Yes, Whitey, in his messed up, sociopath's mind, wanted to send the message that HE was the only low-life allowed to murder and terrorize the city that put every cent he ever made in his pocket. He wasn't going to sit around while The Strangler was eating meals and sleeping with a roof over his head, paid for by the taxpayers of Massachusetts' dollars. So, he orders his hit, and like usual, it was carried out without a problem. What a nice guy, huh?!

But Bostonians are the proudest people you can find, as well as some of the smartest. The best universities and hospitals are found here. The lower and middle-class citizens work harder than any others I've seen anywhere else. We love our state's history, the good and the bad, we love our diverse heritages, despite the segregated city boroughs, we love our food like Sam Adams beer and New England clam chowdah, and we especially love our professional sports teams! Thankfully, they have returned the love by providing countless championships in all four major sports: baseball, basketball, football, and hockey. I wouldn't permanently live anywhere else. Nope, I'm a proud patriot from head to toe. But call me a "Masshole" only if the weight of your head is something you're looking to shed.

When we arrived back at my house in Franklin, Russ peeled the skin gloves off me, and I scanned them into the computer where I saved the images. We discussed our plan throughout the night, leaving no stone unturned and no detail overlooked. This was going to be a dangerous mission.

"Are you sure you're up for this?" Russ asked me with a serious look on his face.

"We can pull it off. It's not every day I feel good about torching a building, but I know I can handle it," I answered honestly.

The plan was simple; I would start a fire and leave Reed's fingerprints behind for arson investigators to discover. Russ expressed obvious concern after I recently had come close to burning my summer home down to the ground. I did my best to reassure him, and he seemed satisfied for the time being. My biggest worry, besides the safety of others, was making sure I wasn't spotted in the process. I wondered what Eve would think about what I was doing and the kind of person I was becoming. What would she say? Wherever she was, I hoped she was watching out over me as closely and lovingly as she did while she was still alive. She was my miracle, and that was exactly what I needed to pull off the stunt I had planned.

Chapter 8

Richard Reed did, in fact, live in his sister's apartment, as we were informed. It was a dumpy old colonial house converted into four different units. He and his sister lived on the first floor with her boyfriend and his two big pit bulls, nasty ones with the kind of big, dangling balls I despised. I don't just detest dog balls, but all animal balls. There are a few weird things that really bother me that might seem silly to someone who knows me, and my alter ego. Monkey genitals and their bare, oddly colored asses are another one. I mean why are baboon's rear ends that radiant blue color?! They practically glow, like a smurf with a spotlight up his ass.

Horses in general freak me out too because I was bitten by one at a petting zoo once. For no reason at all, as I stood checking out a woman in a short skirt leaning over the fence petting another horse, some cunt mare behind me bit me right on my shoulder! The solid right hook she received in return got me kicked out and forever banned from Southbridge Animal Farm. I also had a very traumatic acid experience in a barn full of horses when I was in my twenties, that contributes to my equine enmity as well.

My buddies and I were visiting a friend of ours, who was house-sitting for someone, even though she was strictly forbidden to have any guests over. After discovering that the four of us had each dropped a couple hits of "Mad Hatter" LSD, she invited us over to entertain her on what was looking to be a long and boring night. The homeowners informed her they would return sometime after midnight, but they returned earlier than expected, ruining all of our acid trips. We ran out the back door of the house before being spotted and headed across a vastly sprawling and poorly-lit front lawn towards a huge barn. Pulling the barn's front door open, me and my three hallucinating, yet giggling, friends slipped inside. We were four fools, completely oblivious to the primal horror being sheltered and waiting for us in the damp darkness we had just sought refuge in.

We shuffled around trying to find some kind of light source, but a good five minutes had passed with no luck, then five minutes more. Our laughter eventually turned to silence, an unsettling silence that quickly replaced naive amusement with the kind of doomsday panic that only a bad trip can inflict. That's when I heard the spine-tingling sound that paralyzed me where I stood. A loud, exhausted *HUFF* noise penetrated straight through my ears, then it reverberated and resonated deep inside the bone marrow of my cranium. It was accompanied by a gust of warm air as it wafted around my neck and head, instantly demanding each and every hair on my body to stand on end, and they complied. The stench of rotten fruit mixed with gingivitis-plagued morning breath rushed up and into my nostrils, instantly choking me while taking my breath away. The images of what had just made its terrifying presence known are too brutal to describe. The psychedelic visuals that are what one typically seeks when taking LSD did exactly what you pray won't happen during your trip: they turned from innocent to satanic. I knew, as I'm sure my friends had also suddenly realized, that my life had reached its end. What I had just heard was The Reaper's arrival, ushered in with the unmistakable stench of death. There was no mistaking it: my time had come.

My friend, whose nickname was "Hoover," was the one who, at last, found and flipped on a light switch. Standing eye level with me, weighing more than a ton, was one wide-eyed, frightened, and pissed off Clydesdale stallion! I am not ashamed to admit that I screamed like a little girl. I released an echoing shrill that was exactly the opposite of what the enormous beast in front of me wanted to hear. Of this, I was certain because his sinister, glossy eyes, that were the same hypnotizing shade of black that can only be found on the horns of Satan himself, suddenly swelled and locked onto mine. He returned my scream of dismay with one of his own, only much louder and longer. Rearing back, he bicycle-kicked his front legs and massive hooves towards me. The stable door prevented a successful assault, though it sent tremendous rumbling sound waves through me that almost knocked me on my ass.

As the other giant horses followed suit and acted in the same manner, I then realized that I wasn't the only one who's manhood had suddenly been tossed aside at discovery of the barn's occupants. All four of us were frantically screeching and glancing in all directions, our arms sticking straight out to our sides, fingers spread wide apart like lightning bolts were animating us!

I don't recall who, but one of us sprinted out the door, and the rest of us followed. As we continued running across the dew-dampened lawn, our screams were heard inside the house, and the downstairs lights all suddenly turned on. We also set off the motion lights that illuminated the front porch and walkway.

Hoover was the fastest and reached the perimeter fence first. It was a fence made of thick, wooden railroad ties linked together by three parallel rows of black wire. Unfortunately, Hoover's speed would prove to be his peril once he grabbed the top wire with both hands. His plan was to hurdle himself over, but three thousand volts of electricity meant to stop the horses from escaping put an abrupt end to his evacuation. Again, the air was filled with an awkward, awful man screams. I'd like to blame it on the LSD, or the sheer panic-stricken state the rest of us were in as the reason we all made the same humiliating mistake shortly after. Whatever was to blame, we all found ourselves lying on our backs in the mud, staring up at a cloudy night sky, desperately trying to catch our breaths after having the wind knocked out of us as the homeowners and our friend all watched in disbelief from the front porch of the house. It was one embarrassing nightmare after another.

So that is why I hate horses. I also dislike those wooden nutcrackers you see around the winter holidays, but I'm not going to explain why not now at least. I am not scared of any them, they just make me really uneasy. Nothing scares me anymore after Eve's passing, but animal balls, horses, and nutcrackers are what cause this serial killer's discomfort. Kind of funny isn't it?!

The type of apartment Reed and his sister lived in was common in Dorchester and, lucky for me, there was a condemned vacant lot three blocks away from their residence. Russ and I drove around the outskirts of Boston for six consecutive days until we finally decided that run-down, cockroach-infested apartment building would be the perfect one for me to set on fire. It was a crack house used by the local drug abusers and pushers, and one less crack house was something Dorchester desperately needed. On our reconnaissance mission, we estimated the distance between the crack house and its neighboring buildings was far enough apart to prevent any flames from carrying over by the wind and spreading. We factored in the average wind speed during the evening hours, and everything seemed to be safe enough. All we needed to do in preparation was clear the building of any squatters and ensure they were gone long enough for me to do my business inside. Russ came up with the idea.

The Boston police did a great job in protecting our beloved city, but there were instances when they opted out of responding to 911 calls. These included calls placed complaining about individuals lingering around known drug houses because, if officers did respond and cleared the premises, those individuals would simply wait for the police to leave before returning. How could we draw homeless drug-addicted vagrants out of the one place they felt safest? What could we use to bait them with, so they stayed out of harm's way? Russ' plan provided a simple enough answer. We would use something they desperately needed: money.

Russ proposed we recruit one other person to help us, someone he knew from working in the soup kitchens. His idea was to park a van down the street from the abandoned building that contained valuables in the back. We would lure them out using the van as bait. Russ got his homeless friend, who I'll refer to as "Danny," to relay a message to the occupants inside the crack house. His story would be as follows: he and one other man hijacked a box truck full of brand-new televisions, laptops, and cell phones earlier that day. Before his partner paid Danny and dropped him off, he had taken a call on his cell phone and got into an argument with the caller. Danny overheard him saying he would have to leave the truck parked outside his house overnight and meet the buyer of the products in the morning instead. Little did his partner know, but Danny knew exactly where he lived, and it was not far from the crack house. After getting dropped off, he used some of his money to rent a moving truck and planned to steal the already stolen goods, but he needed a few extra hands to do it quickly and not get busted. That was going to be his pitch, we just had to hope it was good enough to peak their interests.

I searched the internet and found a cheap box truck for sale and paid cash for it using a fake I.D. After I had the truck, all I needed to do was load it. Of course, I wasn't going to fill it full of expensive electronics. Instead, I went on a shopping spree at Sav-Alot Warehouse and bought food items, packages of socks and underwear, as well as healthcare products like soap, shampoo, and vitamins. Russ and I packed the merchandise in unmarked cardboard boxes and taped them shut. I even slipped a couple boxes of Evinall in them, hoping at least one person might take it and clean themselves up. I also hoped that when it was discovered, there were no valuables in the truck, the looters would be satisfied with the items I substituted regardless. Otherwise, Danny would have to make haste and get his ass out of there.

With the truck loaded, I drove it with Russ following me and parked it about three blocks away from our target house. The back latch had a padlock on it and was reinforced with chains and another lock. With our bait in place, it was time to get our helper up to speed on everything.

We decided to carry out our plan on a Saturday night, the reason was, maybe fewer people would be at the target building on a weekend night. Russ had to work, but that afternoon he and Andy met me near Andrews Square. I was introduced simply as Russ' "friend" as they both entered my pickup truck. Danny sat in the front and immediately I felt his presence. I feel bad saying this, but he did, in fact, look and smell very much homeless. Perhaps he would take a shower and get a new change of clothes after we paid him for his help. Russ and I went over the plan three times and made him rehearse his lines about ten. For a man living on the streets, he was quite witty and smart. I understood why Russ chose him and my heart went out to the man.

When we finally felt we had everything memorized and were confident in Danny's understanding, Russ said goodbye and left for work. It was approaching dinner time, and he was in high demand. That made me wonder if Danny was hungry. I asked him, and he stared down at his feet, a frown on his face seemed to point out the obvious had hurt his feelings. Immediately, I apologized for being naive and felt my face flush from embarrassment. There was one of those chain steakhouses close by, and that was where we went. I treated him to a nice big dinner, which he inhaled faster than I'd ever seen a person eat before in my life, and then we headed back to the box truck.

It was dark out as we sat there for a minute before I made one last request. I wanted Danny to signal me, as he exited the condemned building so that I knew he successfully managed to get everyone to leave. There was a Patriots hat on the back seat that he reached back and grabbed, putting it on. He looked at me, lowered his head, and tipped the hat, indicating our signal was decided.

"Well good luck and please be careful," I said with a nod.

"Thank you, I will be," he reassured me.

I parked my truck a block away from the house and got ready. Richard Reed's skin gloves were in the metal briefcase, carefully wrapped in wax paper material to protect them. After I had them on, I put my ski mask on the top of my head and watched out of the windshield for Danny to appear. A few minutes later he came walking down the sidewalk and entered the house. He was in there for twenty minutes when I finally started to worry. Did they not buy his story? Were they beating him up or worse, had they killed him? Maybe he was doing drugs with them, but Russ assured me that Danny was clean. Whatever was happening, it wasn't happening fast enough. Finally, the front door opened and out walked four men. Danny was the last one out and, as they walked down the porch steps and turned, heading in the direction of the box truck, Danny lifted his hat up, ran his fingers back through his greasy hair, and put it back on, giving me the green light.

I pulled my ski mask over my face, got out of the truck, and went back to the toolbox in the bed of my truck. There was the five-gallon container of gasoline I had filled up earlier and a couple of rags next to it. Lifting the container with one hand, I grabbed the rags in my other and hurried across the street. I hustled up the porch steps and kicked the door open and walked backward from room to room, pouring the gasoline in one constant line until I came out the front door again.

I also doused the staircase until I reached the door to the second-floor unit. This one was locked, but thanks to termite damage, it splintered easily at the latch when I kicked it, and I was inside in no time. The apartment had disgusting, old, stained mattresses lining each wall, forming a square in the middle of the living room. It reeked of human waste, and I became nauseous.

I stood in the center of the main room and placed the gas can down. There was about one gallon left in it, and so I twisted up one rag and snaked it down through the nozzle. Next, I removed my leather gloves and went about touching windows, doorknobs, the railing heading back downstairs, the areas around the kitchen and bathroom sinks, and then finally the front door. Nobody said this was going to be a sanitary job. I took a Zippo lighter out of my pocket, lit it, and tossed it in front of me straight through the main doorway. If anything, the fire investigators would find that and get the fingerprints they needed.

With a *WHOOSH* of energy, a flame took off and retraced the trail I had left. As long as the first floor caught fire nicely, the rest would follow suit, and the whole structure should burn as planned.

Nobody was in sight as I sprinted back across the street and over to where my truck was parked. I sped off down the road in the direction of the box truck. It was still there, right where we had left it. The truck faced me as I passed, and I could see movement in the back. Shadows were bending, as they rummaged through the cargo, illuminated by a distant streetlight a few hundred yards away. It was done! I yanked off my ski mask and deeply inhaled a breath of much needed fresh air. My whole body felt electrified. Wow, I actually enjoyed that! It was getting scary how much committing the same crimes I punished my victims for became easier and easier for me to carry out. What if there was another Nero out there somewhere, hunting behind the night shadows, watching me commit my sins and planning to hunt down and eventually kill me? Such atrocious deeds were precisely what I was taught throughout my entire life NOT to do. It felt so wrong yet so incredibly right. The feeling I had was unlike anything any drug gave me. It was a feeling of power, even more than that of being filthy rich and successful. This was a new high I experienced, and I absolutely loved it!

Chapter 9

Two days after the fire had left the condemned building in a charred pile of soot-covered rubble, Richard Reed was formally arrested for arson and taken into custody. Russ forwarded me the story in an email that was titled, "Congratulations." Two months after that, Reed was sentenced to ten to fifteen years in prison. We got the bastard! His prints were discovered on the lighter just as I knew they would be, and Reed couldn't provide an alibi. His sister was out with her boyfriend, so Reed must have been home alone while I was setting him up.

It felt so good taking down a loser like Reed. He had been living a double life, much like I do, but had caused pain and suffering to the innocent. Justice had been served.

The next person I targeted was so big, so bold that his downfall sent a clear message to all the other non-contributors in the city that nobody was beyond the law. Well, nobody besides me of course! One question lingered in the back of all the free felons' minds living in the Boston area, as well as it did in mine; "Who was going to be next?"

Joseph Yoder was the answer to that question. He was as corrupt and deceitful as a politician could get, and yet he managed to carry out his dirty business unscathed, hiding behind a phony smile much like the other city councilman. I knew he had some pretty impressive names in his pocket, and I was extremely eager to set him up.

Yoder was also the proud owner of an off-the-beaten-path piece of property that Russ and I referred to as "Amphetamine Acres." There was an abandoned, powder blue farmhouse with a sun-scorched, tar and gravel, sunken roof set at the end of a long, twisting, dirt driveway. Fractured window shutters dangled crookedly from the sides of most of the broken windows. The chimney had only three-quarters of its original form still intact, as the top layers of brick had crumbled off and plummeted to the ground below decades before Yoder acquired the lot. Most of the paint was cracked and flaking on all the wooden shingles; baked and beaten off by the scorching suns of summers past. Concord grape and poison ivy vines sprouted and crept up the foundation. They relentlessly snaked behind the shingles, causing them to lift apart. Crabgrass, ragweed, and dandelions encompassed the two-bedroom dwelling and sprawled outwards in all directions. Some maple saplings even popped up inside, just below the windows where the sun's rays penetrated long enough for them to grow! The entire structure was one strong breeze away from completely collapsing.

It sat on a hill overlooking Route 95 in Foxboro, Ma thirty miles outside of Boston. Every day, thousands of commuters unknowingly sped past rows of wooden stables, settled just thirty feet away behind a thinly wooded area, that housed hundreds of ostriches inside. Where the last row ended, a barn containing feed and hay also housed several more of the largest birds on Earth.

But the house, stables, and barn were all just a cover for Joe Yoder's crystal meth laboratory. I've been chomping at the bit to take the scumbag down, ever since he ridiculed my life's work while going off on a drunken tangent at a charity dinner event, we both attended years ago. He claimed Evinall robbed sick and vulnerable addicts of their lives, in my greed- motivated ploy to get rich. I totally despised the man.

His name would be on the ballot of the election taking place a few months after Russ and I had added him to our target list. That meant he was out making the rounds of public ass-kissing to assure his re-election. Tracking him down at a pro-am golf tournament, I approached him and announced he was positively getting my vote, extending my hand outwards. He hesitated for a moment as if waiting for me to say more. I stood there smiling until I finally received his firm handshake. The feeling of my powerful grip around his much smaller hand gave me instant gratification, so I applied a bit more pressure, and he suddenly realized who I was.

I proposed we should let bygones be bygones and he agreed, vigorously shaking my hand up and down while thanking me for my support. I made sure to say, "No, thank you, Joe," before retracting my hand. It almost seemed too easy. The poor sucker had no idea what was just stolen from right under his nose, nor what was inevitably coming his way. I would have given an arm and a leg to see his face when the police apprehended him and read him his rights.

Yoder's family had owned that ranch for generations. It was previously maintained by one of his uncles, who he hadn't spoken to in almost twenty years. This is why it baffled Yoder when he inherited the property after his uncle had passed away. Not knowing what to do at first with the run-down farm, Joe got the idea of converting it into a narcotics factory, inspired by a popular television show he watched. He paid top dollar to hire a crew of men who never asked questions and always kept their mouths shut. They built a basement in the barn, ventilated it with exhaust ducts, set up workbenches, and installed the security cameras around the perimeter. Two 'cooks,' who made the methamphetamine, set up the lab equipment. Joe loved the fact he could monitor everything right from his cell phone, and he kept a very close eye on his smoothly run operation. Finally, he purchased two hundred ostriches, from a breeder in Georgia, and had them shipped up to Foxboro. If anyone ever asked, he raised them for their meat, hide, and feathers.

Inside the barn were two rows of stalls lining the left and right-side walls. A staircase going down to the lab was centered in the middle of the floor. To conceal the existence of the basement, a twelve by eight-foot steel slab was positioned over the lone entrance, using a bulldozer to move it around. Then, to hide the metal plate, a six-ton pile of bird feed was dumped on top of it. It was pushed aside in the morning to allow the cooks and guard to enter the lab, and then back over the plate in the evening when the kitchen was closed. To the average person, it appeared to be a typical farm with nothing standing out of the ordinary.

The night before I raided the place, on October 29th, Russ and I spent hours scoping out the area and rigged up sixteen separate cakes of fireworks, strategically placing them about the property where they would attract the most attention. Ten rows of twenty stables ran along the far-right side of the field, and most of them were occupied. The last thing I wanted was for a rogue, roman candle ball to land near one and ignite the hay inside. Our reconnaissance mission went smoothly, and Russ and I agreed I should be able to infiltrate the lab with a moderate amount of difficulty. It wasn't a walk through the park, but it was definitely doable. We counted six men and eight security cameras I needed to get past. It was all about careful planning and precise timing, two areas that I excelled in.

At approximately 5:15pm, I drove my black pickup truck down an old access road that ran parallel to the highway. Then I pulled off the side and onto the shoulder where I left it. Acres of conservation land lined both sides of the road until finally ending where an electric fence marked the beginning of Yoder's property.

My backpack was stuffed full of useful items like wire cutters, night vision goggles, smoke grenades, and duct tape. I was ready for anything! I made it over the fence by climbing a nearby tree, that had a large branch overhanging the other side, and jumped down where Yoder's land began. Hustling in a crouched position to a cluster of trees, that was the last line of cover available before reaching an open field of dead grass, I came upon a sprawling meadow. It was about thirty yards wide and led right up to the barn. Bales of decomposing hay were scattered all around outside, and several broken-down wooden carts littered the area as well. Six cameras were attached to pressure treated timber posts around the perimeter, with two more mounted on opposite ends of the barn. Those posts were the only new lumber on the property. The rest of the wooden structures showed blatant signs of rot, as the stable doors looked like they were ready to fall apart at any moment.

I took my position, wearing my black ski mask, with a gas mask dangling around my neck, hugging a chilly, knobby, red maple tree. Peering through night-vision goggles, I scanned the area for the patrolling guards. All-in-all I had counted four armed men; two patrolling the perimeter, one at the barn door, and the last guarding the two cooks in the basement. Six men total meant twelve eyes I needed to avoid while taking out each guard one at a time. I made one last equipment check and tightened the straps on my backpack before removing the pair of leather gloves I wore to protect Yoder's mitts.

The gentleman defending the barn door was about twenty yards away from me. Try to picture Willie Nelson's corpse decked out from head to toe in camouflage Bass Pro Shop apparel, with a mouthful of sunflower seeds that he would spit out every twenty seconds or so. This was effortless to him since the number of teeth remaining in his head was less than a dozen. He would stop whistling, what I believe was Rick Astley's "Never Gonna Give You Up!" and spew a wad of shells out through a gap in the front of his teeth.

Willie was built on a tiny frame, standing no more than five feet six inches tall. If he weighed a hundred and fifty pounds, then I weigh ten thousand. That was the menacing force Yoder hired to protect his illegal operation. He had possessed unrivaled martial arts skills, or maybe he could transform into a giant mutant because he posed absolutely no physical threat whatsoever. I tucked my long-sleeved black cotton shirt into the waistband of my matching black sweatpants. In my right hand, I held my trusty machete. My combat boots were tied tight, and I was ready to go.

Waiting for Willie to turn the corner and walk out of sight, I silently approached the side of the barn, where a wooden power breaker box was attached. Just as I was about to throw the switch, it started to snow. It was October 30th and already snowing. That's New England for you.

The power outage sent a message to Yoder's cell phone and, within two minutes, Willie's phone rang. On the opposite side of the barn, I heard him answer and, judging by his stammering, it was obvious his boss was not happy. I quietly made my way back around the corner to the left side of the barn, where I knelt behind one of the old, crippled, wooden carts and waited for my opportunity. After another three minutes, the two patrolling guards arrived, jogging down the dirt trail.

"What the fuck is up with the power?" the goon on the left asked Willie, placing his hands on his knees, trying to catch his breath.

"Shit, the boss called and said it's not an outage," he replied.

The two sweaty guards looked at each other confused and asked Willie "So what's that mean?"

69

"It means somebody's cut the power numbnuts!" he shouted.

At that moment I sprang out and yelled, "Yeah, ME!"

With one swipe I beheaded the guard on the right. Just as the other drew his pistol, I grabbed his arm and swung it around his back, bringing my blade up to his neck. I took him hostage before he could even fully comprehend what was happening.

There we stood, Willie with his 9mm aimed at me, as I was pressing my machete into his colleague's throat. It had to have been the cold chill of the razor-sharp blade on his skin that made him drop his gun. Then, just as Willie started to say, "Now let's not do anything stupid," I shoved my hostage forward as hard as I could, causing the two of them to collide. In a panic, Willie accidentally fired his gun, and the shot grazed the side of his partner's face, just as they both fell to the ground. The one guard clenched his arms around his head as he lay face down, pinning Willie on his back beneath him. I quickly plunged my blade through the center of his back and into Willie's chest. They both squirmed for a couple of seconds and then died. Oddly, I could not help but think of those little plastic swords, with pineapples and cherries, that are put in Mai Tais.

Pressing my foot on that dirtbag's ass, I pulled my machete from the short stack of corpses and wiped the blood off on the back of his pants. This went smoother than I thought. I checked my watch, it was 5:48pm. I had the pyrotech timers set to go off at 6:15pm, a perfect time to draw as much attention as possible from local authorities. The only thing left to do was to get inside the meth lab and plant Yoder's prints on a few surfaces, and then my work would be finished. Lifting my gas mask up I thought, "Eve, if you're feeling angelic, now would be a great time to watch over my crazy ass!"

Inside Willie's front pants pocket were the keys to the bulldozer that was parked behind the barn, as well as the key to the lock on the barn door itself. There was no need for that because the plan was to smash through the doors, move the pile of feed to expose the meth lab's entrance, and drop two smoke grenades down to clear the place out.

I ran and hopped on the bulldozer then started it up. The controls were simple enough to operate in the fading evening light, and once I turned it on and faced the barn door, I thrust it into full throttle and surged forward like a charging bull. Wood splintered and tumbled down around me, as I plowed through with ease. The two dozen ostriches that were in the stalls inside were frightened by my sudden, unexpected entrance, as they began squawking and ruffling their thickly feathered wings.

Next, I lowered the bulldozer's bucket until it sat about three inches above the ground to account for the thickness of the steel plate. It took two trips back and forth to push most of the feed pile off, exposing the metal plate. Dropping the bucket flat on the ground, I caught the edge of the steel slab and slowly pushed forward until the staircase was revealed. Suddenly, a bullet whizzed by my head followed by another, that ricocheted off the blade of the bulldozer. I jumped down off the machine and took cover behind its rear, where I was out of the line of fire. I pulled my backpack off, dug out two silver smoke grenades, pulled the pins, and lobbed them over the front of the bulldozer and down the stairwell.

Up to that moment, everything had gone exactly as planned. What happened next would prove to be one of the few moments in my life that I wish I could do over. As the guard and cooks stumbled around the smoke-filled drug lab, one of them knocked over a Bunsen burner while temporally blinded by thick, suffocating smoke. The entire basement laboratory quickly went up in flames, trapping the three criminals in a fiery pit just below my feet. In an attempt to contain and possibly smother the fire by sealing the lab shut with the metal slab, I got back into the bulldozer and was about to start it up when *BOOM!* An explosion from the lab blasted me right out of the seat, knocking me to the floor. I had nearly been knocked unconscious, but luckily, there was plenty of bird feed nearby to break my fall.

I had to get out of there and fast. All I heard was a deafening, high pitched ringing sound in my ears, as my vision struggled to become clear again. I pulled myself up on a nearby stable and staggered my way toward the doors I drove through. The heat was so intense! Flaming chemicals spewed up and out from the basement, like a science fair volcano, igniting the hay that was all over the ground. It wouldn't be long before the whole structure was engulfed in flames. My sweatshirt was glowing from all the little curling bits of cotton singeing from the blast. The gigantic birds were barking frantically and kicking at the rotted, wooden doors until one of them burst open, and a tremendous ostrich barreled down the center aisle making his escape. The others followed suit, and one-by-one they broke out of their stalls in fear induced panic, as the fire spread quickly throughout the property.

The thick smoke billowed everywhere making it almost impossible to see my hand in front of my face. Breathe, the key was to breathe. It's amazing how much oxygen fire consumes. Suffocation from smoke inhalation claims more victims than the actual flames. I finally found my way out of the barn. I gasped for air but covered my mouth with my sleeves to try to filter out the smoke that swirled around outside with help from a flurry-filled October night breeze.

EEEEERRRRREEEE.......BOOM!

The firework displays I had staged, had been set off.

REEEEEEAAARRRRTTT...BOOM!

Suddenly, the whole ground rumbled and shook around me! Looking ahead, I saw a stampede of squawking ostriches charging frantically right toward me! The majority of the two hundred birds had broken free and were running rampant. Sprinting as fast as I possibly could, I bolted across the field towards the tree line. I felt the massive fowl prancing past me, darting left and right, screeching and screaming. It felt like I was running with a herd of dinosaurs!

Taking cover behind a tree at the last moment, I barely managed to avoid getting trampled. One of the birds ran straight into the electric fence and got stuck. It fluttered and flapped its wings as it violently kicked its powerful legs. After landing a few solid kicks to one of the fence posts, it freed itself and fell, taking three rows of electrified wires with it. She jumped back up on her feet and ran off, disappearing into the conservation woodlands before her. The other ostrich saw the new opening in the fence and made a run for it, easily hopping over as they proceeded in the same direction. Once the herd had moved past me, I also ran and jumped back over the fence and headed off in the direction of my truck.

Next, I heard a loud squeal and smash come from somewhere in the distance. At first, I thought the fireworks were the source of the sounds, but then I heard it again and recognized it as cars colliding with each other. The herd had crossed the access road and ran directly onto route 95! Oncoming cars didn't react fast enough to the dreadful scene that was suddenly sprung upon them. Instead, they swerved and collided into each other. The flames chased the animals off the ranch and led them directly into rush hour traffic, on one of the busiest highways in the Boston area.

A tanker truck, filled with recycled cooking oil, jack-knifed and tipped over, spilling a riptide of nasty, smelly, oil all over the highway, making the already wet pavement even more slippery. Car wrecks were happening all over the place, and terrified drivers and passengers witnessed dozens of massive, feathery, birds get absolutely destroyed, as they were struck by out-of-control vehicles. Some rolled onto the hoods of the cars and spider-webbed windshields. Others were pulverized with a *POOF!* of feathers when they met the grills of pickup trucks and tractor-trailers. Broken glass, feathers, blood, and cooking oil covered everything. The fiery, flurry-filled, night sky provided a beautiful backdrop for the incredible carnage.

I stood behind a fallen oak tree and watched in horror as the "Devil's Night Disaster" played out before me. The fireworks finally stopped, not that they were needed anymore. The whole ordeal lasted about twenty-two minutes, but it seemed to have lasted a lifetime. Eighty-four automobiles were damaged, three hundred gallons of cooking oil was dispersed, one hundred-and-six ostriches were massacred, but it was the two human lives that were lost that would haunt me for the rest of my life.

Andrew LaPlante and Lindsay Pastino were best friends since they were toddlers, and now they shared an apartment in Quincy. They were not lovers though because Andrew was gay. He came out of the closet to his inner circle of close friends a week before, but he was terrified to make the announcement to his parents. Lindsay, being the supportive friend she was, offered to go with him to make the revelation to his parents over dinner at their house. They were driving there in Andrew's big blue Dodge pickup truck when the disaster struck. The two friends were joking and laughing about the worst possible scenarios as only best friends did. Lindsay pulled a tube of cherry red lipstick out from her pocketbook and instructed Andrew to pucker up. He smacked his lips together as she applied the makeup. They laughed, and both agreed that he looked better in it than she. Andrew sat forward admiring himself in the rearview mirror when Lindsay screamed.

BAM!

A nine-foot, three-hundred-pound flightless bird exploded on the grill, then rolled up across the hood, indenting an impression into the windshield. Panic most likely caused Andrew to jerk the wheel to his right, because the speeding Ram truck swerved abruptly, and then barrel rolled over and over again before coming to a stop up against a tree.

The truck looked like an accordion, and its two passengers were smashed and compacted inside. Gasoline and oil leaked out quickly, and then a fire suddenly ignited that originated from the engine block. It was only a few minutes before the roaring flames consumed them both. Their screams and squeals haunt my dreams to this day, as I witnessed firsthand, two innocent victims lose their lives due to the catastrophe I had set in motion.

Lost in a surreal nightmare, I made my way through the thickly wooded forest to the dirt embankment where I left my truck. Climbing in, I tossed my masks, machete, and backpack on the passenger's seat. With my eyes clenched shut, I rocked back and forth in my seat, letting out a deep sigh of disbelief. That was definitely not how I had imagined the night would end. Tears streamed down my cheeks, as the distant sounds of police and emergency sirens signaled it was time for me to get a move on, so I drove away and headed home. I would have to do a lot of soul-searching before fighting crime on my own again.

Part 2

Chapter 10

The remnants of Hurricane Marco were dissipating as it shifted back out over the Atlantic, off the coast of northeast United States. The overall damage it inflicted was minimal throughout Massachusetts, though it caused several flight and shipping cancellations and delays. One of those ships was a cargo ship named "Gypsy Wind" which departed from the Port of Libreville, Gabon two days earlier. She had docked six hours later than scheduled, in Boston Harbor, due to the storm. Its workers and passengers eagerly disembarked, but none of them were happier and more anxious to step foot on solid ground than Brutus Boone and Jacob Stills and with good reason. The two seasoned criminals were escorting a very precious delivery to their impatiently waiting boss. Their trip to East Africa was extremely taxing on the two thugs. They spent a total of six days on a dangerous excursion into the sweltering jungles of the Congo to locate a remote primate conservation site. There they followed strict, extremely detailed instructions to obtain a specific specimen. The return trip made the flight there riding in coach seem much more appealing. Cramped sleeping quarters and turbulent seas provided more nauseous misery than anything they imagined.

Brutus walked ahead of his much smaller partner in a thoughtful attempt to shield him from the imminent scorn they were about to receive.

"Where's the freight manifest?" they were greeted with.

Brutus quickly pulled a yellow piece of paper from his jacket pocket and placed it into the equally massive hand of his employer. He unfolded it, scanned it quickly, and for a moment seemed to be pleasantly satisfied with the report.

"You know the transportation arrangements I made clearly stated that you were to meet here at 6:45am, not 12:38pm right?" the man in charge asked, calmly looking at his watch.

"Boss, the hurricane... it was the captain's decision to sail around the storm. I told that stubborn prick to stay the course, but he refused and locked us in our cabin because he felt threatened. He said we were acting aggressively because Jacob and I..."

"Enough! Just gather your belongings and get the fuck in the van before I show you aggressive!"

Silas Wilde was as intimidating and as physically powerful as were the apes he spent most of his life researching. Standing six feet six inches tall, and weighing just under three-hundred-pounds, he was frequently mistaken for a professional football player or wrestler. Primates were his passion in life though, and he worked as the head primatologist at the San Diego Zoo for fifteen years until he was disgracefully terminated. A fellow co-worker reported to management, Wilde's inhumane and unethical experiment methods.

An investigation performed by management supported the claims, and criminal charges were pressed. The charges were eventually dropped, however when it was discovered the police had tampered with a piece of the collected evidence. The entire ordeal made him an outcast, even without a conviction, and left him no chance of obtaining a respectable career in that field again.

Silas moved to the opposite side of the country, hoping to leave his tarnished reputation behind, but before he did, he sought out his revenge. He followed the man who filed the original complaint home one day and brutally beat him to a pulp right on his own front steps. Fearing for his life, no new charges were filed.

Silas approached one of the ship's crewman and handed him the freight manifest. A forklift sorting cargo then carried a wooden crate over to Silas's white van and carefully loaded it in. Neither the frigid rain nor the ship's tardy arrival prevented a little sinister smile from briefly appearing on his face. He finally had everything he needed to move forward with his most brilliant project yet. Nothing stood in his way at that time.

Inside the van, Brutus and Jacob sat in silence as Silas hopped in the driver's seat and drove away. They were well paid for their efforts as they were promised, but there was something about the man they worked for that made them quite nervous. It wasn't his enormous size, given Brutus easily passed as his body double. It wasn't the intense look he always had nor the multiple scars that encompassed his shaved head, like those made from wearing a crown of thorns, that made the two men squirm in their seats either. The reason for their uneasiness was what he had sent them halfway around the world to retrieve and the thoughts of what he might do with it. There was a creature in their van, a mere few feet behind them that could curdle milk with just one glance: A full-grown cannibalistic chimpanzee with half of his face missing.

During his first year working as a member of San Diego Zoo's primate research team, Silas was given the task of observing eight male chimps in a family of twenty. He studied the hierarchy of the group and its chain of command. The alpha in the group was a twenty-eight-year-old brute named Tonka. Only a few times a year was Tonka's position challenged by one of the younger adults in the family, but he held onto his crown firmly, and his reign seemed secure for the foreseeable future. That was until Silas noticed intense frustration growing inside the teenage male, they called Cain. Cain established his dominance over the other six males, and when he finally grew to full-size, he was slightly smaller than Tonka. Adult chimpanzees are extremely powerful when fully grown. Compared to an adult human they are easily two to three times stronger. Silas predicted in his reports that a power battle between the two males was inevitable.

Cain decided it was his time to step into the ring with the undisputed champ, one day during summer vacation when the zoo was at its busiest. The commotion was heard from the opposite side of the park as onlookers watched in horror. Squaring off, they screamed and beat their fists on tree trunks and the fake stone walls. Cain quickly overpowered his opponent and landed a dozen well-placed punches to his face and throat. Tonka tried to retreat, but Cain relentlessly chased him down and continued to hammer away with a flurry of devastating punches that the staff later learned caused severe brain hemorrhaging. When at last the onslaught was over,

Tonka laid sprawled out and motionless in the shade just below the visitor's viewing window. Never before had any brawl ended with the death of one of the contestants. Cain did not seem content with his victory, however. What happened next caused all those who witnessed to gasp in utter disgust and shock. After catching his breath, Cain sat in the shade beside Tonka where he tore open his belly and ate his insides.

Cannibalism is not completely unheard of in the chimpanzee world. In the Central African jungles, neighboring families sometimes have turf wars were members of the winning party choose to celebrate by consuming the flesh of the losers. But such behavior never takes place between family members, much less by the typically tamer chimps who live in captivity.

Cain was tranquilized and separated for closer observation. CAT scans showed no brain abnormalities, and the blood work produced not a trace of sickness or disease. With no logical explanation for his disturbing behavior, he was eventually allowed to rejoin the group, but his return was seen as a threat, and his authority was immediately challenged. The other males joined together and launched surprise attacks on Cain, but somehow, he managed to hold his own. Both adult and adolescent family members threw rocks, food scraps, and even feces at him. As the frequency of the fights grew, so did the level of intensity. The belief shared by the zoologists and primatologists was eventually the battling would stop, and things would return to normal. They were all terribly mistaken.

Silas was the one who routinely delivered the freshly chopped produce for the chimps' breakfast each morning, and Cain was usually the first one to eat. So, the morning he failed to appear, Silas knew something was wrong, and it was he who found him in the corner of the habitat after all the other chimps were corralled inside for a headcount. Cain apparently was ganged up on overnight. They savagely pulverized him and left him for dead, and when Silas saw the way his body was positioned, he was certain Cain wouldn't survive. On his back with both arms crookedly bent upward covering his face and head, Cain remained motionless in a large, red, muddy puddle. Bloody bite marks were visible up and down his entire body. His genitals had been partially bitten off, and so were two of his fingers. The top half of his right ear was not just missing, but never recovered, suggesting that it had been consumed. But the most terrifying and serious of all his injuries was what they had done to his face. Both the top and the bottom of his mouth were chewed off, exposing his upper and lower gums and teeth, resembling a ghastly joker's grin.

It wasn't until after he reached down to carefully lift up his torso that Silas heard a faint whimper escape from behind Cain's clenched teeth. The unexpectedness of the moan caused Silas to pull back quickly. Unable to blink for several moments, he stared in awe that anything could have survived such a vicious punishment. But he was alive, barely. A pop-up stretcher was brought in, and Cain was carefully placed on it and then carried off to the veterinarian's office. The surgery lasted eight hours and, thanks to the remarkable efforts of the doctors, he survived.

Silas made it a point to visit the recovering patient as often as his busy schedule allowed him to. He could not help feeling guilty and even a little bit responsible for what had happened. It was not during one of his shifts, but they were all under his general supervision, and he had observed the tension between Cain and the other apes build up over the months prior to the attack.

Cain was moved to a more suitable animal intensive care facility not far from the zoo. As days turned into weeks, small signs of improvement began to show. Progressive movements in his arms and legs were optimistic signs. His head was almost entirely bandaged up with only a pair of sedated eyes visible. Everyone was curious as to what he would look like once the wrappings were removed. The doctors reported they had done everything in their power to repair as much of the damaged tissue as was possible, but there was only so much they could do. Cain breathed with the help of a respirator and was fed through tubes for the first three months. After that, physical therapy helped strengthen his arms and legs again. The long journey down recovery road was just beginning.

The deformed chimp never again saw the inside of the San Diego Zoo due to his gruesome appearance. Even though curiosity may have spiked ticket sales for a short while, his presence would suggest unsafe living conditions and present more questions than the

Zoo's staff cared to answer. When Cain finally walked without any assistance, the animal curator, Walter Freeman, gave him up for adoption. By then, Silas developed a strong bond with Cain (since he seemed to be the only person who wasn't bothered by his disfigured face) and he decided he would be the one to adopt him.

Most of Cain's head was covered in scars of all shapes and sizes. His eyes appeared devoid of life like the lights had been turned off upstairs. A cold unsettling stare held Silas's gaze as Cain appeared to be constantly grinning with his protruding gums and big yellow teeth. Most people couldn't stomach the sight of the mutilated creature, but Silas was not an average person. Not only did he not mind, but he was also excited to call the nightmarish primate his friend, as they both grew to trust each other completely.

Ten years passed, Silas and Cain became inseparable. Then disaster tore into their lives without warning. The criminal charges brought against Silas meant the two of them would be separated if he was found guilty, so Silas arranged for Cain to go back to the jungles of the Congo and stay on a protected private reserve with an animal trainer he knew well from his years studying abroad.

William "Will" Shepherd was rumored to have trapped every species of man-eating predator that lived in Africa, and no matter what the task called for, his talents could always be purchased if the price was right. He received a seventy-five-thousand-dollar compensation for the fifteen months he had Cain in his care. During that time Shepherd drank heavily, and his behavior became more erratic than usual. Caring for the four-foot, one-hundred, and fifty pounds, knuckle-dragging freak became a nuisance to Will because he had to make special accommodations for Cain, keeping him separate from the other apes inhabiting his land as per the special request from Silas. It became a full-time job for him, and gradually the sight of Cain began to enrage Will. One night he tranquilized the Cain, strapped him down on a wooden workbench, and used a chainsaw blade file to grind all of his teeth down into cone-shaped, pointed fangs. He told Silas he did it for his protection, to intimidate the other apes and guarantee his safety. His demonic makeover had been completed, and he was ready to strike fear into the hearts of all who were unfortunate enough to cross paths with him.

What was the significance of his return to Silas now? Wouldn't he live a better life roaming freely in the jungles of the Congo? What bizarre plans could Silas possibly have for the gruesome ape? Those questions left Brutus and Jacob completely speechless as Dr. Silas Wilde explained the answers in detail as they headed west through the whipping rain on the Massachusetts Turnpike.

Chapter 11

The rain continued without much letting up for the sixty-five-minute drive from Boston Harbor to exit 10 off the Mass. Pike. Silas, Brutus, and Jacob were on their way to a secluded farmhouse nestled on a ten-acre spread in the rural town of Oxford, Ma. Silas had purchased for a reasonable price, due to the repair work it needed. Silas and Brutus had a ten-year history working together on several previous instances ranging from routine illegal firearm dealings to week-long poaching excursions in both Central and South America. Jacob was a newly hired helper, but Brutus knew him well and had vouched for him after Silas had surprisingly wasted one of his closest hands for what he thought was an inexcusable comment, opening the new position on his staff.

Brutus witnessed the shocking execution first-hand months earlier when Silas suddenly returned to the farm in a rage of unchecked emotions. He was working on the barn renovations with Bobby "The Mouth" Lawler, a sarcastic, wise-cracking mechanic who could fix just about anything, and two other hired men. One was Tony Catalozzi, a compulsive gambler who lacked the collective patience most professional gamblers possess and whose short temper accompanied his long criminal record. And then there was Mack Chestercove, an auto body shop owner who was always getting in over his head and biting off more than he can chew with loan sharks and bookies. The four men worked on converting the large barn that sat adjacent to the main house into Silas' new research laboratory, as well as a domicile for an occupant not yet revealed to them. They called Bobby "The Mouth" because he never knew when to keep his shut and, in more times than not, he found himself squaring off with an insulted co-worker, random civilian, or at times, the occasional police officer who was tired of the thug's smart-ass remarks. Brutus didn't mind Bobby's obnoxious comments that much though, he mostly found it amusing to watch just how far he could push someone's buttons before making them snap.

Silas was last seen replacing loose floorboards on the house's front porch that afternoon before he came thundering down the driveway with fire in his eyes. In a blind fury, he paced back and forth, punching his massive fist into his hand and swearing under his breath. Moments before, Silas's German Shepherd, Poe, charged past the underground electric dog fence while chasing a rabbit, and he followed it down past the dirt driveway and out into the main road. The rabbit darted across, narrowly missing the antique Corvette that came speeding around the corner. Poe was not so lucky. The owner spun wildly to a stop, fifty yards down the road and sat for a moment before suddenly speeding away from the scene. Silas furiously detailed the incident, gritting his teeth and occasionally rubbing his hand across his sweaty brow. Everyone knew how much Silas loved that dog and so there stood his audience, glancing back and forth at each other in an uncomfortable silence until "The Mouth" finally spoke. He made one fatal comment which apparently pushed Silas over the edge.

"What did you say it was? A 1969 Stingray? I bet it had a 427 running on three hundred and ninety horses..."

In his defense, it wasn't even close to the most offensive thing he had ever said, just a dumb statement with terrible timing.

Silas mentioned the specific make and model of the car, so someone could, perhaps, identify the owner. But Bobby's remarks were utterly unacceptable.

"What the fuck did you say?" he stopped pacing and was standing with his back to his audience. "What the FUCK did YOU just say?!"

He slowly turned to face Bobby, who was standing about ten feet away from him, directly in front of the barn doors. "I just finish telling you Poe, MY DOG, was brutally hit and killed by some spineless coward, who didn't even have the decency to own up to his unforgivable fuck up, and all you can think of is what kind of car it was? You, ignorant grease monkey maggot!"

Silas drew his trusty .44 magnum from under his left arm and fired once directly into Bobby's belly, causing a blast of burgundy innards to splatter across the freshly painted gray barn doors he stood in front of. Silas watched for a second as the last choking gasp of life escaped Bobby "The Mouth's" mouth before spitting at his feet in disgust. He then placed the open end of the gun's barrel directly under his nose and smirked as he sniffed the fumes from the discharged gunpowder. Slowly, he lifted his cold gaze upward while he kept his head down and shifted his dark eyes back and forth between his onlookers, waiting for any other to dare make an additional comment. Once he decided his point was made, he walked past his astonished employees and disappeared into the barn for a moment. He returned shortly afterward carrying a shovel he handed to Mack and gave him a look that said, "You know what to do," and Mack did.

Mack hurried off to bury the trusted guard dog under a huge weeping willow tree in the front yard that was Silas's favorite. Tony waited for Silas to turn and start walking back toward the house before running over and dropping down at Bobby's side. Tony frantically tried to adjust Bobby's body, propping his chin up a little as he then performed CPR to the obviously deceased Mouth. With each chest compression, a tall narrow stream of blood erupted from the hole in Bobby's stomach like a tiny crimson Old Faithful. Brutus covered his face with his hand and let out a loud groan of disgust at the sight, which caught Silas's attention. He turned around and gazed upon the macabre scene unfolding before him. Tony relentlessly tried his all to restore life to his fallen comrade, methodically counting repetitions under his breath as the body jolted and continued squirting blood everywhere with each unsuccessful pump.

Suddenly, a roar of laughter broke the chaotic silence as Silas keeled over, clenching his arms across his own stomach while he belly-laughed maniacally like nothing any of them ever heard before. It startled Tony, and he stopped his efforts and moved away from the corpse with a look of embarrassment on his sweaty face, though he dared not make eye contact with Silas. He wiped off his forehead with the back of his wrist in defeat barely able to fight back the tears. Brutus, disturbed by the brutal display of cruelty and amusement he had just witnessed, shuffled over and grabbed Tony by his elbow. "Come on now, let's go get some blankets and clean this mess up," he said.

From that day forward, Brutus and the rest of Silas's hired henchmen would tread lightly when it came to the love of animals their boss possessed. Clearly, they meant more to him than his fellow man. There were rumors about genetically modified chimpanzees that Silas was accused of tampering with, but nobody really knew for sure just what had happened behind the doors to his laboratory back in San Diego. The papers only described the conditions of the lab after a search warrant was served and the premises were invaded. Most of the data was destroyed or removed prior to the seizure suggesting that he had been tipped off moments before. Still, there were remnants of machines and devices left behind that didn't meet the health codes in medieval times, which set animal rights' organizations off on a ruthless witch hunt. Silas was forced out of Dodge after his acquittal with an angry lynch mob hot on his tail, but not before he managed to ship off what he salvaged from his lab to his old friend Will Shepherd.

Will was the actual poacher who originally captured all of Cain's family members back in Central Africa years ago and sold them to the zoo. Silas quickly made a name for himself after he was hired in San Diego for his magnificent work with the most difficult of specimens. His dedication to his job, along with his immense build an equally impressive strength, demanded respect from all who knew or worked beside him. Some of his coworkers shortened his name from Dr. Wilde to simply "The Wild." A name which the media outlets gobbled up once the official charges were pressed against him. Secretly, Silas liked the name though he acted as if it was overkill.

Just as the rain finally eased off, the white Sprinter van turned off the main road and pulled onto the muddy dirt driveway of the farmhouse. Halfway to their destination, Brutus nudged Jake sitting next to him, casually motioning with his head over in the direction of Poe's wooden grave marker, and widened his eyes as if to say, "Let that be a reminder of the kind of man we work for."

Jake shuddered.

As they approached the end of the long windy driveway, the silhouette of a man wearing a cowboy hat sitting on the porch's hanging swing came into view.

"That son of a bitch," Brutus and Jake simultaneously thought.

What the hell was Will Shepherd doing there? The tall, slender man in the slightly worn blue jeans and brown leather jacket stood up from the swing and stretched long and loud as if hinting he had been waiting there a little too long for his liking. He wasn't foolish enough to believe that Silas cared though. Nobody who worked with "The Wild" past or present was foolish enough to think they dictated what he should do, nor in the manner that he should do it. No, it was always crystal clear exactly who was in charge when working with the doctor.

"Hey! The Wild is back and looking to cause some trouble, excellent! What took Y'all so long, the weather or the lazy union longshoremen?" asked Will as he came down the steps to greet us.

"A little of both I would say. How was your flight?" Silas replied.

"Muy bueno mi amigo. Thanks for the first-class seat. Can't beat those comforts on a fifteen-hour flight! And the fake I.D. and passport worked perfectly as usual."

Brutus and Jake exchanged a glance wondering why Will got to fly first-class and not them.

"Don't mention it. I have no problem paying for the professional services you always provide. You've met most of my required demands thus far and delivered as usual. So how about we open him up and kill the suspense?"

"No problem Boss, I know you must be anxious to see your old pal," Will replied, as he hocked a loogie to his side.

As Silas walked to the rear of the van, Will, glanced at Brutus and Jake and whispered, "He always talks like a robot with a stick up its ass huh?"

The three men tried not to laugh too loudly.

Silas, Will, and Jacob tried to pry the edges of the wooden crate with crowbars as Brutus retrieved a key hanging on a hook inside the barn door. He jogged over to a Bobcat loader on the side of the barn and climbed in it. After the engine warmed up, he drove it over and positioned the machine with the forks pointing into the rear of the van. Slowly, he slid them underneath and lifted the crate. Their attempts to remove the outer wooden casing had failed, so the creature inside had still not been seen. Brutus gently withdrew the precious package, under the intense watchful eyes of his employer, and set it a few feet in front of the open barn doors. Will and Silas again began prying at the creaking edges of the crate until at last the sides popped open and fell to the soggy ground.

The four men stood in an awe-struck silence, gaping at a beast unlike even the most ungodly nightmare could conjure up. Sitting with its head down but eyes looking up (bearing an uncanny resemblance to the face Silas made after shooting Bobby Lawler) a low monotone grumble was slowly and painfully heard seeping from his chest and throat. This was a primitive, demonic, revenant summoned forth by the one equally twisted soul who could possibly love such a blunder of nature: Dr. Silas Wilde. How could he proclaim so much love for such an atrocity? As if the scars covering the majority of his gnarled head and the absence of both upper and lower lips weren't enough to strike horrible fear into one's soul, Will, had successfully filed his teeth down into razor sharp points!

Brutus and Jacob earlier sat and listened to Silas describe the chimp as a magnificent ancient soul, who was simply misunderstood and had never been given his fair chance in life. He tried to paint a picture as best he could over the duration of the ride from the dock to the house of the two of them connecting on this unparalleled level, none of his colleagues could comprehend. Neither of his two passengers was remotely close when trying to picture it themselves.

When Brutus and Jacob reached their destination at Will's preserve in Africa, he had already caged the animal and sedated him in preparation for the return trip home. They had flown to Africa, ventured out into the treacherous jungles of the Congo, tracked Will Shepherd down on his well-hidden preservation, escorted the animal to the cargo ship waiting in Gabon, and then sailed back across the Atlantic through a hurricane without even laying eyes on the animal! All that was to assure a safe delivery back into the care of the animal's rightful owner. It was clear how much Silas loved him, but the real question remained: Was the feeling still mutual?

As he stood there in plain sight before them, there was no doubt remaining; Cain was the scariest thing either of his two wranglers ever saw. Even scarier was the fact, The Wild had not begun his real work with him yet! Silas described his plans to weapon train the animal. Weapon train, as in firearms training! He explained the training would not stop until Cain was capable of accurately firing automatic pistols and sawed-off shotguns, hitting targets with both his hands and feet. He also showed them pictures on his cell phone of the different masks he custom made for Cain, that would hide his horrible mouth, but Brutus and Jacob were painted with devilish frowns and ghoulish whimsical smiles. Silas finally revealed he planned on committing armed robberies, with Cain serving as his backup and lone partner. It was all one great big abominable conspiracy that only The Wild was crazy enough to conjure up.

Brutus drove the loader into the rear of the barn, where a custom cage had been fashioned for Cain. Alongside it, a fenced-in connecting tunnel was built for him to travel through. The enclosure occupied about half of the ground floor while the other half served as Silas's laboratory. Walkways covered both sides of the walls and on the left, a ramp led to a loft that was open for Cain to roam freely in. The entire second floor was also enclosed with a chain link fence. The interior was furnished with mahogany and oak tree structures as well as a maze of intertwining, hanging vines, providing his accomplice with a very comfortable and accommodating new home.

Once the men aligned the cage with the entrance of Cain's new dwelling, Silas motioned for Brutus to stop and shut off the machine. Silas didn't break the fixed stare he held on Cain, not even for a moment. His old friend appeared not to recognize him, but Silas knew that was impossible. They had only been separated for about fifteen months. Silas thought Cain was probably still groggy from the time-released sedative Will had administered, that was strong enough to wipe him out for nearly three full days. It was a high-risk chance Silas took; giving Cain enough sleep medicine to knock him out for the majority of the two-and-a-half-day ship ride. The reasons were understandable.

First of all, Cain was illegally shipped to Africa abruptly after Silas received word, he was to be criminally charged with intentional animal cruelty and conspiracy to commit a terrorist act, very serious charges! Silas scrambled to get Cain out of America before Cain could be seized in the investigation and used against him as evidence. One look at his disfigured appearance guaranteed a guilty verdict from any jury.

Secondly, the sanctuary he spent the past year and a half on was run by another wanted felon, also with disturbing charges on his rap sheet. Will was somehow a master at slipping under surveillance and through airport security and customs though. He did it for years, and Silas had absolute faith in his abilities. Using his connections in the West African black market, Will, secured a safe passageway for Cain by obtaining false customs permits claiming that the animal was on its way to the Franklin Park Zoo located just outside Boston.

The six-hour delay in the trip caused obvious concern, given the dehydrated primate passenger was already on borrowed time. Positioning a wheelchair in front of the opening of the cage, Silas attached an IV to the overhead hook. Will used a pair of bolt cutters to remove the padlock and then carefully lifted the latch. Cain's breathing seemed to hasten at the sound of imminent freedom. Silas reached out and slowly swung the metal door open, completely exposing the four men to the heinous beast. Jacob stepped back behind Brutus, who for a man standing six-feet-six-inches tall and weighing as much as a small bear, felt no larger nor more ferocious than a field mouse once openly exposed to Cain.

Cain didn't make any sudden movements though. He motioned weakly with his arm as if calling Silas to enter the cage with him, and then completely lifted his head and he stared eye-to-eye with his amazingly calm friend and caretaker. What could only be described as a smile revealed just how gruesome his mouth really was. Most of the top and bottom lips were missing, exposing protruding gums and pointy yellow teeth. What remained of his lips were greyish-brown scar tissue fragments that resembled torn pieces of sausage links, or quivering skinless worms crawling about his face. The sight almost made Brutus faint as he swayed back, bumping into Jacob.

"Easy big guy!" Jacob yelled, fearing the squeamish giant might crush him.

"Sorry, I'm not feeling well. It's probably just ship lag or motion sickness," he replied attempting to save face.

"Or maybe it's because you're scared shit of our fuzzy little friend here, huh?!" Will sarcastically proposed. "Seems the big boy is a little light in the loafers Silas. I'm surprised he survived the trip out to my reserve. Why, a few more hours of whining, swatting bugs and complaining about the heat and humidity and I would have tranquilized his ass too."

"Like hell, you would have!" Brutus spoke up, squaring off in front of Will, who despite being half his size, was not intimidated by the brute. He had been around long enough and taken down many ferocious foes, both man and beast, in his day. Jacob was quick to step in the middle before either could throw a fist. Surprisingly, Silas wasn't the one to squash the split-second squabble as he typically would. Instead, he continued staring gaily, transfixed on his drug-clumsy friend. He reached out and accepted Cain's encouraging gesture and stepped one foot inside the cage with him. Leaning down, Silas threw Cain's arm behind his own neck and over his shoulder and proceeded to carefully lift his companion up to his feet. Standing fully erect he was four-foot two inches tall and weighed around a hundred and fifty pounds.

Another moan escaped the chimp as Silas escorted him out through the opening and guided Cain down into a sitting position in the wheelchair. The sedatives were wearing off, and the excitement rose his adrenaline level. Not even the incredible Dr. Wilde could predict how a sea-sick, grouchy chimpanzee with a violent, traumatic past might act under such circumstances. He carefully and quickly wrapped two leather straps around Cain's wrists and secured his arms to the chair. Cain didn't seem to mind since his attention focused on Will, who had quickly fastened a tourniquet band around his right bicep. With one hand holding a butterfly IV needle and the other now fishing for a suitable vein beneath a thicket of coarse black hair, Cain slowly seemed to piece together what was about to take place. Before he could react though, Will, pricked him and shouted "Voila!" as he slapped a piece of medical tape over the needle. Cain erupted, eyes rolling back, sneering his devilish teeth and tongue at him. Kicking his legs wildly he almost toppled completely over in the wheelchair. Brutus and Jake were called over to assist, and the four of them pinned Cain's legs back and strapped them down. Brutus could not take his eyes off the infuriated ape, and he was certain the faces he witnessed him make would haunt his dreams well into the foreseeable future.

"There, now just try to relax my old friend. You'll feel back to your old self in no time." Silas injected another mild sedative into the IV line and made a promise to Cain he would stay with him from then on in order to closely monitor his health as he settled into his new home. There was no rush, no set schedules. They took all the time they needed for Cain to regain his strength, to overcome any motion or sea sickness, and then Silas and Cain worked on rebuilding their undeniable bond as they set into motion the diabolical dreams of a brilliant madman.

Chapter 12

Following Silas's instructions, his four employees enjoyed the following week off after the reunion at the farm. Will Shepherd was the only one who stayed to help with Cain's transitioning from life on the African preserve to life in his new home since he was the one who cared for him for the previous year and a half. Will, the poacher, greedily accepted a hefty envelope of cash, and he happily fulfilled all the doctor's demands much to Silas's approval, but not to his surprise. Will, always came through no matter how challenging a task he was appointed. Cain showed encouraging signs of his regular self and the old friends used sign language to communicate with each other.

Given Cain's violent and troubled history, in addition to the abrupt manner that Silas had sent him away, it was a matter of much concern whether he would harbor any animosity toward his old counterpart, but despite the prolonged voyage home, Cain perked up by the second day, and his appetite returned to its normal healthy state. Silas made him an impressive arrangement of his favorite produce and set it out for their first breakfast together. Papayas, cantaloupe, mangoes, and kiwi were treats Silas gave Cain for accomplishing a new challenge or consistently completing a regular task over their first ten years working together, and so this was a great treat and loving gesture the chimp fully understood. Will watched on from a distance as the two long-time friends shared the delectable dish of produce, smiling and laughing as they tossed pieces into each other's mouths. This could have warmed the poacher's heart a little if not for the grotesque sight of Cain's mangled mouth, opened wide with his tongue hanging out over his piranha-like teeth.

After the seventh day, Silas told Will he was confident enough with Cain's transition and health and dismissed him back to his African abode. Will took what little he had brought with him, wished the doctor luck, thanked him for his generous compensation, and was driven back to Logan Airport by a man he had never met before, but who had a very familiar face. He wasn't surprised when a black Lincoln Towncar with tinted windows approached the farmhouse to pick him up since Silas spared no expense when accommodating him in the past. The driver looked more like a politician or a secret service member rather than a chauffeur, and Will suspected he was someone the doctor trusted, which pleased him even more. Silas held Will in high regards, and the feeling was mutual, despite whatever wacky plans he had for that chimp. The two had always worked well together in the past and surely would again in future endeavors. As the car pulled down the driveway, Will hung his head out the window and shouted, "The Wild is back!" and pumped his fist in the air though Silas ignored him as he closed the barn doors tightly behind him.

When the seventh and final day off had arrived, Brutus called Silas to report in for duty. Again, he was told they were all to take another week off. A week later the same instructions. During the third full week off the group of unsettled workers were noticeably disturbed by the unexpected idle time.

Jacob sat on a bar stool beside Brutus in a strip club they met at in Boston's north end, the Italian district. The amazing restaurants and erotic dance clubs made that area of the city Brutus's favorite and whenever he was needed that is typically where he was found.

"You think we've been replaced?" Jacob innocently asked him.

Before Brutus could respond, Mack leaned back and shot Jacob an angry look.

"Don't be retarded. He wouldn't go through the trouble of replacing all of us," Mack replied, as he watched Brutus' face, waiting for confirmation.

The four had found refuge at The Barking Spider Gentleman's Club, a somewhat upscale establishment compared to the others around the city. It was a running joke that nobody ever witnessed any patrons coming or going yet somehow, they were always busy. Brutus, Jacob, Mack, and Tony downed cold beers and snacked on bar peanuts for the fourth consecutive day. Even the bartender noticed the troubled look each wore as they ignored the occasional propositions from the working ladies and kept to themselves at the front bar.

Brutus was popular with the ladies who danced at the club because of his muscular build, well-kept short black hair, dark features, and prominent dimples. The wad of cash he pulled out of his pocket when paying for the rounds didn't hurt his cause either. Though he wasn't there this time seeking company or looking to stuff dollar bills in the dancer's orifices, he was there because it was a good distraction from the pressing issue of why they weren't working and bringing in the money like they had been promised. The other three men looked to him for answers since he knew Silas and worked with him the longest and, for the most part, was second in command unless Silas instructed otherwise. But this time, Brutus had no answers for the sudden hiatus.

"Who'd a thought we'd be complaining about sitting on our asses, pounding brews, and looking at some fine-ass bitches?!" Tony blurted out. "Has Will left town or is he still lurking around?" he asked any who posed a possible answer.

"Silas mentioned to Jake and I that he was planning on sticking around long enough to make sure Cain got properly situated. How long that will take is anybody's guess. From what I've heard that old poacher doesn't like to stay in any one particular place for too long, except if it's at his spread in the jungle, where nobody in their right mind would go looking for him... except us."

Jacob looked at Brutus and forced a fake chuckle, shaking his head.

"So, The Wild must have paid him a pretty penny to fly his ass back to the states and hold him up on the farm for the duration of his stay," Brutus said.

"I'm just getting sick of the fucking guessing games," Mack grumbled. "Are we still going to finish the repairs on the rest of the house or what? When he first brought us on, he said that the job was for complete renovations of both the barn AND the house. I've got bills I gotta pay. What, now that he's got his fucked up little organ grinder, he's forgotten about the deal he made with us? I hate getting dicked around! I'd love to nothing more than to drive up there,

94

and..."

"And what?!" Brutus snapped back angrily. "Are you seriously going to sit here and play us all like fools by claiming you have the balls to tell off Silas Wilde to his face?! You wouldn't be able to push a single word of disrespect out past your foul mouth without shitting your pants. And if you had half a brain floating around inside that lumpy ball of shit that sits upon your neck, you'd know by now that bitching to me is a waste of time. I don't even pretend to be able to predict his next move. For someone who seems to fly by the seat of his pants, he sure as shit has everything figured out in some crazy, masterful plan. You want to know what he's got up his sleeve or feel like filing an official complaint? Then by all means be my guest. Just don't say I didn't warn you when he snaps you in two just like that," Brutus said snapping his fingers.

"And that goes for all of us. Forget about that hand cannon he keeps strapped to his side. I've seen him whip five Colombian drug-traffickers at once just because he found out they had moved one of the traps we'd set. Didn't break anything or threaten Silas in any way, they simply moved the trap about forty yards from where we had set it because it was on the edge of their marijuana plantation, and they didn't want anyone fucking around hunting or trapping on their land. Silas, that crazy prick, walked straight into their village, with the trap in his hand, and when the first machine gun-wielding farmer approached him, he belted the poor fucker right across the face with the trap, knocking his ass out instantly! He didn't even say a word to them as the other four surrounded him and tried their best to take him down. Silas basically went around in a circle, clobbering them one-by-one as they watched in awe of his speed and strength while he took down the whole damn group. I'm telling you, that man ain't nothing to fuck with. So, you go give him a piece of your mind all you want Mack, we'll be here planning your funeral."

Mack slid his bar stool out and hopped to his feet, eying Brutus for a moment, who was now eye level with Mack even though he was still sitting.

"Haha! Or you could settle for another kind of ass kicking right here if you're up to the challenge," Brutus said as he held up his right arm and flexed his enormous bicep a couple of times and then kissed it, smiling.

Brutus and Silas had almost identical, massive arms that were too big for most t-shirts and stretched out the sleeves of the ones they wore. Brutus liked to wear tight-fitting shirts or muscle shirts to show off his beefy build while Silas had the tendency to wear button-ups, solid shirts, or long-sleeved flannels.

Mack was upset but not suicidal. He was a little over six feet tall and also in great shape, but he was no match for Brutus, and all four men knew it.

"Go fuck yourself," Mack mumbled under his breath as he turned and headed for the men's room. Brutus sent Mack stumbling forward with a playful shove that carried a clear message, "Don't test me."

Jacob jumped up and in the middle of the two slightly buzzed men to prevent things from potentially escalating, but they didn't. Mack collected himself and sulked away to the opposite end of the club to relieve himself and lick his wounded ego.

Tony sipped the last of his beer, placed the bottle on the bar and turned to face Brutus. "He does have a point though. We were all promised three to four more months of steady work on the farm, but we've barely done half. I'm not one to stir shit up, but if he doesn't need us anymore, he should let us know so we can find work elsewhere. I'm worried if I do that and then he calls for us to come in, he will be pissed that I went somewhere else and never offer me work again. And I mean come on, that guy pays better than anyone around. I'd hate to lose the opportunity. What do you think big guy?" His reasons and concerns were legit. Brutus thought for a few minutes until Mack returned and rejoined them.

"If you need some cash, I've got you covered. Just let me know how much and I'll front you. Any of you," Brutus said, raising his voice so that Mack and Jacob heard as well. "If you need a cash front you ask me. If you're seriously worried about your employment future with Silas, all I can say is I have never known the doctor to go back on a deal. That man's word is as good as you'll find, and he prides himself on accomplishing all he sets out to do, no matter how crazy it may seem. If he hired you to remodel that farmhouse and convert that barn into a mad scientist's dream laboratory, then he will hold true to his promise. I'd say he's just got a hard-on for that chimp and wants to spend a little quality time with it so, unfortunately, our work got moved to the back burner for the time being. I'm not worried, and none of you should be either. I'll call him after Mack buys the next round and see what's up," Brutus said with confidence, successfully hiding the hesitation he had about confronting their employer.

About twenty minutes and twelve fluid ounces later, the four men settled their tab and made their way outside. Just as Brutus pulled his cigarette pack out of his coat pocket, a familiar and welcoming sound suddenly brought them to an abrupt pause. Brutus's phone rang. It was Silas's ringtone. Standing below the red awning in front of the gentleman's club, he dug out his little black flip phone and answered it, "Yeah we're all together, all four of us. The Barking Spider, about an hour away. Will do Boss, see you soon."

Brutus smiled and announced they were back in business, secretly relieved he didn't have to make the call confronting Silas after all. He instructed Mack to leave his truck at the club where they would pick it up later. The four newly re-energized criminals filed into Brutus' big, blue, quad-cab, super duty pickup truck and peeled out of the club's parking lot.

"What did he say?" Tony asked eagerly.

"He said it's back to work and we've got a busy night ahead of us. What that means is anybody's guess," Brutus replied.

None of them were concerned as long as their unwanted vacations had finally come to an end.

It was just about 7:00 pm when they arrived at the farmhouse. The house was dark, but they saw the lights in the barn were on. Typical Dr. Wild, hard at work as usual. Parking the truck in front of the barn doors and next to Silas's van, Brutus shut off the engine and let out a loud sigh of relief.

"You pansies ready to get back to it or what?!" he said, slapping Jacob on the back and laughing.

"Damn right! Let's go see what boss man has been doing with that mutant in there," Jacob said with a smile.

Mack and Tony seated in the back quickly exchanged glances at that comment, both recalling the serious nature of the subject. Even sitting in the truck with the windows up, outside the barn, easily twenty yards away from where the doctor most likely was, even at that distance it didn't seem safe to joke about Cain or call him names. Brutus noticed the two, swapping uncomfortable looks in the rearview mirror and then slowly turned his gaze to his right, toward Jacob.

"Be careful big mouth. There's plenty of room under that willow tree for another grave to keep old Poe company," he warned Jacob, who regretted his comment as quickly as he uttered it.

"Okay, let's do this," Brutus said as he opened his door and exited the truck.

The four men entered the barn and stopped dead in their tracks when they were in full view of the enclosure. There they stood, shoulder to shoulder, gazing at the cage door that sat wide open in front of them. Where was Silas and more importantly, where the hell was chimpanzee?!

"BOSS?" Brutus yelled.

No answer.

"HELLO?"

Again, no answer.

All four men were on high alert looking for Cain. Suddenly, the sound of an empty tin can rattle, broke the silence as one came flying out from the left somewhere and rolled to a stop in front of them. They all jumped, even Brutus.

"Where are you, Boss?" he called once more only to be answered with silence again.

Then, all at once, there was this tremendous commotion overhead that sounded like the roof was collapsing in. All four glanced up to see Cain dangling by his feet while holding what appeared to be two 9mm pistols in his hands, wildly aiming and firing in all directions!

Brutus dove to his right and rolled to a crouching position underneath a metal examination table. Jacob and Mack bumped into each other before they took cover behind Silas's desk. Tony couldn't move, however. He stood terrified in place, and in shock. The ceiling was about eighteen feet up, and Cain was hanging from the rafters that were about four feet down from the peak. He released his grip and did a forward flip before landing just feet in front of Tony. Poor Tony was physically shaking as he stared at the masked ape, who was now pointing his weapons directly at his face. Cain wore a mask made from a canvas-like material that was white with a big frown painted on it in black paint. There they stood, staring at each other until suddenly, the unthinkable happened. Cain squeezed the triggers.

The three other men gasped and clenched their eyes shut for a moment, not wanting to witness their co-worker and friend with holes blown through his astonished face. But a scream caused them to look up as Tony did an about face and sprinted out of the barn miraculously unharmed. Just as he made it to the door, Silas entered and grabbed him, wrapping both of his arms around Tony tightly as he laughed.

"What the fuck?! He tried to kill me!" was all Tony could get out.

"Oh, come on now, they were only blanks! He's just getting used to handling them for now. We'll start with the actual target practice as soon as he can maneuver about with a little more ease," Silas announced.

Guns?! As in plural?! The room full of veteran criminals were all at a loss for words. Silas was actually trusting this animal with guns! Brutus's and Jacob's worst fears they conjured up on the long car ride from the docks to the farmhouse were coming true. Actually they were being trumped. This was worse than anything they imagined, and despite the fact Silas informed them of his treacherous plan before, it was still horribly incomprehensible. Yet there it was; a full-grown chimpanzee wielding Glock 9mm handguns and handling them quite well, to be honest.

Tony was shaken to his core as Silas made a half-hearted

attempt to comfort him, rubbing Tony's arms up and down vigorously. Silas, a few moments later, pushed Tony away from his chest and looked him in the eyes and stated, "Oh come on now, it wasn't that bad. I hope this doesn't hinder any potential friendship the two of you might have."

Tony couldn't believe what he heard, but he was too shaken to speak.

"Cain, come here and meet the rest of your family," Silas commanded with a clap of his hands. He walked away leaving Tony still frozen in his tracks and placed his hand out for Cain to give him the guns. Cain made a sort of chuckling, snorting noise from behind his mask before gently placing the pistols in Silas's hands.

"Now I would like to formally introduce you all to our new friend here." Silas went around and properly introduced each of his men to Cain. "Now that Cain is a member of our family, he is to be treated with the same respect you give me. I expect you all to assist in coaching him and bringing him up to speed as often as needed. What you just witnessed was what we have been working on over the past few weeks. My goal is to have him fully capable to accurately fire different guns, with both his hands and feet, within the next month. With hard work and dedication, I know we can do it. He will only be using blanks, for the time being, so he can get used to the sound as well as used to the kickback and rate of fire for the different caliber weapons. Once he shows that he is ready, I will begin training with him personally by harnessing him into a custom-made backpack carrying tote, and the two of us will run multiple obstacle courses as a team. Ultimately, he will provide cover in four different directions for me while riding on my back, freeing up my own hands so I can rob and pillage as I please. Any questions?"

You could hear a mouse fart it was so quiet in the barn. Silas looked around, and when nobody spoke up, he nodded and said, "Very good then. I've made a list of supplies that we are going to need to build the ranges out back, as well as a grocery list for the house. There's nothing but fruits, canned tuna, and bottled water so buy enough to stock up for the next couple of weeks. The two finished bedrooms upstairs will be shared by you four so partner up, I don't care who sleeps where as long as none of you snore loud

100

enough for me to hear in my bedroom at the end of the hall. There are four full-sized bed frames, box springs, and mattresses in the basement that you will have to assemble, so I suggest doing that first before you go shopping because I don't want to have to listen to you banging around after I retire to my room. Anyway, I want you all to stay here Monday-Friday for the next couple of months at least while working on finishing the house renovations, both inside and out, the firing range, and obstacle course outside. I even bought a home gym and free weights that are in the basement, so we can all keep in shape. So, start with beds then go start purchasing the supplies I mentioned."

He reached in his back pants pocket, removed his wallet and then a black credit card that he handed to Brutus with a wink. "Have a good evening, I'll see you all in the morning," he said as he turned and exited the barn with Cain following closely behind.

Tony and Mack agreed to put the beds together while Brutus and Jacob left to grocery shop. As they pulled off the dirt driveway and onto the desolate paved road, Jacob looked at Brutus and asked, "Have you ever heard of an ape, or any animal for that matter, that was able to responsibly use a firearm?"

"Shit, I've seen squirrels that can surf, a toucan that plays the piano, and even a dog that could hula-hoop... but a chimp with a gun, now that's a new one to me. I suppose anything is possible, as long as there's somebody motivated enough to put forth the effort in training one like the good doctor is. A heads-up that he was running about, with those Glocks full of blanks, before we came back would have been nice though. And I'm sure Tony really would have appreciated it, there's no way he left that barn wearing clean underpants!"

"Well if he did, it's okay, I shit mine for him!" Jacob said.

"Ha ha! I hear ya, buddy. Ah well, let's just focus on the work we have ahead of us and keep our heads down unless he requests that we do otherwise. I just hope I don't have to deal too much with Cain myself, that creature sure is something ungodly. Ugh..." Brutus said with a shiver.

"Agreed. Let's go get some grub as quickly as possible, we still

101

have to go pick up Mack's truck from The Barking Spider, and we should do that before we get the food and building materials, so we can load up both trucks," said Jacob, dangling Mack's keyring up in the air.

"Oh shit, I totally forgot about that. Alright, we'll do this quick, I'm sure everyone is just as hungry as we are," Brutus replied.

"And tired. I feel like I could sleep for a week straight. If only I can manage to get some rest without envisioning that chimp's face whenever I close my eyes. Now that will take some practice."

"We have a little bit of a drive until we get to his truck, grab a few Z's right now. I'll wake you a few minutes before we get there," suggested Brutus.

"I appreciate it, man. This is why I don't drink during the week typically, wipes me out," said Jacob.

"I've heard stories about chimps whose owners let them smoke cigarettes, cigars, and even drink alcohol. Imagine our new coworker shitfaced!" Brutus laughed at the visual he was imagining and slapped the steering wheel.

"Oh God, that's all we need; a drunken demon chimp dropping down from the ceilings launching sneak attacks on us!" replied Jacob.

The two shared a good laugh for a minute then quieted once the seriousness of the issue sank in. Was it that far-fetched? Going forward after the day's events, no outrageous scenario would be taken lightly, nor would any idea of their employer be out of the question. Anything was possible with that man, and he meant business.

After ten minutes, Jacob eventually drifted off into a light sleep as Brutus hummed along and played air drums to a Lamb of God song playing on the radio. He was glad to be back to work again despite a tiny shred of doubt and hesitation that had been planted inside of him with the arrival of Cain. Brutus trusted his boss though and hoped it was nothing more than a little paranoia. After all, what could go wrong moving in with a mad scientist plotting some terrorist acts with a cannibalistic, psychotic, gun-toting ape?

Chapter 13

It was just past 10:00pm when the two pickup trucks returned to the farm. Brutus and Jacob purchased as many supplies as they could fit into the beds of both trucks and then loaded up the back seats in both with groceries. Overall, they made fairly good time, considering the multiple stops and time spent shopping at Shop & Save, and at the Home Headquarters Warehouse. The two exhausted errand boys were pretty heavy footed for the normally forty-five-minute drive on the Mass Pike, taking them just under thirty minutes to reach the farmhouse. They unloaded the plastic grocery bags on the kitchen table and floor. Silas, Mack, and Tony were heard overhead, probably finishing up assembling and making the beds. An empty twelve pack of summer ale provided the explanation as to why it was taking so long putting the beds together.

Once all the food was put away, Jacob placed a couple frozen pizzas in the oven before calling dibs on the first shower. All four men had a few changes of clothes they kept in the house for nights they worked there late or were too drunk to drive back to their own residences. Silas did a great job filling the house with all the standard necessities: bath towels, toilet paper, cleaning supplies, televisions, beer, and he also bought most of the furniture from one of those massive, warehouse-style, Swedish furniture stores, though not everything had been completely assembled. Put that on their to-do list.

Upstairs, Brutus found Mack and Tony in one of the bedrooms both sitting upright on each of the beds watching the news on the small flat screen TV that sat on top of the dresser.

"Food's here?" Mack asked over-eagerly.

"Yup, pizzas are in the oven, twenty-two minutes. Just about the time, it will take you two lazy turds to help me unload the building supplies and lumber from the trucks," Brutus informed them.

"Awe c'mon. Can't that shit wait until morning?" Mack whined.

"Absolutely not. I take it you weren't paying attention to the weather. Rain's coming and should be here before midnight. All we have to do is unload everything into the barn and lay it alongside the wall out of Silas's way. We can move it again tomorrow if he isn't happy with it being there. So, get off your asses and let's move," Brutus said, kicking their boots over to the sides of their beds.

Reluctantly they laced up and followed him downstairs and out into the cool night.

Most of what they had purchased was lumber; specifically, 2x4s, ten boxes of framing nails, a couple of large rolls of burlap, paint, and a dozen pieces of both sheetrock and plywood. They moved with haste as they emptied Brutus's truck and then moved on to Mack's. As they carried the items inside the barn, Tony constantly kept one eye looking up, fearing for another ambush. Noticing his state of discomfort, Brutus went over to the light switches on the wall and flipped on the only two that were in the down position, illuminating the upstairs where Cain slept. The sight of him unconscious in his hammock-like swing ushered in a wave of relief for Tony, who received a head nod from Brutus before he switched the lights back off. They all did their best to keep the noise level down so the creature could rest.

Once Mack's truck was almost empty, Jacob conveniently appeared from the house and made his way down the porch steps and over to the empty trucks where his help was no longer needed.

"Just in time, ya good-for-nothing..." Mack half-jokingly mumbled.

"Pizza is done in five minutes," Jacob replied.

"Well, at least you're good for something. I'm starving!" Tony added to the ball busting. "Did you make us fresh baked chocolate chip cookies too Chef Boy-You're-Gay?"

"Keep it up, and I'll cover you in fruit slices while you sleep and then release the beast. I'm sure he'd get a kick out of watching you turn into a six-foot vagina again," Jacob shot back.

"Don't you girls ever get sick of teasing each other?" Brutus asked as he went back into the barn to make sure everything was in order before calling it a night. Taking a quick mental inventory of all the supplies, he tried to envision what Silas had planned to build. He had an idea in his head of how Silas might want to design the shooting range, but as for the obstacle course, he was clueless.

What type of exercise regimen did he have in store for he and Cain? He had already begun doing rigorous exercises and lifted the free weights in the basement almost daily. Silas stated he wanted to eventually carry Cain on his back in some type of backpack holster, but that's one hundred and fifty pounds of squirming, sweating flesh and bones that will be weighing him down! It's a hard sight to imagine, but Brutus knew in due time, he would bear witness. Very few men possessed the power, athletic ability, and the endurance to pull off such a feat, never mind the balls to do so as well. Brutus also knew better than to doubt the doctor and, occasionally, he thanked God for pairing him up on the same team and not the opposing side of the Wild's.

Silas appeared shortly after Jacob and didn't seem to mind the supplies spending the night in the barn and out of the rain. He informed them that the use of the barn's two large front doors would not be allowed after the following day and that he wanted to board them up using the plywood. The side door would be the single way in and out from then on because the next day they would be installing a security system to monitor both the house and barn. Arming the large double doors and monitoring them would be a pain in the ass and so the side door was a much more reasonable solution. Most of what was being said would have to be repeated in the morning, however, since all four of his hired hands were daydreaming about the pizza that was cooking inside. Sensing he was losing his audience, Silas switched off the lights in the barn and said, "Alright, let's go get some hot food and cold beers."

As the rest of them made a dash for the porch, Silas turned and glanced up one last time at the soundly sleeping Cain and smiled. "See you tomorrow buddy," he whispered and then closed the door behind him.

After the men devoured the pizzas, the rest of the crew took turns showering and eventually called it a night. Brutus and Jacob shared one bedroom, and Mack and Tony shared the other. Silas had the master bedroom at the far end of the upstairs hall, complete with his own private bathroom. Jacob heard him get up and flush the toilet a few times before he fell asleep and as he lay there, Jacob wondered if his boss could sleep. Silas went about in somewhat of a dream-like state ever since Cain arrived. Jacob pictured Silas lying wide awake in bed all night staring at the ceiling above with that sinister smile he saved for special maniacal situations. Jacob also wondered if the guys in the other room were asleep or if they were having trouble too, despite being exhausted from all the craziness and excitement that surrounded them. Jacob knew Brutus was out, he was snoring like a bull. Eventually, the moonlight that shined through the small gap in the center of the window's curtains was blocked out by the approaching storm clouds, making the room pitch black. Eyes open or eyes closed, it made no difference, and soon, everyone was fast asleep.

By 7:30am the men gathered around the dining room table and were served a pleasantly surprising big breakfast by their host. Silas was the first one up, so he prepared bacon, eggs, home fries, toast, and coffee for his temporary guests. He explained to them previously, they were only his employees during the workday, in the evening and early morning they were his guests, and he was a very accommodating host. When they finished, it was back to business as usual. Silas told the guys to meet him out in the barn in ten minutes; enough time to prepare Cain's breakfast.

The rainstorm had passed overnight, and the sun was already breaking through the scattered, lingering clouds. The men changed into clean work clothes and headed outside. Tony and Jacob sat on the top porch step while Brutus claimed the wooden rocker. Mack was on the hanging wooden swing, kicking his feet as he swayed back and forth. They made small talk about the weather, the delicious breakfast they shared, and the Red Sox. Silas finally came to the front door and yelled for someone to open it for him. Brutus hopped to his feet and let him out of the house as he carried a deep platter of fresh produce.

"Man, your new employee eats like a king," Brutus said with a smile.

"Nothing but the best for my men," Silas responded.

Following him into the barn, they were greeted with welcoming hoots and grunts from the highly alert chimp. Just like the days back in San Diego, he wanted to be the first to eat and never missed a meal.

"Anybody want to feed him? It's a great opportunity to bond with him," Silas asked with no takers. "You're all going to have to eventually. I want you all to be trained on how to handle him in case a situation arises when I'm not around to do so myself. Sort of like a life insurance policy for our friend. The sooner you men start to participate the better and smoother things will go. So, let's have it, who's it gonna be?"

To everyone's astonishment, Tony spoke up, "I'll do it."

The others glared at him in admiration for his newly developed pair of testicles. He took the platter from Silas and walked over to the door of the cage. In the center, there was a horizontal opening big enough to slide a tray of food through, like in jail cell doors. Tony picked a piece of cantaloupe with his hand and slowly offered it through the opening. Cain scrunched his nose and smiled in satisfaction before reaching out and taking the offering. Once it was determined by the trembling, Tony he hadn't lost his hand in the process, he too made a quirky smile as he dished out more fruit.

"There ya go! See, nothing to be afraid of. I spent a good ten years molding and conforming our friend here to do as I command, behave the way I taught him, and respect those who treat him with kindness. As long as we're all on the same page with what are acceptable behaviors and what are not, then we should all get along just fine," Silas said as he smiled at Tony and Cain.

Cain was a fast eater, and his meal was gone within five minutes. Satisfied with his feat, Tony turned to the others and smiled proudly. "Not bad huh? And I even managed not to shit my pants," he said sarcastically.

Silas walked over to the wall where the supplies had been piled and scanned them over as he slowly rubbed his hands back and forth over his bald head. "Hmmm. I think I'm going to have Brutus and Tony install the surveillance equipment while Jacob and Mack get to work on making dummies. Brutus, all the cameras and equipment are in the den in the box that's sitting in the corner. If you need assistance, use the internet and if that doesn't help, come find me so I can tell you what a moron you are. Jacob and Mack, I will build one dummy to show you how I want them made. Make about fifteen for now and when you're done come find me. Any questions?"

Four heads shook, and they all went their separate ways.

Mack dragged one of the metal tables over to the center of the room and covered it with a drop cloth. Jacob retrieved two large tool bags from the container in the back of Mack's truck. Silas disappeared outside and returned with a wheelbarrow full of basketball-sized watermelons. "Cain would have a heart attack if he knew what we are going to be using these for," he stated.

He put them aside and grabbed one eight-foot and one four-foot long 2x4s from the pile and placed them on the table forming a cross. "First use the circular saw to cut the tops and bottoms into points. We are going to be staking them into the ground and today will actually be a good day to so since it's still a little soggy. Nail the cross together and then grab a piece of plywood." Silas did so as he instructed.

The plywood was placed on the table and Silas pulled out a permanent marker from his pocket. Carefully, he drew the outline of a person about five-feet tall, only he made it without a head. It was flat at the neck, and they would soon learn why he wanted headless targets. "Cut this out and use it as a template. Once you have the body cut out, nail it to the wooden cross with about six to eight inches of the top point of the cross sticking up from behind the body. Next cut a piece of burlap wrap and give yourself enough to cover a watermelon. After they're stuck in the ground securely, pierce the watermelon down on to the top point and wrap the burlap tightly around it. There is a box of wire fasteners you can use to fasten the fabric to the fruit. Once you're ready, take them out to the trail in the backyard where you'll see orange plastic ribbons tied randomly throughout the woods. I placed them where I want the dummies to go, so go around and find them all. When you're done, come find me." His instructions were a bit peculiar but very clear.

Jacob and Mack went to work.

"You find everything okay?" Silas asked Brutus when he entered the kitchen. Brutus nodded unconvincingly. He and Tony were reading the illustrated instruction manuals for the surveillance cameras. Motion detectors, night-vision, high-definition wireless cameras... these things had it all. Brutus had electrical experience, and Tony was tech-savvy, which is why they were selected for the task.

"How long do you think until it's up and running?" Silas asked.

"We will have it done by the end of the day. Going with the wireless setup was a wise choice," Brutus complimented.

"That's the only kind of choices I make," Silas replied. "If you don't need me, I'll get out of your way and let you go at it. I'll be out back if you need me." He left and returned to the barn, where he nailed the plywood over the barn doors. When he was done, Silas took some of the supplies out to the rear of the shed and began constructing a shooting range out back. About three hours had passed, and Jacob and Mack were ready to take the dummies outside. Silas stopped them before they left the barn and requested one last favor. He wanted them to take the paints he had in a steel tool cabinet and paint smiley faces on the burlap. Shrugging their shoulders, the two men did as he asked and painted fifteen white faces with blue eyes and blue smiles on the cloth cutouts. Once the paint dried, they headed out to find the destinations for each dummy.

Mack came up with the idea to take a five-foot steel pry bar with them to make a hole in the ground with first, before attempting to drive the wooden spikes down using just a hammer alone. Jacob carried the dummy while Mack held the bar and a sledgehammer as they made their way to the edge of the forest. Jacob walked through the foot trails until he came across the first orange marker. It was about twenty feet off the trail in the overgrown brush of the woods. Mack held the pry bar up straight while Jacob hammered it down until it was embedded deep enough. The dummy was placed in the hole and staked in firmly. At last, Mack and Jacob impaled the watermelon and wrapped the burlap bag around it with the face looking outward. It took almost forty minutes to set up one target.

Mack and Jacob had to pick up the pace. They didn't want to spend the whole day walking back and forth, banging holes into the rocky soil.

By mid-afternoon, Brutus and Tony finished securing all the cameras on the farmhouse and were working on the barn. They installed four more on each corner of the barn, just below where the rafters overhung the walls, and another two inside to keep an eye on Cain. Brutus finished up and double checked the positioning and angles while Tony sat at Silas's desk and installed the software on the computer and cell phone. Soon, the entire system was up and fully operational, and they did it all a few hours faster than they originally estimated. Silas was very much pleased with their work as he went from viewing the monitors on his computer to his phone. No matter where he was, he was able to keep an eye on things.

"Have you heard from the other two?" Silas asked.

"Not since lunch. They came in for about ten, fifteen minutes, made a couple of sandwiches, scarfed them down, and went back out. The appeared very unhappy for whatever reason," Tony explained.

"They're having trouble setting up the dummies. Why don't you two head out and give them a hand?" Silas insisted more than he requested.

"You got it, boss. We'll see you in a while," Brutus answered.

The sight of Brutus alone coming down the trail to lend a hand was like a godsend to the two exhausted, blistered men. There were six more dummies to place, and Brutus offered to hammer them all. Tony jumped in and held the bar as the brute pounded away like a caveman on crack. Jacob and Mack stood close by and felt the ground vibrating beneath their feet with each thunderous thump of the sledgehammer. He pounded one in and immediately moved on to the next, hardly taking a moment to catch his breath. The mosquitoes served as great motivators to get the job done quickly since they went out there without applying any bug spray. Those last six dummies went up in an hour, much faster than Mack and Jacob had done, but they didn't care about being shown up, they just wanted to get the hell out of there.

Walking out of the woods and coming into sight of the farmhouse, they saw smoke rise from somewhere behind the house. Then the aroma hit them, steaks! The good doctor manned the grill and prepared yet another tasty meal for his workers. As they approached, he greeted them and said, "Who likes it medium and who likes it rare?"

The men were parched, they could barely get any words out!

"Go get cleaned up quickly and meet me back here at the picnic table. And make sure you grab plenty of waters from inside," Silas instructed.

They did as they were told and washed before joining him at the picnic table for plate-sized porterhouse steaks, grilled asparagus, and potato salad. For the duration of the meal, they sat in silence as if speaking would take away from their enjoyment of the mouthwatering meal. It wasn't awkward though, it was peaceful, and there they sat dining like family, as the sun descended toward the horizon, setting in front of the pink and lavender evening sky.

Chapter 14

Early Saturday morning, Silas heard a vehicle pull down the dirt driveway and come to a stop beside his house. He was alone, and it was as quiet as a morgue around the farm. The sound of the automobile approaching, and parking was enough to wake him up, and he threw the blankets off and sat erect in his comfortable king-sized sleigh bed, curious but annoyed. He listened quietly and intently, and the moment he heard the car door open and shut, he reached for the gun in his nightstand. Not the .44 magnum he typically carried, this was a .38 snub-nose that packed enough punch to stop an intruder dead in his tracks while conveniently fitting in the bedside drawer. The hardwood floor was cold on his bare feet as he stood and quietly walked over to the window to investigate. Pulling back the hanging curtain he spotted the culprit; a black Lincoln Towncar with tinted windows. He knew the car, knew who drove it but did not know what that person was doing at his house at 8:00am on a Saturday.

Shaking his head in disbelief, Silas walked over and returned the gun to its drawer. He opened his closet, stepped into a pair of running sneakers, and threw on a hooded sweatshirt. The sweatpants he wore to bed were warm enough to wear downstairs, though a recent November chill seemed to linger longer than he cared for. Silas looked in his dresser mirror and shook his head like a dog drying itself off, in an effort to wake up and come to his senses. What was the purpose of this unexpected, unwanted visitor?

He made his way downstairs, then through the living room and into the kitchen where he stopped in front of the outside door. On the opposite side stood a well-dressed man in his late fifties, with salt and pepper hair and a matching beard, staring in at Silas from behind a pair of dark sunglasses.

"What a tool," Silas thought to himself before opening the door to greet him.

"Well, this is unexpected. You campaigning early this year or are you lost?" he said to his visitor.

"We need to talk, it's important," the man replied.

Silas turned to his right and picked up the cell phone that was charging on the counter beside him. He held it up in front of the man and waved it back and forth.

"I don't feel comfortable doing your kind of business over the phone. You can't read a person's body language over a phone call, and it can be hard to tell if they're honest or if they're just plain full of shit."

Silas didn't like this at all. "Are you implying something? I hope for your sake you're not suggesting that I am untrustworthy or guilty of deceiving you."

The man backpedaled a bit, "Well no, I didn't mean you specifically, just whoever I happen to be dealing with. It's more personal face-to-face, and that can be very reassuring in this particular line of work. You know, a firm handshake looking whoever you're dealing with directly in the eye? That's what I meant by body language."

Silas stood perfectly still, locked in a death stare for one very long, very awkward, silent moment. He seemed unimpressed. Finally, he spoke, "What's my body language saying to you right now?"

The man's brain raced as he recalled the brutal stories he heard about the doctor and the reasons why he was nicknamed "The Wild."

"I guess it's saying... well I know you weren't expecting me but..." his words trailed off for a moment as he realized Silas didn't break his stare.

"Ah Jesus Christ, I'm sorry for dropping in on you. I didn't think it might seem like I'm here looking for trouble because I'm definitely not! I want to talk to you about something your friend Will Shepherd and I discussed when you had me drive him to the airport a few weeks ago. I didn't mean to intrude, and I certainly don't mean any disrespect."

Silas finally blinked and slowly smirked. It was humorous to him just how spineless some people truly were. They tried to come off as confident and fearless men until he called them out and stood up to them. Then they melted right in the palm of his hand, turning softer than puppy shit and willing to do anything to avoid a confrontation. What a coward this guy was. It was to be expected though, he is a politician after all.

Silas met Joseph Yoder about three years before when he ran for the first time for the state representative position. He accompanied Brutus to a private meeting where Yoder requested the talents of the hired thug in helping rattle the cage of the man who ran against him. Yoder's competition spread vicious allegations about drug trafficking, and it looked as though it was the end of the campaign road for him. Miraculously, an anonymous tip led police to his running mate's office where a laptop filled with child pornography, allegedly belonging to Yoder's competition, was seized and the man was arrested. Silas sat in the meeting and watched Brutus reassure the man days before, he need not worry, the state rep's seat was basically his. Brutus was, needless to say, a man of many talents. Yoder still owed him big, but sooner or later the day eventually came when the big man called in that favor.

Brutus was recruited by Yoder to be the head of security for his side business, the crystal meth lab he owned in Foxboro. The money was good, but not as much as Silas paid him and besides, drugs were a dirty, violent business he wanted nothing to do with.

Silas stepped backward and invited him in. He already regretted his previous decision to invite Yoder over to see his new base of operations, but Yoder had practically begged him over the phone, and eventually, Silas caved. Yoder suffered a huge blow to his meth business the previous October when his lab and most of the ranch which served as its front burned to the ground. It seemed they were raided, most likely by rival drug manufacturers, though none of the product was taken.

During the sabotage, a fire started and quickly consumed everything. Three of his hired guards were murdered, their fatal injuries appeared to have been inflicted by a large blade such as a machete or a sword. His two cooks and another guard were burned alive as they weren't able to escape the fire. By the time the smoke

114

literally cleared, six of his men lay dead, and the entire lab was buried under a mountain of charred wood. Since then, Yoder looked for a place to start up again and set up a new shop that was equally as covert as the last. Once he caught wind that The Wild had purchased farmhouse property out in the sticks, he was eager to come and check it out for himself. Silas would never agree to cook crystal meth there, but for some reason he still allowed Yoder to come under the condition he chauffeurs his guest, Will Shepherd, back to Logan Airport.

But there he was, almost four weeks later wanting to discuss a conversation he had during his car ride with Will? Silas wondered what could possibly be so important they must speak in person yet could wait a month before bringing it up. He glanced at the clock over the refrigerator and then back at Yoder. "You've got three minutes, go."

"Your friend told me vaguely about your interest in taking up a new kind of action. I admit I was prying a little because, well I just love a great business opportunity. He didn't reveal much, but from what I've gathered, you've partnered up with someone who's damn good enough for you to have him escorted all the way back from Africa. He also mentioned you will be doing some training here, but he wouldn't specify what type. I know you have firearm connections and you're preparing for something big. Now hear me out. My ranch going under has really hit me hard in the wallet. There are boatloads of money in the meth trade, which is why I got into it in the first place, to fund my campaign and support my expensive tastes. But ever since I lost it, I've been really up shit's creek. I'm desperate and will do anything for the chance to rebound and make some quick cash. I realize that cooking here is out of the question, so I ask you this: do you have any need for a groveling politician in whatever it is that you're planning?"

Silas hated beggars. He despised politicians. And he really detested anybody who went around sticking their nose in other people's business. Yet for some reason, he wasn't about to grab this jellyfish in front of him by the back of his neck and toss him to the curb, not yet anyway. He had a lot of pull around the state, and someone with that kind of political influence was not the worst person to have in his corner. He sat a moment longer pondering.

"Tell me what you think I'm planning, I'm curious," Silas said.

"Honestly, I thought of two possibilities: you are going to be making one big transaction, guns perhaps, and the buyer is overseas, like in Africa. The other is your planning to heist something even bigger. What? I'm not positive. Maybe a specific armored truck carrying something heavy, I'm only guessing here. So, am I close?"

"No," Silas replied. "You're a little warm, but you haven't hit the nail on the head yet. You've got me wondering; what role exactly did you see yourself playing in any of those scenarios?!" Silas asked with a laugh.

"I know, I can't exactly be the getaway driver in a robbery or anything where my identity might be exposed, but I'm a man with an abundance of resources, no lie. You name it, and I bet I could locate it for you. Just try me," Yoder proudly proclaimed.

"Okay hotshot. Do you know what lacrymatory is?" Silas asked.

"Lacrymatory?" he repeated. "I haven't the faintest idea. Does it go by another name perhaps?"

"Sure, tear gas," Silas said.

Suddenly, Yoder's eyes lit up. "You bet your ass I can," he exclaimed. "How much it costs I don't know, but what I do know is this ex-military guy who can locate practically any type of munitions, and he just happens to owe me a favor. I introduced him to the lawyer who saved him from making a twelve to fifteen-year bid for trafficking so, lately he has been laying kind of low, only dealing with close acquaintances, like yours truly."

For the first time during his visit, Silas was interested in what he heard. He had asked the people he knew if they could locate the gas canisters for him without any luck. It was such a crucial part of his plan to rob a bank, without it so much could go wrong. Could Yoder actually get his hands on some? There was only one way to find out.

"I'll tell you what, you do your thing and nail this down for me and I'll buy three cases, thirty-six canisters. You do that, and you'll have greatly increased your chance of being a player in my plan.

That's the best I'm going to offer until I see whether or not you're full of shit. CALL ME as soon as you hear anything, do not stop by again. Your three minutes are up, please, see yourself out."

Yoder opened his mouth but then held back whatever it was he was going to say, realizing he had overstayed his welcome. Instead, he stood, nodded, and then smirked at Silas before walking out the front door. Watching him drive away, Silas thought for a moment how great it would have been if he could get a state representative to personally deliver three cases of tear gas to him! What's this world coming to?!

Silas recalled the incident at Yoder's ranch the year before. The media called it "The Devil's Night Disaster," and it was a pretty big story since some of the animals got loose and caused a big pileup on the highway. How he avoided catching any legal shit for that was beyond his understanding. Did he say six of his employees died then? That's all he had guarding his meth factory?! Dr. Wilde questioned his judgment on that one. Two of the men were cooks, so that meant only four men were on duty protecting his big money-making investment. It was no wonder moments ago he practically squirmed on his belly begging for a bone. "If he's all talk and falls through on this, I'm chopping him up and feeding him to Cain," Silas said to himself.

The next bone he picked was with Will Shepherd. What the hell was he thinking, discussing business with a man he only just met? He didn't know anything about Yoder or what kind of history he and Silas had together. He had to have thought he was someone who could be trusted since Silas hired him to be Will's driver. It just so happened that Yoder asked to come by when Will helped him out and he figured two birds, one stone. It seemed like a no-brainer. Besides, Yoder drove around in that stupid Towncar looking like a livery service, and Will didn't know he wasn't unless they got into some intimate conversation, which they obviously did. That rubbed Silas the wrong way. You don't discuss other people's business like that, he never did anything like that before to Silas's knowledge. He would lay into him the next time they crossed paths. Will was always up for a good fight and Silas was happy to give him one.

The following evening, while Dr. Wilde read old notes in his lab,

117

his phone rang breaking the silence and startling him. It was Joe Yoder, and he had good news. The packages could be obtained as early as Wednesday. For five thousand dollars they were as good as his. They would even come with free delivery since the man getting them felt it was less risky for him to personally make the drops and see them safely arrive at their location, rather than meeting up in some dark parking garage to do the exchange. Silas couldn't believe his ears! This was a dream come true. The only hang-up was now he had to cut Yoder in on the action. He wanted to be a part of the plan somehow, but Silas didn't need the help. He thought of offering Yoder a payout to settle the debt. Yoder said he would stop by sometime after the package was delivered to discuss the agreement. "Great, now he's going to want to know every last detail and will want to see the lab and all its contents. He sure is a pain in the ass even if he was about to come through huge for him." Dr. Wilde thought.

Silas had to lay down clear ground rules before any agreement was struck between them. He was both anxiously awaiting Wednesday's arrival and dreading it at the same time. "Everything will work out," he kept thinking.

On Wednesday he might just have a few beers before Yoder arrived to take the edge off. He hoped that would do the trick!

Chapter 15

Monday and Tuesday came and went with little to no excitement at the farm. The men returned to work and completed two side-by-side shooting ranges behind the barn. Brutus and Jacob took turns feeding Cain his breakfast. Mack and Tony stayed up later than the others Monday night drinking beer and watching television in the living room. Silas worked closely with Cain showing him how to properly put on his own gas mask so that it was snug but safe. He also let him carry the two unloaded Glock 9mm's around with him while they were inside the barn. There were no more surprise attacks though, and things around the farm were uneventful.

Silas was awake at dawn on Wednesday, fully dressed and fed, and ready to take on the day. Yoder told him to expect the delivery before 8:00am, which seemed early but the man making the delivery wanted to get it over with as early as possible. There was still an hour to kill so Silas kicked back in his office chair and played solitaire on the lab's computer. When he became bored with that, he pulled out an envelope of cash and counted the stack of twenties and fifties frontwards and backward just to be sure. It was all there, five thousand dollars in crisp bills.

Finally, he heard someone driving down the driveway. When they shifted into park and turned off the engine, Silas rose from his chair and walked outside to greet the man who delivered the little silver canisters of joy to the eager doctor. He looked more like a member of a motorcycle gang rather than an ex-marine, but Silas was never one to judge. The man with the thick black beard wearing a black handkerchief around his head extended his hand and formally introduced himself, "Jeff Clark, and you must be Silas."

"Pleased to meet you and thank you for driving out here personally, I really appreciate it." Silas gave him a firm handshake and made eye contact to show he was sincere.

"Follow me," said Jeff, who walked to the rear of the white box truck with lettering on the side that read "Premier Chimney Sweep." He flipped the latch, rolled up the door, and hopped up and into the back of the truck. A large drop cloth with dried paint spots on it covered the dangerous cargo. Jeff pulled it off and there they were, three full cases of tear gas just for Silas! He could barely contain himself as he reached in and caught a grip on one. Jeff slid a case that perfectly slowed to a stop right at the edge of the truck. Then he and Silas carried the other cases into the barn and placed them beside his desk. Dr. Wilde handed the cash envelope over, and his new acquaintance counted it quickly and nodded his head with approval. Again, they shook hands, this time exchanging goodbyes, and as quickly as he had appeared, Jeff Clark was gone.

Like a small child on Christmas morning, Silas unwrapped his gift and ran his fingers across the tops of the silver and black gas canisters. "What a beautiful sight." he thought.

After admiring the delivery a few moments longer, he packed up the box and carried them one at a time in the house and stashed them in the basement out of the way. When he came back upstairs and entered the kitchen, Brutus and Jacob stood awaiting the good news.

"We are in business boys," Dr. Wilde announced.

"Awesome! Who woulda thought that of all people Joe Yoder would come through in the clutch?" Brutus asked.

"I know, I'm still amazed he pulled it off so quickly without any hang-ups. Now if I can only convince him to take a generous payout to call it even, rather than make him part of our plan and give him a slice of the pie. He had dollar signs in his eyes when he stopped by Saturday, let's hope he's calmed down a little by now." Silas clung to a tiny bit of hope he could be persuasive enough to change the crooked politician's mind. He didn't wait long to find out.

At 10:30am, the black Towncar pulled down the driveway and parked in the same spot it had a few days earlier. Out stepped Yoder looking as tacky as ever, wearing another cheap black suit and politician's crooked smile. He looked like a daytime television game show host, the kind that laughed at his own jokes. Strolling casually around the front of the car and up the porch steps, he didn't knock assuming his presence was already known. Silas greeted him at the door and invited him in.

"You look pleased. I take it everything is just peachy?" he asked already knowing the answer. There was no doubt he had received confirmation from Jeff the deal went down smoothly as soon as he pulled off the property.

"Things are just fine," Silas said, doing a great job of hiding his excitement. "Thank you again, you really pulled through as promised, I won't forget that any time soon."

"Should we talk business here or somewhere private, the barn perhaps?" Yoder asked calmly.

"Here is fine. We'll talk in private here," Silas replied, giving Brutus and Jacob a look.

The two men nodded and left the house.

"So, let me do the talking here if you don't mind," he continued as he turned his focus back to Yoder.

"By all means, it's your house."

"I'm not sure what you're thinking my big project is at this moment, but I need to make one thing clear: this is my project. I formulated the whole thing precisely down to the tiniest detail, leaving absolutely zero room for error. You must realize that suddenly throwing in another participant, with his own pros and cons, his own opinions, and his own motives greatly add to the human error factor. I can't make adjustments or a roster change this late in the game, it just won't work. Instead, I'm giving you twenty grand and my most sincere thanks for helping my cause. And let's not act like this will be the last time I make a play, I assure you that you will be included in another project in the future. Here, take the money, you earned it." Silas held out a very fat, manila envelope as a hopeful peace offering.

Yoder sat staring at it for a few silent seconds. "You don't hear "no" too often huh? It must be nice to be boss," he stated as he reluctantly took the payment. At the end of the day, money was money, and Yoder was hard up for some, the sooner, the better. He hoped if he was made a partner in Silas's big move, he would get at least twice that amount. The envelope was a little bit lighter than he anticipated, but he was in no position to be picky. Besides, he didn't even know for certain what type of job it was. All he had were wild theories and scenarios bouncing around his head, and it became clear that was all he would have to settle for. There wasn't going to be any sharing of details by the man sitting across from him, the man paying handsomely for his efforts as well as for his silence. It was the cold, hard truth he had to swallow and be satisfied with it.

"Can I offer you a drink?" his host asked kindly.

"Sure, anything with suds would be great." Far be it from a politician to talk business without alcohol involved. He was handed a cold summer ale and took three big gulps before setting the already half-empty bottle down in front of him. "How are things around here? Have you finished with the renovations?" Yoder inquired.

"For the most part, all of the major tasks are done. The barn is 100%, and I'd say the house itself is at about 80% complete." Pausing, as if lost in thought, Dr. Wilde considered his next question before deciding to ask it, "Would you like to see something spectacular?"

Yoder's eyes widened from a suddenly rejuvenated morale. "Sure, I would! What have you got?"

Silas walked toward the door and waved his hand, signaling for Yoder to follow. The curious politician grabbed his beer and hopped to his feet. Outside were Brutus and Jacob smoking cigarettes sitting on the tailgate of Brutus' truck. When Silas walked past them, he gave a wink signaling all had gone as planned. They weren't surprised, their boss was used to running the show however he pleased.

As the barn door opened, Dr. Wilde stepped aside and held his arm out, extending it into the doorway and welcoming his guest to explore at will. Yoder accepted the invitation and walked past his host and entered. He was expecting something like a few expensive cars or even a racehorse there to impress him, but not what his eyes saw. Such a clean and organized laboratory didn't seem to fit the outside appearance at all. Nobody would suspect such a drastic transition from one extreme to another. A rural colonial-style barn hiding an immaculate research lab on the inside. Silas nudged him forward and pointed up at the domicile above. Cain stood at attention, wondering if he was in for some kind of delicious treat.

"What in God's name..." Yoder's words trailed off, lost much like his ability to comprehend the need for such a creature. "He's... yours?" was all he could muster up.

"He doesn't belong to me or anyone else. He lives here freely, a partner and friend to us all. Life for him early on was difficult, to say the least, which is why he is confined in there, for his own safety and peace of mind," Silas explained as if giving a tour at the zoo. His guest was dumbfounded and suddenly very uncomfortable.

"Nice," he said. "You're a fortunate man. Listen, thanks for the talk and the cash, as well as the tour. I've got a meeting this afternoon that I have to prepare for. Would you mind showing me out?"

The primatologist witnessed true primitive fear and discomfort. Panic slowly reared its unwanted head and sent Joe Yoder running for the hills!

"Of course, I wouldn't be able to forgive myself if I caused you to be unprepared for your meeting," he sarcastically replied.

Yoder didn't care if he was laughing on the inside at him, as long as he headed for the door, he didn't give a shit. Silas ushered him out and turned to him with an inquisitive look on his face. "So, now, do you still think you know what my plan is?" he asked knowing the answer.

"Between the pile of cash, I now have in my pocket and that...thing in there, I don't give a flying fuck what you're planning. I hope everything goes off without a hitch and I wish you all well. You have my number if any future endeavors present themselves and you want my assistance. Until then, take care my friend" Yoder said, holding out his hand.

The Wild shook it tightly and smiled.

Yoder beeped his horn as he turned off the dirt driveway and onto the road, and that was the last time he was in person for a long time. Another surprise appearance to the farmhouse would never be a concern to Silas again. Cain proved himself more useful than previously believed. Perhaps it was time to really put him to the test. Yes, it was time to take off the training wheels and see what that magnificent being was capable of, time to break out the sawed-off shotguns and chill the champagne.

Chapter 16

The day after Jeff Clark and Joseph Yoder visited the farm, the theme for the household was boot camp, and Dr. Silas Wilde reported in for drill instructor duty. He set his alarm for 6:00 am and had the rest of his housemates up shortly after. A light breakfast of coffee and bran flakes was consumed with haste because Silas ordered them to report to the barn no later than 7:00am wearing loose-fitting pants, t-shirts, and sneakers. From the sound of it, he was planning on making them run, but where and for how long was anybody's guess. Much of what went on inside the mind of Dr. Wilde was a mystery, even to those who knew him best, like Brutus.

Jacob had on navy-blue track pants while his three coworkers wore sweatpants. They had either long-sleeved shirts or sweatshirts on since the mornings were chilly, and the downstairs heat was turned off each night before they went to bed. Sitting facing the window that overlooked the porch and part of the driveway, Mack watched as Silas walked over to his van, opened the passenger door, and pulled a medium-sized cardboard box out. He turned, shut the door with a bump from his rear end, and headed up the steps and into the kitchen. Without saying a word or even acknowledging any of the men, he opened the box using a utility knife and reached inside. "Now that's more like it," he exclaimed with a smile.

He held up a large, camouflaged t-shirt that was a perfect fit for him, but instead of wearing it, he tossed it over to Brutus. He bent and rummaged around a little before holding up three more shirts. "Let's see..." he said, reading the tags, "extra-large. Here you go Jacob, and double X for Mack and Tony."

All four stood and exchanged confused glances, probably wondering what the shirts had in store for them. They swapped what they wore with the dark green camo tees and waited for instructions.

"You've got about ten minutes until 7:00am," Silas reported, pointing to the clock above the refrigerator. "If you have to use the bathroom, do it now because we're going to be outdoors all day. Lock up the house on your way out and meet me as planned in the barn."

He opened the refrigerator and took out a plastic container of chopped melons and then went outside. Tony looked at the others and said in a serious, low-pitched monotone voice, "He's hunting us. He's going to fucking hunt us down like dogs and..." he ran his finger across his neck making a slicing noise.

"Well lucky for me, all I have to do is run faster than the slowest one here," Brutus said, patting Mack on his shoulder.

"Haha, ha...fuck off," Mack countered.

Once they took turns relieving themselves, they filed outside, and Brutus locked up as instructed. They entered the barn and immediately saw Cain standing in the center polishing off the last few pieces of fruit. Silas sat in his desk chair lacing up a pair of rugged outdoor boots. His jacket was on the back of the chair, which he removed and put on as well. Why was he wearing a nice, warm jacket while his men only had matching t-shirts to keep them from catching pneumonia they wondered. As it turned out, they would rather have not learned the answer to that question.

"I hope you boys are up for a good workout. Ready to get those heart rates up?" Dr. Wilde asked clapping his hands together. "Today is going to be a day for learning as well as exercising. You will be learning the lay of the land as you all will scatter and choose different hiding spots to take cover in. Cain and I will be learning how well you are at becoming invisible in what we will pretend to be hostile grounds. The two of us will practice communicating with each other quietly as we hunt the four of you down, one at a time. Whoever is caught first is on kitchen and garbage duty for a week. The last one to be found gets their choice of a cash prize or the privilege of picking out what we have for dinner every night next week. Once you pick a spot you cannot move, you stay in your original hiding spot. Chances are you will see us before we find you so if I find out any of you break my rules, I promise I will break you. This is an important drill, and I want all of you to take it as seriously as I am."

He paused for a moment and pulled at a piece of string that was around his neck. It was a coach's whistle. "When I blow this the first time, that signals the exercise has begun, and you all will sprint across the backyard and throughout the trails in search of your cover. You technically got a bit of a sneak peek, when you set out the dummies, so I hope your memory is good and you recall what trail lead where. You are also not allowed to touch or alter the dummies in any way either, leave them be. Use them to remember where you are, where you came from, and where you're going. If you get found, you will hear the whistle first, followed by me calling your name and where you're hiding. One more final note: when I said that the two of us are hunting you, I meant it. We will be armed with several airsoft guns. Cain mostly will use the pistol, possibly the rifle if I feel like he can handle it, and I will be using a pump action shotgun. They might not be real bullets, but they leave marks when you get hit. Always be aware of your surroundings and stay sharp. I will be learning a lot about all of you today and how you operate in high-stress situations when you are at a significant disadvantage. I need leaders who don't crack under pressure. I'm testing you on many different levels so take this as seriously as you would any other job I assign you. If you want to prove yourself to me, this is your chance. Any questions?"

Brutus raised his hand and asked, "What are the borders as to how far away we can hide?"

"Good question, I'm glad you reminded me. You are to stick to the trails and not venture more than twenty yards on either side of them. There are plenty of hiding spots out there, so I feel that's fair. Otherwise, you could take the fuck off, and I'd never find you. Oh, and the last person standing won't have to worry about getting shot at when we do find you, so that should be even more motivation to win. Okay, head outside and stand side-by-side up against the side of the house facing the woods. I'll be right there."

Silas directed them out, and they did as they were told. He and Cain came out of the barn about five minutes later carrying their guns. The guns looked realistic and would fool most people who weren't familiar with real ones.

"We will turn our backs, blow the whistle, and I've set the timer on my phone for seven minutes so you'd better haul ass. You all ready?" Silas asked as he stood with his shotgun strapped around his back, holding Cain's free hand.

A couple "yes sirs" and head nods let him know his prey were ready to begin. Biting down on the whistle, Silas turned with Cain facing the house and blew one long hard whistle and held it for about ten seconds.

He heard the thudding of their feet on the lawn before they reached the tree line. Once they made it there, he heard leaves rustling, twigs snapping as the sounds became fainter. Silas checked the timer, five and a half minutes. Cain seemed to be cooperating remarkably as if he fully understood what was going on and was obeying the rules he had just heard. The Wild let go of his hand and held his hand out flat, telling him to remain with his back turned. Silas suddenly jogged over to the barn and stepped inside for a minute before coming back out with something in his hand. It was one of the masks he made special for Cain. This one he hadn't shown him yet, not sure how he would take it. There was the mouth of a chimp painted on the white canvas material, but there were black stitches running up and down, back and forth through the top and bottom lips. The level of detail Dr. Wilde had achieved was remarkable. It looked like a real chimpanzee mouth that was sewn shut.

Holding it out for him to examine, Cain's appeared unimpressed, and so Silas slipped it over the ape's head and then pulled it down over his mouth. Much like how Native American braves would apply war paint to intimidate their enemies, Cain's mask would surely have a similar effect on the men he was hunting. Silas chuckled to himself imagining their faces if Cain was able to sneak up and startle them. Hopefully, none of them had weak hearts!

The timer went off, and again Dr. Wilde took the chimp's free hand as he jogged toward the far end of the property where the grass stopped, and the forest of maple, birch, and pines began. There were two possible trails to choose from about thirty yards apart. They chose the one on the left, and the pursuit was on.

For forty minutes Silas and Cain surveyed and patrolled a

winding network of trails, sometimes straying off to investigate a possible hiding spot but finding nothing and no one. A few times they backtracked to a trail they passed by on the first trip around, making it harder and harder to memorize where they were going and where they'd already been.

Silas kept a space between himself and Cain of ten to fifteen paces to cover more ground and increase their range of sight. They used sign language and a number of different clicks and chirps to communicate and, for the most part, they were on the same page. They headed down one of the trails they went back to and after ten minutes of traveling down it, they caught their first break. A patch of weeds called fiddleheads had sprouted in the center of the trail, and they were recently stomped on. "A rookie mistake," Silas thought to himself. Half of a footprint, a medium-sized one, was visible. It was too small to be Brutus's and probably Mack's as well, so they were certain either Jacob or Tony had traveled that way. They ventured a little farther down the path before coming into view of a formation of large granite boulders, that sat just about twenty yards out in the thick of the forest. Silas made a motion for Cain to stay down while he waited for him to circle around and take a closer look. Like a good soldier, Cain obeyed.

Moving slowly in a crouched position, The Wilde walked in a sweeping motion, closing in on the pile of massive stones. He felt he did a fine job representing his nickname. Thankfully, the majority of the forest floor off the main trails was covered in dead leaves, pine needles, and ferns; all of which made no sound when walked on. When Silas was about twenty feet away, he caught a glimpse of a camouflage pattern set in contrast to the blue-gray stone behind it. He didn't see a face though, since whoever it was had burrowed in the center of the rock formation like a tick.

Dr. Wilde turned and faced Cain, who was growing impatient from staying idle too long. He signaled that he spotted someone and pointed to the spot. Cain returned hand gestures asking what to do next. Silas instructed him to quietly move around to the opposite side of the stone hideout and carefully climb and take a position in a tree that overshadowed the boulders. The ape gave a sign he understood and followed his master's instructions. Showing virtually no effort, the chimp made it up a maple tree and onto a limb that was fifteen feet up, with such ease Silas watched in jealous awe. He scaled up so quickly using only one free hand to grip the trunk since he held the gun in his other. Snapping out of it, Dr. Wilde signed to Cain asking him if he had eyes on their target, to which he responded, "Yes."

Silas held up his right hand in the shape of a gun and gestured to take the shot. This was a great chance to gauge how comfortable and accurate he was wielding a pistol about the same size as the Glock 9mm and how accurate his aim was.

Cain scooted his body a little further down toward the end of the tree branch and got into position. He lowered and dropped his legs below the branch and then sat on it, rather than standing still while aiming. It proved to be a wise move. Cain sat and held his arm out straight as he aimed while he kept perfectly still. He released a deep sigh, and then came the shot.

"AHHHH MOTHER FUCKER!" Jacob screamed in pain.

Silas blew the whistle and called his name. Jacob emerged from the rock formation rubbing the side of his neck where a red welt was already very visible. He met up with Silas, and they waited for Cain to climb down and join them. When he finally made it over to the two men, Jacob did a double take and stared, speechless, at the masked assassin. He didn't know what to make of him.

"Nice shooting partner!" Silas congratulated the chimp.

"Did you see him up above you or were you completely unaware of his presence?" he then asked Jacob.

"I thought I heard something move in that general direction, but I was looking around the ground, not for an aerial assault! Well played. Who else have you ambushed besides me?" Jacob asked.

"Oh, my poor man, you're the first. Sorry but you're the biggest loser today. I hope you cook better than you hide."

"Are you shitting me?! I thought Brutus would be the first one out since he's so damn big. Shit..." Jacob moaned, still rubbing his neck.

"Head back to the house and get washed up. When you're done, get to making dinner. There are pork tenderloins in the refrigerator you can bake. Peel and make mashed potatoes and use up the rest of the carrots. I have a feeling I might know what direction the others headed off in. We've covered the majority of the trails leaving only one more area we haven't checked yet. We should be back within the hour."

Jacob did as he was told and headed off in the direction of the farmhouse, massaging his neck and mumbling profanities. Silas rubbed Cain's shoulder and congratulated him again for an excellent job, for getting into position without being noticed and for such a precise shot. The ape had a wide smile behind his mask.

Doubling back, the two hunters came to a small clearing in the woods where three trails intersected. They had already been down two, so they set off down the final remaining path, scanning left and right, up and down in hopes of stumbling upon another helpful clue. It took less than ten minutes before they found one. A cigarette butt tossed to the side by the only man who smoked, Brutus. It was an Indian Gold, his brand, and it was wet, meaning it was recently left behind. "How sloppy," thought Silas. Why would that meathead light one up, sending miniature smoke signals into the sky when he should have been searching for a fool-proof hiding spot? He is a great, dedicated, and trustworthy worker but not the sharpest knife in the drawer," came Silas's rapid thoughts.

Holding the butt in his fingers for Cain to see he said, "Brutus, Brutus, Brutus," and then he held his arms out to indicate a large man.

Cain made a series of positive grunts indicating his understanding. With a sudden look of hope in his eyes, he intensely scanned in each direction. Silas this time held back, and Cain took the lead while heading down the trail. He proved to be a great look-out. Every twenty feet they moved Cain stopped, scanned the woods around them, and listened carefully for the slightest sound. At one stop, the chimp listened for a moment, his head suddenly turned around, and he stared at a huge tree that was root up and laying on its side. It was only a few feet from the side of the trail, but it was large, perhaps large enough to provide cover to an also very large man.

Cain crept forward slowly, gun lifted and pointing ahead of him. He stopped five feet in front of the trunk and listened carefully once again. He definitely heard something moving. Was it Brutus or some woodland creature? Silas was motionless, carefully studying Cain's every move. Then, without warning, the chimp sprang forward and landed with both feet planted on the tree trunk. As soon as he had his balance, he drew his weapon, aimed it directly below him, and rapidly fired off five shots.

"ALRIGHT, ALRIGHT YOU GOT ME! CHILL FOR CHRIST'S SAKE!" roared Brutus. The Wild blew the whistle and called out Brutus' name. Brutus put his hands on the tree and pulled himself up. He was covered in leaves, a smart decision for cover but his deep breathing in and out caused the leaves to rattle just enough for Cain's sharp hearing to pick up. The proud primate headed back over to Silas, who was chuckling as he dished out compliments.

"Great job again buddy! You're one hell of a tracker, I would have walked right by if I was in your position. Impressive job squeezing behind the tree though, Brutus. Next time don't leave evidence on the trail you dope."

Silas reached into his pocket and held up the butt. Brutus hung his head embarrassed. Impressing his employer and receiving his praise was a close second to getting paid. It wasn't often he made mistakes or got reprimanded by Silas. And now, he got one-upped by an ape?! Brutus wasn't pleased with himself, and the discomfort he felt on the inside made him forget the pain on his upper arm and side, where he was hit with the plastic pellets.

"The good news is we already found Jacob, who's back at the house getting dinner ready. Go wash up and get ready to eat. We'll see you there soon," Dr. Wilde told him.

Brutus made no objection and walked back, sulking the whole way.

"Only two left," Silas announced as they picked up right where they left off, heading down the trail.

For a while, they continued the same stop and go method that had worked finding Brutus, but no signs were found. Finally, after a half hour, Silas swapped places with Cain and took the lead again. They made it to a split in the road, and they stopped. Looking down the left trail, there was nothing that a grown man could hide in or behind. Checking the right trail wasn't much better, but Silas did spot one of the dummies a little way down.

The Wild thought if Mack or Tony made it to that point, they most probably choose the side with the dummy since it was more familiar to them. He was right. As he and Cain approached the dummy, something caught the corner of Silas's eye. Up ahead about fifteen yards and ten yards to the left of the trail, something moved up in a giant oak tree. As they got closer, the shape of a man crouching on a tree limb and hugging the trunk became clear. It was Tony, and though he was plain to see once they drew near, from afar he blended in quite well. Not to mention, they didn't search the trees until that point. Tony drew his shotgun and aimed it at Silas, who had the whistle in his mouth. Dr. Wilde squeezed his trigger and let out a loud whistle. Tony almost lost his balance from the spray of yellow, stinging pellets.

"Tony in the tree, come on down!" Silas shouted mimicking a television game show host.

"Alright, don't shoot, don't shoot!" pleaded their latest victim. "I take it I'm not the winner if you fired at me."

"That's correct. Mack is the champ. Do you have any idea where he is?"

"We both headed this way, but he turned off the trail a short way back. There was one big boulder by itself where he turned. When we see that we'll know we're close. Come on I'll show you."

Tony suddenly became the leader of the group. Dr. Wilde was anxious to head home since hunger had set in with ferocity.

After walking for about ten minutes, Tony pointed and shouted "Right there! That's the spot."

Silas put the whistle in his mouth, drew in a deep breath, and blew with all his might. Tony waited for him to finish and then called out to Mack, "The game is over Mack, you won! Show yourself!"

A rustling noise coming from directly behind them, on the side opposite the bolder, made them jump and spin around. The ground was covered in dead leaves at first, but suddenly it moved and up stood Mack. He was laying on his back and had simply pulled the leaves over him. He must have figured hiding in plain sight was the smartest move, and he was right.

"Nice job!" praised Silas. "You were right under our noses when we first walked by. No offense, but this morning I had picked you to be the first one out of the game. Way to prove me wrong, enjoy it because it won't happen ever again," The Wild said with a smile.

"Thanks, I honestly was just exhausted from running, and I collapsed at that spot and figured if I was going to die, I might as well start burying myself to save someone else the trouble."

They all burst into laughter as they walked back to the farm.

It was just after 6:00pm by the time they cleaned themselves and sat down to enjoy the first meal Jacob prepared for them. He did a great job, as they all agreed, and hoped the rest of the meals he cooked for them would be as delicious. They shared funny stories and laughed together, something that became a more frequent occurrence. They were starting to feel like a family, and they all sincerely enjoyed it since it had been ages if ever, they had each experienced the feeling. They raised their bottles of beer for a toast, and Brutus proposed, "To Dr. Wilde, thanks for being the greatest employer, the best host, and an even better friend. Salud!"

Chapter 17

Saturdays were quiet around the farm since the men went back to their own residences for the weekend. It was the perfect time for Silas to give Cain intensive one-on-one attention, training, and care. His ability to operate the airsoft pistol was inspiring. He had been handling the empty Glock 9mm's on a regular basis for a few weeks now. It was time to step it up a notch and see how he did with something a little more powerful: the sawed-off shotgun.

Silas had a pair of them he introduced to Cain inside the barn. Cain took hold of the one Silas offered him and examined it. It was heavier and a little more cumbersome than the svelte 9mm pistol. Despite showing care and noticeable respect for the firearms, Cain had a bad habit of peeking down the hole of the barrel. Dr. Wilde corrected him by placing his hand around the chimp's wrist somewhat tightly and lowering the weapon away from his face while firmly saying, "No Cain."

The curious ape eventually stopped looking into the barrel of the pistols, but there was a new kind with two bigger holes he could peek into at the same time! The temptation was too much, and after holding it for less than a minute, he turned it around and brought it up to eye level. Silas, this time, wrapped both his hands around the chimp's and said in the same tone only louder, "CAIN, NO!"

Cain was not a fan of this behavior. Being reprimanded by his teacher and friend in such a manner not only upset him, but it also embarrassed him. He directed an evil glare at Silas, and he grunted but finally gave up and held the gun properly.

For the first half of the day, Cain had the gun in his possession, carrying it around the inside of the barn wherever he went. He fully understood this was something special, a precious gift from the man he trusted most, and so he took good care of it. Dr. Wilde gave him plenty of space, keeping mostly to himself at his desk downstairs, but always closely observing his primate pal to ensure he didn't mishandle the gun again. Silas was pleased when lunchtime arrived without there being any repeat offenses. This encouraged the doctor to take the experiment outside again to test the chimp's abilities.

Directly behind the barn were the side-by-side shooting ranges the men built. Forty yards long was a reasonable distance to start with. A section of a wall built four-feet high on the left side and three-feet high on the right. The shorter side was built for Cain to stand in front of. A small wooden box was beneath the three-foot wall to boost his height, so he could rest his arms on the top of the wall and keep him steady as he aimed. The left side was for Silas to do the same. He demonstrated for Cain until he got the hang of it. At the opposite end of the range, there was what looked like a miniature clothesline, running horizontally with four different targets to aim at. They were made simply out of two squares of plywood on top of each other with targets painted on each.

Dr. Wilde loaded live rounds into the clip of the 9mm for the first time and handed it to the chimp, then he pointed to the targets and gave the command: "Fire!"

Silas decided he would stick to that one prompt from then on until it was fully understood by his student. Cain held his arm out aiming for the target and fired, showing the same impressive poise he had with the airsoft pistol. His shot was off the mark, but it still found the corner of the target. Silas got into position behind Cain and wrapped his arms around him, taking hold of his hands and helping him aim. There was very little resistance, almost as if he welcomed the help. When Dr. Wilde had the sight centered on the bullseye, he squeezed the ape's index finger, and they hit just two inches away from their mark.

"Good boy!" he praised his pal.

Cain loved positive reinforcement and wanted more. He remained arms stretched outwards waiting for The Wild to repeat the same routine. Again, they hit the target, this time a little closer to the center, and again he was a good boy. A few more repetitions and then Silas backed off, leaving him to take aim by himself. Cain hesitated for a moment until Silas gave the command, "Fire!"

An impressive shot hit one inch away from the center!

They continued for a solid hour with the Glock 9mm, and then Dr. Wilde introduced a second identical pistol to the routine. He demonstrated first how to aim both, and then fired ten rounds from each. This really excited Cain, as he eagerly held out his open hands asking for the guns. It took him a full clip, fifteen rounds each before he honed-in his accuracy. But he did it, and he was delightfully good!

They practiced for another hour until The Wild was satisfied then they moved on to the sawed-off shotguns. Repeating the same drill, they started off with one at first to get the hang of it. Silas loaded two twelve-gauge slugs into the breakaway barrel and then took his position behind his student. They aimed and fired once, but the recoil made Cain jump back into Silas's broad chest, and the chimp let out a yelp. Silas stroked his back and used a calm voice to tell him it was alright, but Cain was trembling a little too much. He couldn't aim steadily if he wanted to.

Cain took a break and sat in the grass on the side of the wall and watched as his teacher practiced his own shot. After loading and reloading about ten times, the chimp decided there was nothing to be afraid of and walked over and squeezed in front of his instructor. Silas smiled in relief that Cain's fear had vanished. Reaching up and taking hold of the guns, the chimp fired a couple of shots. Much to Dr. Wilde's satisfaction, the target had taken both hits relatively close to dead center. Again, he reloaded the powerful gun and this time instructed Cain to fire on his own. He steadied after shaking for just a moment and shot twice, splintering the plywood to pieces.

"Good boy!" was Cain's reward, and he was glowing with a newly discovered confidence and talent.

The rest of the afternoon was spent getting used to firing different combinations of the four guns. The better his aim improved, the more he wanted to keep firing. Seeing an opportunity, Dr. Wilde had Cain sit up on the lower side of the wall with his feet dangling out in front of him. He walked around to the front and grabbed hold of one of his feet and placed the sawed-off in it. Cain quickly glanced up at his master, as if he was both crazy and brilliant for thinking of that. The chimpanzee gripped, with his wonderful primate foot and its opposable thumb, and slowly leaned back and aimed. When the gun discharged, Silas cheered and jumped up and down, patting Cain on his back and head. The Wilde's insanely wonderful vision was slowly coming true! He continued target practice lessons until sunset, then the next morning again and throughout the rest of the day. It became part of their daily routine.

When the men returned Monday morning, Dr. Wilde was so excited to show them the progress, he couldn't keep the goofy grin off his face. His elevated mood was noticed as soon as he greeted his confused workers, who weren't used to seeing him so happy. Before they did anything, they were ordered to meet at the shooting range around back. The men did so and waited for Silas to join them. When Dr. Wilde came out of the barn, he was carrying a wicker basket with a corduroy cushion in it, and on top of it, four guns were lined up. He placed the basket on the ground as Cain jumped up and sat on top of the three-foot wall. Silas loaded the guns one at a time and handed them to his primate pal, the two 9mms in his hands, and the sawed-off twelve-gauge shotguns he held each in one foot. A low murmur from the onlooking crowd suggested disbelief in what they were witnessing. Brutus shook his head and chuckled at the sight before him. Jacob mumbled profanities as he too shook his head and took a couple steps back. Mack and Tony watched in silence since no logical explanation nor positive outcome came to mind.

Like a proud parent showing off the talents of his child, Dr. Wilde gave the commands, and the show began. "Steady, steady. Aim, easy, and... FIRE!"

Four shots echoed at once and rang in their ears. Cain hit and decimated the target with two bullets and two slugs. After a brief silence, Silas cheered and congratulated his student for his superb marksmanship. The four men also clapped in disbelief. The crazy bastard had done it! He taught an animal to accurately fire four guns at once! Absolutely amazing was an enormous understatement. This accomplishment ushered in countless new criminally crazy opportunities the boss had surely already conjured up.

When the show was over, Cain returned to his enclosure with a large platter of produce and a chocolate bar as an added bonus. The four workers went to work. They tackled the list of remaining house repairs The Wild had made and hung on the refrigerator. Brutus replaced a leaky shower head in the master bathroom, Jacob installed a new sump pump in the basement, and Tony and Mack prepared their bedroom to be painted. Silas remained in the barn hard at work on something, but none of them knew what. It wasn't until they stopped for dinner that they discovered what he was up to. Dr. Wilde came into the kitchen wearing a large backpack. This was no ordinary backpack though, he had custom tailored it so Cain could sit in it, with holes for his legs, a hole in the top flap pulled over his head, and buckled him securely in, and even two loops, one on the left and one on the right that were to holster the guns.

"So, what do you guys think?" Silas asked proudly.

"It's great," Tony responded.

"You really outdid yourself this time," was Jacob's answer.

"You're fucking fried," Brutus said, tapping his temple. The others couldn't believe he came out and said what they were all thinking!

"This here is the key to a successful robbery. With Cain on my back, covering me from four different angles, my hands will be free to rob and steal at lightning speed. It's perfect and besides, who in their right mind is going to test a gun-toting chimp?!" he proposed.

The Wild did have a point, nobody would be brave with a deformed, devilish primate pointing two sawed-off shotguns at their face.

"Tomorrow, I'll give it a test run in the woods. Now you understand why I had you scatter those dummies about? Cain and I will see how good we do, firing on the move. If we can do that, then doing it standing before a bank teller will be cake. I suggest you all keep indoors until we finish our practice though, we don't want any stray bullets coming near you."

As Jacob prepared chicken Parmesan with ziti, the image of Silas, standing six and a half feet tall, with a four-foot deranged chimp on his back, gripping four guns as they walked into a bank and demanded money, was a more terrifying scene than anyone witnessing it could possibly comprehend. What was he planning on wearing? Would Cain wear one of the creepy masks Silas made for him or would he be snarling like a rabid hyena? It was a sight he was sure he wouldn't ever want to see, and they were on the same team!

After Silas went back to the barn, the four men sitting at the table sipped their beers and searched for the right words.

"Brutus, has he been planning this for a while, I mean like while he was still working at the zoo or is this a recently thought up plan?" Mack asked.

"Honestly, I think he has been on this for a while, but exactly how long, I'm not sure," Brutus offered up as his best explanation. "He told Jacob and I when we first got back from Africa and mentioned how he wanted to pull off a heist, just he and Cain. We shrugged it off as him just talking out of his ass. We had no idea how serious or how capable of pulling it off he actually was!"

"Can we hold off talking about this until after we have eaten, please? I'm getting sick to my stomach thinking about it, and the beers aren't helping?" Jacob asked.

Tony nodded and said he agreed, and so Brutus kept quiet with his thoughts. Mack got up and began setting the table realizing how lucky they were they didn't have to share a dinner table with Cain, given how much Silas cared for him, treating him more like a son than a pet.

Right as their meal was served by their maid for the week, Jacob, Silas returned and moved about quickly, taking his plate and silverware back out to the barn to eat. "Go on without me," he said. "I've got some work I want to finish up before it gets too late. It looks and smells delicious. Jacob, you're really starting to shine! The meals are getting better and better every day."

Jacob laughed it off but was secretly flattered someone had noticed and showed appreciation for his efforts. He was the kind of person who wanted to be the best at whatever job or hobby he took on, and cooking was no exception. Accessing the food channel's website on his phone for helpful recipes helped enormously. Now if only they helped keep the bathroom clean by picking up after themselves and lightening the load for him. What did he expect though, a miracle?

Dinner came and went, and so did bedtime. Tony was the last

one to fall asleep, and when he did around 11:40pm, Silas still hadn't come in from the barn. Whatever kept him busy had to have been very important. There were only a couple hours of twilight remaining when he did finally retire to his bedroom. Four hours later and he was up and active again. Silas wanted to start his target practice in the woods early because the weather station said they may get showers in the afternoon.

It was just after 7:00am when Silas made his way to the kitchen, wondering if Jacob had or felt like making him breakfast. He peeked in the bedrooms and knew the only ones awake were Brutus and Jacob, so when he reached the kitchen and found it empty with no signs of food or coffee, he was quite puzzled. Silas saw all three of their trucks in the driveway, so they hadn't left. Fumbling for his phone, he pulled it out of his bathrobe pocket and hit the security system app. He checked, and they weren't in the barn either. Where the hell had they gone?

He brewed a pot of dark roast coffee, toasted a bagel, and sat on the living room couch eating and watching the morning news. Just as he suspected, the outlook predicted rain around 1:00pm. The window to the left of the entertainment center overlooked the long front yard and the driveway that ran alongside it. Two figures suddenly came into view. Brutus and Jacob jogged down the driveway, then sprinted toward the house. A sick feeling moved through Silas's stomach as the situation with his dog Poe replayed in his head. Something wasn't right. He jumped up, spilling coffee on himself but ignored it as he ran to the front door and flung it open. "What happened?!" he cried out.

Brutus and Jacob were startled by his sudden appearance, and they slowed down as they approached him.

"What's the matter?" Brutus asked his boss.

"You tell me, where did you disappear to and why were you running back in such a panic?"

"We weren't panicked, we had a race," Jacob answered. "I asked the big man if he wanted to go for a run with me and he agreed. When we got to the driveway, we bet breakfast on a footrace, loser cooks. Why were you in such a panic?!" Jake asked looking at the

141

coffee stain on Silas's white robe.

"I couldn't find you two and, well you know how I have to know everything that's going on. When I saw you barreling down toward the house, my first thought was someone was chasing you. I don't know, I wasn't fully awake yet," he said, feeling awfully foolish.

They laughed at his expense that one time because he almost never lost his cool like that.

An hour later, they were all awake, had eaten the breakfast Brutus made for them, and they were dressed and ready to go watch Silas take off in the woods on his target practice expedition with Cain in tow. The Wild had everything prepared the night before; the guns had been cleaned and loaded, Cain's backpack was laid out, a Fannie pack filled with extra clips and shotgun slugs was on his desk, sitting on top of a map he had drawn of the locations of the dummies.

"How do you load up Cain?" Tony asked his boss.

"Watch and see," the doctor answered.

Silas put on the backpack first followed by the ammo pack. He sat in his comfy, black desk chair and pulled his boots on, tying them tight. "Now it's Cain's turn."

He let his partner in crime out of his enclosure and called him over to the examination table. Tapping on the empty surface, Cain hopped up with impressive ease. Silas retrieved a folding chair that was against the wall and turned it, so its back was against the edge of the table. He sat with his back to Cain, who then very gently stepped one foot at a time into the backpack. Once he was in place, The Wild asked Brutus to pull the top flap over Cain's head and make sure he was buckled in tightly.

When all was said and done, Silas grunted as he stood nice and tall, one hundred and fifty pounds heavier. He picked up the map, folded it, and tucked it into his chest pocket. Next, he grabbed two Glocks and held them over his head. Cain grabbed them with his hands. Then Silas picked up the two sawed-off shotguns and held them by his sides with his elbows bent. The chimp took them both with his feet, keeping all four weapons aimed away from he and

Silas' bodies at all times. They obviously had been working on this. The Wild turned to face his audience and smiled from ear to ear. "How do we look?" he asked, knowing the answer.

"Fucking terrifying and badass!" Mack answered without hesitation.

"Good, thank you. Now, let's do this before we get washed out," Silas said as he stepped out the door.

The four men stood at the edge of the yard and watched as Dr. Wilde jogged with all that extra weight as he headed down one of the trails. Before he rounded a corner stepping out of sight, he turned back and waved to the guys, who stood there amazed at how strong and psychotic their employer truly was. They waved back and gave him thumbs up in support of his mission, admiring his determination. When he was out of sight, Tony broke the silence, "Who do you think is going to die first out there?"

Answering at the exact time, the three other men all replied, "Silas!"

Chapter 18

Dr. Wilde's legs burned, and his quads and calf muscles cramped under the weight of a lethal, full-grown chimpanzee. More squats would have to be incorporated into his daily exercises. Silas came to a familiar split in the trail and stopped there to catch his breath. Up ahead where it split off to the left, he saw the fifteenth and final dummy they were searching for. He pointed and made the call, "FIRE."

Cain lifted his right arm and aimed at his target from about twenty yards away. Silas covered his ears and watched as his passenger made a great shot, directly in the side of the target's head. He hadn't thought of wearing earplugs, and he paid the price for it.

They located all the dummies and Cain shot them up like a seasoned hitman. Some he shot while Silas jogged, some from a good distance away. He only missed three times with the shotguns because they were a little too far out of range. They were made specifically to deal massive damage at close range. Silas was so proud of Cain's performance, especially in the short amount of time they had trained.

They covered a dozen acres of thickly wooded trails, searched out and shot all fifteen strategically placed targets in under two hours. Not bad considering Silas was on foot, but Cain was not, he rode on his back. Coming to an open area where three trails intersected, The Wild stopped to catch his breath.

"Let's get you out so you can stretch your legs and I can rest mine," he said as he slowly lowered himself to the ground and sat Indian style on the dirt trail. He unbuckled the two straps that held the backpack on and slipped out of it. Next, he unbuckled Cain and helped him out. The chimp was a little wobbly at first, perhaps his legs had partially fallen asleep. The two of them were pleased by the turnout of their target practice, and it showed on their faces.

A rumble of thunder caused them both to glance upward at the darkening sky.

"We'd better get a move on," Silas said.

He grabbed the four guns and placed them in the backpack, securing them in with Velcro straps. Once again, he put the pack back on and reached for Cain's hand. The chimp and the doctor walked back to the farm holding hands, and just as they reached the end of the trail it began to rain. Silas escorted Cain into the barn where he shut him in his home. He put the guns in the wicker basket and slid it under his desk. His rumbling stomach told him it was dinner time and so he headed out the door then hurried up the porch steps to avoid getting soaked.

Jacob had prepared shepherd's pie, and it smelled good in the oven. Silas arranged Cain's fruit-filled dinner and brought it out to him. He didn't stay because he was too hungry himself and wanted to eat as soon as the food came out of the oven.

"How did it go out there?" asked Jacob.

"That is one gifted animal. He's got sniping skills if I've ever seen some. He only missed three shots out of about thirty. I'll take him out back again once more, but after that, it's the real deal," the doctor stated.

Jacob stared in shock at what he just heard. "The real deal?" he asked Silas.

"I'm not messing around. I have everything planned out, and I believe he will be ready. The sooner I do a test run in real life setting the sooner I can move forward onto the bigger jobs. I'll find something easy, like a Mom and Pop liquor store or a check cashing business," The Wild explained with confidence.

"You're going to be putting your life in his hands," Jacob said as if making that realization as he was saying it. "I hope you know what you're doing. I don't doubt you, boss, I'm just concerned for your safety."

"Thanks, but I have everything under control. We make an awesome team, and we're going to kick some serious ass out there!"

Brutus, Mack, and Tony went to the casino for the evening, so it was only Jacob and Silas who remained for dinner. They changed the subject and engaged in casual talk about politics and the first placed Red Sox, but Jacob's mind kept going back to the Silas and Cain holding up a bank.

The last five minutes of dinner they sat in silence until Silas got up with his empty plate and put it in the sink. He headed to the living room, but when he got to the doorway, he stopped with his back to Jacob. "He's ready I said, I know it," the doctor said, in a low voice and then turned to give Jacob a look before heading upstairs.

After Jacob tidied up the kitchen and dining room, he took a cold beer out of the fridge and sat on the couch to watch a game on television. He had only enjoyed one beer and one full inning of baseball when Silas came back downstairs. "Put your boots on, you're coming with me," he said.

"Not another shooting drill," Jacob thought. He sighed loud enough to be heard and rose to his feet. "What are we up to?" he asked.

"I have to meet someone I don't trust 100%, and I want you with me just in case," Silas answered.

Just in case? Just in case what?! Jacob was full of questions, but all he said was, "Do I need my gun?"

Silas looked at him and pulled his jacket open revealing his, in his sidearm holster. Jacob went to his room and grabbed his gun from his duffel bag and returned downstairs. As he walked through the kitchen, The Wild used a bottle opener on his keychain to open two beers and then handed one to Jacob along with the set of keys. "I want to do this quick so drive fast," he instructed.

"You got it." Jacob walked out behind his employer and locked the door. They got in the van and sped off.

They drove on side streets, avoiding the center of town and highways. Silas instructed where and when to turn until after fifteen minutes, they pulled into a long driveway in the neighboring town of Douglas, Massachusetts. Jacob had no idea what business Dr. Wilde conducted out there, but whatever it was they had privacy. The driveway was a half of a mile long! The lights inside the little ranch house they approached were off except one, that came from a lamp in the living room's bay window. An expensive, black, European sports car sat at the end of the driveway and Jacob eyed it in admiration.

"You stay here and wait. I'll let you know if I need you. I'm probably being paranoid but just keep your eyes open," Silas said and exited the van.

It was practically dark, and there were no outside lights on at the house. A man with shoulder length hair and a thick push-broom mustache opened the door and glared at Silas, then inspected the van. He was a muscular man despite being vertically challenged. From where he sat, Jacob estimated the guy to be about five-foot-six inches tall, a whole foot shorter than Silas. It was unheard of for The Wild to be intimidated, let alone afraid of another man. And even though this guy was well-built, Jacob had no doubt Dr. Wilde could take him. There must have been a reason why Silas had him come along.

Jacob watched as the two men exchanged words for a moment and then went inside. Still, the only light came from that little lamp in the house. He leaned over to get a better view inside the window, but he didn't see well from where the van was parked. Jacob got out and stretched his legs and kept watch from outside instead. Almost immediately, a swarm of mosquitoes buzzed around him. This meeting couldn't go fast enough for his liking. Aggravated and now itchy, he paced in circles around the van to keep from getting bit.

Suddenly, he heard shouting, and in the window, he saw the silhouettes of the two men. The shorter one seemed to yell while he waved his hands, and Silas stood with his hands on his hips. Then the front door swung open, and The Wild stormed out. The man standing in the doorway looked frustrated. Silas opened the driver's door, reached behind the seat, and removed a brown briefcase. With his head, he motioned for Jacob to come. Jacob walked over and stood next to him, where he saw Silas counting out hundred-dollar bills taken from a briefcase full of money.

"I don't typically do business with this guy, it's his partner I usually deal with. But he said they got into an argument and left before we got here. Some roid-rage lover's quarrel, I guess. I know that he has access to his partner's supply, but he's claiming that he doesn't and told me to leave. The guy's half in the bag and really testing my patience. I'm going to go up there one more time with the cash, and maybe once he sees it, he'll be persuaded to work out a deal."

"Okay, I'll stand out here and watch for his boyfriend coming home," Jacob responded.

Silas closed the briefcase and put it back behind the seat. As he walked back up toward the house, the man opened the door and picked up where he left off shouting. The Wild quietly walked toward him and held up the wad of bills. For a moment, the man stopped and stared, probably trying to estimate how much there was. The doctor pushed the money into the man's chest, and with that, he finally grabbed it. He sneered at Silas but then turned and walked out of sight. In less than two minutes the drug dealer was back holding a brown shopping bag that was crumpled shut. He handed it over to Silas who unrolled it and peered inside. Dr. Wilde seemed satisfied because he smiled and walked away from the man without saying a word.

As Silas walked down the driveway, the man in the doorway gave him the middle finger. Jacob laughed and got in the van. They were both inside ready to leave, but Silas didn't go, he sat with his hands on the wheel grinding his teeth. Jacob waited for him to turn on the engine, but it didn't happen. Instead, The Wild dropped a bomb in Jacob's lap. "I want you to go in there and kill him now," he said in a casual manner like he was telling Jacob the weather forecast.

"You what?!" His very perplexed passenger replied. He was completely thrown off by the request though he heard it perfectly clear.

"Go up there and shoot him in the face. You brought your gun, didn't you? What did you think it was for, to appear to be tough? Go do it and get the money back before his partner returns," Dr. Wilde instructed his employee.

"Seriously? What about his body? Are we just going to leave it there?" Jacob didn't believe his ears.

"Yup, right there where his deadbeat boyfriend will find him," Silas said in a tone as cold as ice.

Jacob's heartbeat fast in his chest. He had committed all different types of misdemeanors and felonies before, but he had never murdered anyone, especially not for such an insignificant reason. Jacob thought about when Brutus first told him about the job and how good the pay was. He informed him they could be ordered to do anything from moving weapons to moving animals but no matter what, the compensation would always be worth it. Jacob wasn't an experienced hitman. The only thing he ever killed with a gun was deer hunting with his uncle as a kid. This was not how he had imagined his evening would go.

"What are you waiting for?! MOVE!" Silas roared, causing Jacob to literally jump off his seat.

Jacob stepped out of the van and removed his pistol from the glove box where he had placed it. Holding it behind his back, he walked up to the house. Before he could knock, the door swung open and the man gave a surprised look when he saw Jacob standing there.

"What the fuck is it now?" he asked.

Jacob hesitated for a moment and glanced over at the van, where saw The Wild staring at him. If looks could kill, he would have expired right then and there because his eyeballs attacked Jacob, who unexpectedly found it hard to breathe.

"Well, what the fuck is your malfunction asshole?!" his voice was getting hostile. Then the man noticed Jacob was slightly turned to his side as if trying to hide something behind his back.

"What the fuck?" he reached out and grabbed Jacob's right arm and yanked it out from behind his back. Jacob tried to control his arm and take aim at him, but it was too late. He had a hold on him with his powerful fist and tried to get the gun from out of his hand. The two men in the doorway intensely and frantically wrestled for control of the gun.

"Why you motherfucker! You're a dead man!" the drug dealing

149

homeowner shouted.

They pushed and pulled each other's arms, but Jacob was overpowered. At last, the man pried the gun away from his hand as they both stumbled trying to get their footings. Standing just an arm's length away, the man raised the gun and pointed it right in Jacob's face. *POW!*

The blast was loud and echoed throughout the surrounding woods. Jacob's eyes were closed when the gun went off, and he heard his life end. But suddenly, he heard a thumping noise at his feet. Opening his eyes, the man lay before him, face down, with the entire backside of his head missing, as the bitter cold, New England, evening air summonsed swirling ghosts of steam to vacate the warm exit wound. He spun around and saw Silas standing behind him with his .44 magnum in his hand, a look of utter disappointment in his eyes. Jacob couldn't believe he was alive. Dr. Wilde couldn't believe Jacob messed up such an easy kill. Jacob searched for the right words to say but couldn't come up with anything. He was trembling from the cold weather and the ever-colder ease Silas had just displayed killing a man.

"Get in the van," The Wild spat as he pushed past him and stepped into the house.

Jacob did as he was told. Once his boss returned with the money, he started the engine and drove back down the extensive driveway.

"I'm sorry, I don't know why I froze like that," Jacob said sincerely.

Silas glared at him and said: "Now you know why I prefer working with a chimp."

Chapter 19

Not a word was uttered about the shooting to the other guys when they returned from their trip to the casino. Jacob and Dr. Wilde returned to an empty house, and the two of them went to their separate rooms after an awkward drive. Jacob was rattled by the incident, mostly because Silas murdered a man for no reason other than he briefly gave him a hard time. He was a cold-blooded killer, and he was insane. How many people had killed in his lifetime? The possibilities made Jacob sick to his stomach. And when did he start using steroids?

A month had passed since the men moved into the farmhouse, and since then, exercise equipment had been assembled in the basement, which they all used from time to time. Silas usually woke up first around 7:00am and went down to get in a workout before breakfast. He was the biggest and strongest of them all, even bigger than Brutus. Did he really need steroids? Did he really need to kill that man? Did he really intend to commit armed robberies with the chimp as his partner? It all just seemed like total madness that only got more and more bizarre as the days passed.

The following morning Jacob woke up to the sound of Brutus snoring like a buzz saw. He hadn't heard him come in the night before, but he sure smelled the booze radiating off him. He smelled like Cpt. Morgan's asshole. They must have hit the complimentary drinks provided by the casino and hit them hard. Jacob wondered if that was a good sign of Brutus' winnings or a bad one.

It was 7:40 am, and Jacob couldn't fall back asleep with the big brute making all that noise, sounding like he was gargling and struggling for air. He threw the blankets off, swung his feet around and planted them on the floor. There, by his feet, on the rug separating the two beds, was Brutus's jeans. A round bulge was protruding from the front right pocket, and a few fifty-dollar bills lay on the rug next to his pants. Jacob picked them up in one hand and the jeans in another. He didn't want to leave his friend's money laying out like that, so he reached into his pocket to remove his wallet. It wasn't his wallet that formed the lump in the pocket, however. Instead, there was a wad of bills thickly rolled and held together with an elastic. "Holy shit!" Jacob thought to himself. Did his slumbering buddy visit the casino or hold it up?!

He glanced at the large mass of sleeping drunkenness and made sure he wasn't being watched before removing the elastic. Fifty, one hundred, fifty, two hundred, fifty, three hundred, and on and on it went. Jacob counted out over sixteen-thousand dollars in fifties and hundred-dollar bills. What a night the big moose had! He added the two bills from the floor and secured it tightly in the roll with the rubber band before tucking it back into Brutus' pocket. Placing the jeans back on the floor under his roommate's bed, he leaned over to check if his eyes were shut. "You had one helluva night huh?" he whispered, regretting not going with them after his night in hell.

Jacob assumed the role of house chef after losing the outdoor hunting game, but he actually enjoyed the duty. He received praise for his culinary creations from his co-workers much to his delight. Mack especially raved about his abilities, though not around Silas. Ever since Dr. Wilde made a remark about him needing to use the gym in the basement more frequently, Mack tried to eat less in front of him. After he and Brutus, Mack was the next largest of the group, but he was slightly overweight and self-conscience about it.

Jacob found Mack already awake and sitting at the kitchen table when he entered.

"How was your night? Obviously not that good if you returned here to work," Jacob joked.

"Actually, pretty awesome. Me and Brutus cleaned house. He won a bit more than I did, but we both were running the blackjack tables for most of the night," he told Jacob.

"No shit? Good for you. What are you going to do with your winnings, save it or buy your old lady something nice?" Jacob asked. He knew Mack was single.

"Later today I'm meeting up with an acquaintance of mine to pick up a new piece. A combat SMG, real nice little smoke show.

It'll cut you in half in seconds," he replied as he pulled a folded picture of the gun out from his pocket and handed it to Jacob.

Mack loved guns and moved his fair share in his time. Typically, he carried a .50 caliber Desert Eagle in his sidearm jacket holster that was more than enough to make an enemy drop a hot one in their shorts. He must have some big job coming up if he felt the need to upgrade to a submachine gun.

"How much does that set you back?" Jacob asked.

"Ten large for the piece, five more for the extra clip and ammo," Mack informed him.

"Wow, cutting people in half doesn't come cheap these days huh?!" Jacob joked again.

"I just want something that will do the trick without having to necessarily pull the trigger, and other than a combat shotgun, the SMG seems to be the best at getting your point across to anyone possibly considering drawing on you."

Jacob looked at the image in his hand and agreed, he would hesitate long and hard before he challenged the likes of that gun if it was aimed at him. His stomach still hadn't settled after witnessing the previous night's events, so he trembled just slightly.

"You ever want to beef up your belt just let me know. I can get my hands on all kinds of firepower with a wide range of pop. Just say the word, and I'll hook you up."

"Thanks, bro, I appreciate that, and I will take you up on that offer when the time comes to super-size my own. Have you eaten, or did you just have coffee?"

"I'm just nursing this cup. My stomach ain't feeling too hot. Fucking Brutus and his Green Giant shots. I don't even know what they put in those fucking things, but he just kept ordering round after round. He said it was like drinking The Incredible Hulk's piss. Why I thought it would be wise to drink all night is beyond me, but I'm certainly not feeling incredible."

"I'll make you my special omelet, guaranteed to cure even the worst hangover." Jacob got to work fixing his groggy friend's breakfast as the room fell silent for the time being. Finally, Jacob mustered up the nerve to ask Mack "Did you know Silas has been juicing?"

Mack looked up but said nothing. He stared at Jacob, and selected his next words carefully, "Not that it's any of our business, but yes, I know." It remained quiet again for a couple more minutes before Mack added, "If you're wondering why he's doing it I'll tell you, if you keep it to yourself. Got it?"

"Sure. I don't talk, you know that."

Mack sipped his coffee and looked across the living room in the direction of the stairs. Nobody else was awake or at least coming down from the second floor. He returned his gaze to Jacob and told him, "He's doing it for Cain."

Jacob cocked his head to the side a bit as his forehead wrinkled in confusion.

"What I mean is he's making sure the roids are safe enough to give to Cain. He's doing one cycle, for now, to test them out before giving them to the monkey," Mack said in a low monotone voice as if reading an obituary out loud.

His words stunned Jacob. Was he serious?! Silas planned to give a full-grown chimpanzee with a violent, cannibalistic past *STEROIDS?!*

"Listen, kid, keep your mouth shut and your opinions to yourself if you value your chin. You have no idea what he's capable of, and even though we've only known each other for less than a year, you seem like a good guy. I'd hate to be digging a hole underneath the big willow tree for you because you let your mouth get the best of ya." he said in a fatherly tone.

Jacob was twenty-eight years old, about twenty years younger than Mack, but had viewed himself as his equal up until that moment. Suddenly, he felt like a kid warned by an adult not to play with matches, and he very much disliked the sensation. But he knew Mack was right and only looking out for him. Mack had been around longer and surely had witnessed more of Dr. Wilde's madness than he had. Jacob felt vulnerable.

Jacob blurted out his next words before he even realized it, "He killed a man last night."

Mack's eyes enlarged. "Excuse me?" he responded.

"Yeah, we went for a drive, and he met up with some muscle-head who sold him the steroids. Before we left though, he shot him in the face," Jacob said, feeling as if he was ratting to the police. His face flushed as the last words left his mouth. He felt Mack stare at him as he looked down and then to the stove, flipping the omelet in the frying pan.

"He shot his dealah?" Mack asked slowly, with his Boston accent strongly coming through.

Jacob nodded, Mack, shook his head in disbelief. "Are you sure?"

"Of course, I'm fucking sure! What do you think I'm making this up? Or don't know what it looks like when a guy gets his face blown through the back of his head?!" Jacob felt his heart begin to race.

He realized his volume had risen and suddenly Brutus was heard from across the room saying, "Whose face was blown through the back of their head?"

Jacob and Mack looked on as the big guy stopped in the doorway between the kitchen and living room and pulled a t-shirt over his massive torso. After that, he ran his hands back through his dark, messy hair and stretched as he yawned. It was possible he didn't think they were serious or at least weren't talking about their employer.

"Nobody," Jacob offered up quickly. He hoped it sounded nonchalant.

It didn't work. When he looked back at Brutus, who had taken the seat next to Mack at the kitchen table, he realized he wasn't satisfied.

"You're not getting off that easy Jacob. Who are you talking about?" he said ever so seriously.

Desperately, Jacob looked at Mack for help, but Mack sipped

155

his steaming cup of coffee and didn't respond.

"Really, it's nothing," Jacob tried a second time.

Brutus didn't take his eyes off him as Jacob spun around and tended to the omelet cooking on the stove. Placing it on a plate, he handed it to Mack and Mack thanked him while he pursed his lips and gave a look as if to say, "keep your mouth shut."

Brutus caught the look, and his suspicions piqued. "You better tell me what the fuck you two are talking about. And after you do, you can explain why you were going through my pants."

Jacob felt a surge of embarrassment rush over him as the hairs on the back of his neck felt as if they had caught fire.

"Your pants? I didn't... I mean I did, but it's not what you think. I would never..." he stuttered as Brutus watched his every move. "There was a couple of bills on the floor, so I put them in your pocket. I would never go through your shit, you know that."

"But you just admitted that you did," Brutus responded. He was not joking around, and perhaps it was the booze still running through his system, but he clearly meant business.

Jacob had known Brutus for over ten years, but never before had he felt intimidated or threatened by him. Quickly, he made the decision to change the subject and offered up the information he was looking for. "Fine, don't repeat this but when I was with Silas yesterday, we visited a drug dealer and he fucking shot him! Don't tell anyone else, I'm not a fucking rat!"

Brutus made a similar head gesture as if also in disbelief. "What are you talking about? What drug dealer? Who was buying? You're full of shit," he rebutted.

Mack saw the desperation on Jacob's face so, in between bites of his quickly disappearing omelet, he said, "He was buying roids from the guy, and Jacob says he wasted him."

"Roids? Are you sure?" he looked back and forth from Jacob to Mack in disbelief. "Tell me what he looked like."

Jacob went on to explain, "He was short but jacked, a gay guy that lived with another dude way out in the middle of nowhere."

Brutus's eyes suddenly showed signs of life as they lit up.

"Are you positive?!" he asked with a shaky voice. "He killed *that* guy?"

Jacob confirmed what he had already said twice. The look Brutus had, did not make him feel any better about the previous night's events as his stomach turned once again. It was obvious Brutus made some connection.

"Do you know who I'm talking about?" Jacob asked him.

"Well shit, I'm ninety-nine percent positive I do. There's only one queer couple around that deals, and they're supposedly some pretty heavy hitters. Was it a house at the end of a mile-long driveway?"

Jacob nodded.

"Wow, you don't say... Christ almighty! What the fuck..." he answered, his words trailing off.

Jacob grew more concerned but leaned against the counter in silence. Mack kept his head down as he finished his breakfast. Then Brutus seemed to snap out of it and asked, "Tell me exactly what happened. It's Okay, we'll go for a walk, and you can fill me in. You can trust me."

As he walked for the door leading to the porch, Jacob noticed Brutus was barefoot. This wasn't good if his story couldn't wait even a few more minutes, so a pair of shoes could be pulled on. Placing the spatula, he had been clinging to next to the stove, Jacob followed Brutus outside.

It was a chilly morning, and the dew made the ground damp and the driveway a little muddy. Brutus didn't care as he reached out and placed his muscular arm around Jacob's shoulder and pulled him next to him. They walked slowly as Jacob told the story from the beginning. He had just about finished as they approached the huge willow tree. Beneath its hanging branches, at the base of the trunk, was a granite bench hidden by the weeping boughs that dangled inches above the ground. Brutus separated and opened them as if drawing back a curtain, revealing the secret stone seat. With his head, he motioned for Jacob to enter, and so he did, taking a seat on the left side of the bench, leaving room for his friend. Sitting next to him, Brutus turned his body to face Jacob and asked slowly, "You're one hundred percent positive he shot and killed that man?"

"Without a doubt," he replied.

This did not please his co-worker.

"Okay, listen carefully. I obviously don't have to tell you not to repeat this to anyone else. The guy he popped was no joke. I introduced the two of them right around the time you started working with us. I thought he wanted to bulk up and do a cycle or two after we set up the gym downstairs. It wasn't until after we got back from Africa that he told me he planned on juicing the chimp. I honestly thought he was busting my balls and shrugged it off. Ever since Cain arrived, he's been a different person. I knew he had started taking Evinall a while back and I think he's reacting weirdly from it. He doesn't sleep, he sits in his room all night on his computer planning all different kinds of whacked out shit and does rippers, and I mean a lot of them. The cocaine he sniffs is so strong he needs to swab the inside of his nostrils daily with first aid ointment so that it heals. Even I know you're not supposed to mix Evinall with recreational drugs, especially another stimulant. It's been eating away at what little sanity he has left. And now he's adding steroids to the mix... Don't you dare repeat any of this, ya hear?!" he shouted suddenly, realizing the consequences of badmouthing Silas.

There were only two things that struck fear into both criminals: Dr. Silas Wilde and Cain. Jacob was surprised to see Brutus rattled. He reassured him, "You have nothing to worry about. The last thing I want is to piss the doctor off, trust me."

Brutus seemed satisfied. "Well good. But that brings me to my next concern. You say he asked you to kill the dealer first, but you didn't do it? Why?"

Jacob pulled his head back in disbelief. "Why didn't I kill a man I had never even met? Why didn't I kill a drug dealer who had done me no wrong but had delivered on his end of the deal? Oh, I don't know. Maybe it's because I don't typically go around wasting dudes, making unnecessary enemies."

"Yeah, but you fucked up. You fucked up *BIG TIME*," he stressed. "You don't get how Silas thinks. He's so bent on loyalty and trust, breaking his is unforgivable. That's why he uses Will Shepherd and pays for him to fly across the globe, he trusts him. That's why I stressed to you how important coming to Africa with me was because he trusted ME when I vouched for you, and if anything went wrong, I'd be the first one to go, even before you. He has major trust issues, man. Oh shit, this is not good. What did he say to you after you guys left? Tell me everything."

"What the fuck?! Oh God, I don't know... The only thing he said was 'Now you know why I prefer to work with chimps.' That was it for the whole ride back," Jacob said.

"Shiiiit. Not good bro, not good."

"What does that mean?! Who does he think I am, Whitey Fucking Bulger?! May that prick rest in peace, but doesn't he realize most normal people don't just blow other men's heads off for no reason?!" Jacob pleaded.

"That's just it. He was testing to see what kind of man you really were, to see how far your loyalty would go. Would you kill for him without question or hesitation if he asked you to? That's it. He was feeling you out. It had nothing to do with the other guy. He's not afraid that his lover has some serious pull in the Scavito, crime family. That motherfucker could have us all taken out like nothing, but Silas doesn't give a shit. All he's thinking is that you failed his little test. Shit, man..."

Jacob couldn't believe it. How was he to know he would be put up to such a meaningless murder on a whim like that? Just because he wasn't willing to execute some poor fella in his own doorway didn't mean that he wasn't loyal to The Wild. He would never roll or turn anybody in, he was no rat. He needed to figure out a way to redeem himself in Silas's eyes before he terminates HIM, or worse. Jacob asked Brutus, "Did he have you and the other guys do something similar to prove yourselves?"

Brutus rubbed his chin and looked at Jacob. "Not exactly the same, but yes. I'm not getting into it any more than just saying yes. I lived through his little test once, I'm not doing it again here with you."

Jacob's mind raced with possibilities of what Silas had Brutus do that was so unspeakable. Torch and orphanage? Drown a trash bag full of puppies? What could be so bad he was unwilling to confide in him after he just shared his secret? Maybe it was best he didn't know.

The two sat hidden underneath the long, waving branches of the willow tree. A gentle breeze sent another shiver down Jacob's spine, he was getting sick of the feeling. Finally, Brutus leaned back and reached deep into his front right pocket. He pulled out the familiar wad of cash and placed it into Jacob's hands. "Take this and go."

Jacob was dumbfounded. He shook his head. "I'm not taking your money, are you crazy?!"

"You'd be crazy not to! Listen to me, Bud, I'm not asking, I'm fucking insisting. I brought you into this mess, and I'm seeing you out. You take this, and you take off. You're not married, take off somewhere today. Go somewhere nice and warm. Just gather your shit and go."

Jacob became numb from terror. Was he serious?! Was his life in danger simply because he didn't shoot a man in the face for his demented boss?! He couldn't move, and suddenly his breathing seemed almost impossible.

"He's going to fucking kill you! Do you hear what I'm saying? The fact that he hasn't done so already makes me worry he was waiting for me to wake up and he would have ME do it!" Brutus confessed.

"What?! Why would he have you do it?"

"Because I vouched for you, but you didn't come through for him. He wouldn't kill me but rather punish me by making me kill you. His way of sending a message. I'm not fucking around, take the money and split. Leave your shit, get your ass to town and get yourself good and lost. If Will Shepherd was still here in the states, I'm positive he would pay him to track you down and do the deed himself, so consider yourself lucky."

Lucky?! Where the hell, was he going to disappear to? He watched as Brutus stood and peeked out of the branches toward the farmhouse. Then he waved his hand and firmly said, "GO! NOW!"

Jacob was up and running down the remaining part of the driveway before he realized it. Just as he got to the slight bend where the view of the house would disappear, he turned and looked back. There standing on the top step of the porch was Brutus, waving with his hands, shooing him away like an unwanted rodent. He turned and continued down the narrow country road for a solid twenty minutes before the burning in his chest forced him to stop. He was still a few miles from the town where there was no public transportation anyway. His cell phone was still on the kitchen counter, charging where he had left it. All he had were the clothes on his back, sixteen-thousand dollars in cash, and a handful of questions he knew he wouldn't get answers to.

One thing Jacob knew for certain though, Brutus feared for his life, and that was all the evidence he needed to make him believe Silas wanted him dead. The Wilde was living up to his name once again but wouldn't be out and about looking for Jacob since his face had been all over the news. Would he still put a hit out for him? Maybe Brutus or Mack? And if so, how much time did he have before they came for him? Suddenly, his stomach turned for the last time that morning, and he vomited on the side of the road. He didn't typically have a weak stomach, but the sudden stress of the situation combined with the unsuspected workout jogging toward town got the best of him. He needed to find somewhere safe to sort out his thoughts. He needed to pick up a disposable cell phone he could access his emails from since he had all of his contacts saved there. He needed to settle his stomach and clear his head. Most of all, he needed to be sipping a strong drink on a continent besides Africa!

Part 3

Chapter 20

Five months had passed since the "Devil's Night Disaster," during which time I found it nearly impossible to sleep. When I closed my eyes in the silent darkness, all I heard was the horrible screams of the two victims burned to death, with visions of one of the fleeing ostriches that caused the truck to turn upside down in a great ball of fire, much like it did to my life. I couldn't bear to turn on the television over the weeks following the incident because that was all that was on.

The ranch property was owned by a Walter Yoder, not Joseph Yoder. That slime-ball managed to take over the property from his deceased uncle but kept it in his name to avoid any connections. He got off scot-free, and I was not okay with that. But was taking him down, or anyone else for that matter, so important it was worth possibly putting innocent lives at risk? Do all the "non-contributors" pose such a threat to society to rationalize such severe collateral damage? Those were the questions that tormented me ever since the incident went wrong and I saw just how dangerous the life of a vigilante could be.

My home in Franklin is on a lake I have fished in for more than three decades. Growing up in that town was just fine for me since there are multiple bodies of water for an avid fisherman, like myself, to perfect my skills at. The lake my house is on, Echo Lake, is ideal because it is stocked with trout every spring and it is private enough, I can go out on my boat some days and be the only angler on the lake. I lose myself there just by sitting on my dock with my feet dangling above the water's surface, reeling in respectable-sized bass or the occasional pickerel and then releasing them to catch another day. The therapeutic value that a day fishing provides is priceless. I spend my fair share of them in that exact spot, especially when life kicks my ass. At the very end of the dock, centered in the middle of the last wooden plank, are the initials NK + EB for Nero

Karlin and Eve Brooks. I carved it out the first summer we spent in our new home, one perfect August evening when the lightning bugs danced through the air as they should have, and life seemed too good to be true. I love that dock. It has helped me much more than any psychiatrist or antidepressant capsule have.

Russ took the remaining vacation days he had left at his job and kept me company after the Devil's Night Disaster. His boss was not happy, but Russ gets to do whatever he wants since he is pretty much irreplaceable. He works at a four-star restaurant just outside Boston's city limits, in fact, he co-founded the place when he was in his early twenties using the winnings, he received from a short-lived professional poker career to fund it. His success gambling brought him all the way to Las Vegas, where he placed second in the All-National Poker Tournament. The payout made him a million dollars richer, and he did what many young, hotshot, professional poker players do not; he invested it wisely.

After working one-hundred-hour weeks getting his new business up and running for the first five years, Russ was finally able to cut down to more normal hours as the head chef, and his reputation for gourmet cuisine remained impeccable. Eventually, he ended up selling his half of the company to his partner but made a deal to stay on as head chef, so his comings and goings are somewhat regular. Russ makes sure things are running smoothly during weeknights before he heads to volunteer at one of the soup kitchens. On the weekends, he stays the entire night and whenever there is a special event, a VIP customer, or any other situation where everything has to be perfect. People from all over the state come and pay top dollar for one of his beautiful, delicious meals that are rightfully described as art. Russ pours more of his sanity and soul into that place, they had no ground to stand on and complain when he announced his three-week hiatus.

Russ moved in with me for the first month after the tragedy, and as always, my rock was firmly there for me. We spent many moments figuring what went wrong and why, though I will never be completely satisfied with any of the potential causes so long as those two people are still dead. I knew I needed to figure out a way to either get over it or make peace with the situation. It happened, it's over with, and there was nothing I could have done to help them.

Sometimes I envy the people who take Evinall, never having to worry about cravings or anything like that. My own came and went throughout the months of November and December. At times, I wondered why I tortured myself and didn't swallow my pride along with one of the damn pills, but I stayed strong and sober on my own as the winter months came and went, dumping ridiculous amounts of snow all over the state.

Russ spent most of November with me but eventually went back to his own life. I will forever be in debt for his kindness and support. I hope I provide even a fraction of the support he does in return. He too has periods when he struggles with his addiction when I am there to help him. He took Evinall before it was made available to the rest of the public as a test study patient.

The research team at KarlTech kept a close eye on Russ for three months as he showed no significant side-effects and did wonderfully, remaining alcohol and substance-free over the course of the study. Alcohol was never really his problem, but he reported having cravings for opiates regularly, even after months of consistent clean time. Evinall did exactly what I designed it to do and got rid of his cravings. He even stopped drinking coffee, which he told me he never thought he could do.

When April arrived, bringing an end to the frigid weather, I began taking daily jogs around town to keep in shape and to ease my mind. During my runs, I thought about the lives I have intentionally taken and desired the euphoric rush killing another person gives me. The satisfaction of removing that despicable pimp from existence was unparalleled. That was the first time I felt a surge of pride radiate outwards from my heart as though I did society a huge favor. I felt heroic, I felt alive.

Each day I ran and worked out in my home gym, getting stronger and stronger, but at the same time more and more eager. I tasted the forbidden fruit, and I liked it, no I loved it! The only thing that could possibly satisfy would be another taste, another kill. Perhaps I bit off more than I could chew trying to take down an entire meth operation and I just needed to stick to the solo slayings.

One at a time with perfect planning aided by my physical and mental preparations. I could be successful at it again, right?

Where was Russ? I needed his advice. Am I cut out for a double life, adding to the one I already struggle with? Should I have adopted a second version of myself that operates on the opposite side of the law and puts everything I've worked so hard to accomplish at risk? Surely Russ would know.

I picked up the phone and called him. No answer. I paced back and forth in my bedroom. I needed a distraction, so I turned on the television and watched the news for the first time in six months. I wasn't expecting to see my living nightmare still airing, but I definitely wasn't prepared for what I saw. In Framingham, Ma a neighborhood liquor store and check cashing business had been robbed at gunpoint, with the culprits making off with several thousands of dollars. A robbery was nothing out of the ordinary, but what made this one so unique was the eyewitness accounts and descriptions of the suspected crooks.

The first reports depicted a man and a gorilla, both wearing scary masks, walking into the place at 8:10pm, carrying a duffel bag and several weapons. They claimed the gorilla was sitting piggy-back style on the man and waved guns in the air with his hands and feet. The man shouted at the clerk until he finally opened a safe hidden in the floor. After loading the cash, the gorilla shot the store owner in the face with a mini shotgun and they both disappeared as quickly as they came.

Did I hear that right?! How could the gorilla hold on to the man's body if he had guns in both his arms and feet? Was he harnessed in somehow? And who was big and strong enough to carry a gorilla on their back? Not to mention, who the hell pairs up with a gorilla to pull off an armed robbery?!

None of it made sense until a different news channel obtained the surveillance footage and aired it. On the video recording, things became clearer. It wasn't a gorilla involved but a chimpanzee. A little bit more understandable, gorillas weigh up to two hundred and eighty pounds. A big chimp weighs about half of that. A man of great stature could indeed carry one if he wore a backpack carrier.

The human assailant was both extremely large and wore a child carrier. He had to have been about six and a half feet tall and very well-built. On his bald head, he wore a mask which covered his nose, mouth, and chin with a large frown painted on it. It was obviously a homemade mask that sent a very clear message: he was in no mood to be messed with. The chimp also wore a similar mask, but he had a great big smile with pointed teeth painted on it.

The hairy ape on his back was, in fact, carrying three guns, amazing! Whether he could accurately shoot them or if they were real was incredibly displayed right there on the surveillance tape! He sure wielded them like he knew what he was doing, pointing his arms forward at the clerk and his legs to the left and right, covering the two customers in the store and the door simultaneously. That was brilliant, I thought. The man had his hands free yet was being covered from all angles by, what appeared to be, two 9mm's and a sawed-off shotgun. Boy, that was not something you see every day! I had to find Russ.

At last, Russ picked up his phone "What's happening Doc?" he asked.

"What's happening is there's a half man, half chimp robbing liquor stores in Framingham! Have you seen the news?" I asked.

"What's your mom doing causing problems again? Is she that hard up for money?"

Russ knew I didn't have a good relationship with either of my parents, but that didn't stop him from shelling out a tacky momma joke.

"Just put the damn news on, enough with the shitty one-liners," I ordered.

"All right, all right, give me a minute. I just got back from the gym, and I'm still all sweaty. Some of us actually work out when we exercise," he joked.

Russ is a man who doesn't need to lift a single weight to have rippling muscles. He is a natural beast but adds to the intimidation factor by working out and packing on more vein-popping mass. I am taller than him by about three inches, but he is like a bulldozer and one that I'm glad I've never crossed. We both keep in excellent shape, so poking fun at each other is typical when it comes to physical superiority.

"What channel are we watching?"

"Put on channel six and wait for a bit, they're just on a commercial, but they'll show it again," I told him excitedly.

"Okay, I've got it on, another damn Flex Seal commercial. What do you mean half human, half chimp? Were they fused together by the awesome power of Flex Seal? Do you think it's single? I'm going through a bit of a dry spell here..." Russ said, unable to be serious even for a moment.

"I'm serious! You've never seen crazier shit than what you're about to see. This huge guy busts into the liquor store wearing...Oh, it's back on, watch!"

We both sat in silence as they replayed the story again along with the surveillance footage and eyewitness testimonies. The receiver at my ear was silent. Finally, when it was over, I heard, "What in God's name did I just see? Are you kidding me?! Hahaha!" he replied.

"I know, right?! Have we both officially seen it all or what? 'Chimp-man on the loose terrorizing Boston residence, details at eleven," I said in my best news reporter impersonation.

"You've gotta admit though, the guy had it together and pulled it off. I wonder if there was an orangutan waiting outside driving the getaway car." Russ laughed.

"My thoughts exactly. As insane as it was, it worked! He was wearing gloves, so they won't be able to pull any prints. This must be the first time he's ever done something like this, using the chimp as a backup. You would think if it happened anywhere else, even somewhere out in the sticks or in another country, that the story would make national headlines. It sure is hard to be an original criminal these days, but that prick nailed it tonight. He definitely wins the award for "Most Original Heist" along with a sack full of loot. Nobody got hurt, but sooner or later someone will surely recognize the man or chimp or both and tip off the authorities. If he

167

was smart, he would keep his money and retire while he's still on top. Nobody is dumb enough to attempt another robbery with an ape, not around here at least. People are going to be on high alert for a while, and it would be far too risky," I explained to Russ.

We laughed and joked a little more about the story as it created a much-needed distraction from my previous worries, allowing me to end my day on a high note.

The following day I ate my own words as the chimp bandit proved me wrong. Maybe there wasn't someone "dumb" enough to try pulling off another robbery using the same approach, but there apparently was someone ballsy enough to. Not even twenty-four hours had passed when another news story came ripping through the airwaves. At first, I thought they were repeating the liquor store robbery, but then I realized the reporter was standing in front of an Enterprise Bank location in Natick, Ma, the town next to Framingham.

That asshole stormed into the bank just after noon, when some of the employees were on their lunch breaks and held the place up with the chimp on his back again! They weren't wearing some creepy homemade masks. No, they wore gas masks, even the ape! They wore those because, as the video footage showed, upon entering the bank's front door, the man pulled the pins off two canisters of tear gas and threw them inside. He threw one behind the front counter and the other in the center of the main room, hitting one of the customers in the chest who was waiting in line!

Everyone hit the floor as the two of them stood, the fog from the gas swirled around them as he held both of his huge arms out to the side and then lifted them up, yelling something that was inaudible, but then clearly laughing behind his mask afterward. The chimp kept his sights aimed in all four directions like robbing banks was something it did for years.

The video footage was much clearer than the one taken from the liquor store. I could make out scars on the chimpanzee's head as well as the man's. I paused the television and zoomed in on the criminal. He had, what looked like some type of claw or tooth, scars all over his bald head! And there they stood in the center of the bank, admiring for a moment the complete and utter chaos they caused. Things didn't go as smoothly as they did in his first stick-up though, as the situation took a terrible turn for the worst.

The man walked over and grabbed a chair from the seating area near the front door and dragged it to the end of the main teller's counter. Leaning the back against the counter, he stepped up onto the chair and then on and over the counter, as the chimp kept his guns constantly aimed at all who were around them. There were six customers in the bank, four tellers, and the bank manager.

The man seemed to remain silent, as he walked over and grabbed a middle-aged woman, who's maroon business suit indicated she was someone in charge because she held the vault keys. Holding her by the back of her neck, he pushed her on toward the vault. She sobbed and coughed uncontrollably, as she rubbed her eyes still blurry from the gas. But the man prodded her along anyway. He didn't need to say a word, she knew to get the vault open, and the quicker she did so, the quicker he could take the contents and leave.

After lifting his gas mask up, the robber used a hockey equipment bag he had slung over his shoulder and tucked under his arm and filled it with the stacks of cash as soon as the vault door was opened. Bricks of ten and twenty-thousand dollars were heaped into the bag before he zipped it shut. Exiting the vault, he took two lollipops out of a little candy jar from one of the clerk's windows and removed the wrappers from both. He put one in his mouth and held his hand up behind his head, sticking the other one in the chimp's hand. Finally, he crossed back over the counter and headed for the front door. This is where things went south.

One of the customers in the bank happened to be an off-duty police officer, just like in the movies, and he was armed with his service pistol. When the man and ape were about five steps to freedom, the cop jumped to his feet and yelled, "Freeze asshole!" as he drew his weapon on them.

The crooks slowly turned around and saw the thirty-something-year-old, chubby, balding, wannabe hero pointing his gun at them. He trembled a little and blinked rapidly, trying to regain his vision.

That was the telltale sign that did him in. The thief knew he couldn't see well and probably wouldn't be able to place a critical shot. He dropped the bag of money and slowly raised his hands above his head. Just as the officer was probably about to instruct them to drop their weapons and lie on their stomachs, the man took the lollipop out of his mouth and shouted, "CAIN, FIRE!" and he did.

POW! A thunderous explosion from the sawed-off shotgun unloaded and found its target ten feet away, and with devastating results. The poor man's chest was blown wide open, as a mixture of shattered bone fragments and bloody tissue sprayed out from his back, creating a mosaic of mid-section matter on the wall behind him. The look on his face was of total confusion. His arms fell to his side, dropping his gun, and then he collapsed, powerless over the bitch we call gravity. But the macabre mayhem didn't end there. The woman in the maroon suit screamed and came running to the fallen hero's side. She clenched the sides of her head as she screamed, rocking back and forth on her knees over the very deceased off-duty officer. The burglar casually walked over to her, took a few licks from his lollipop, looked up at the surveillance camera, and then down at the frantic woman. His deep voice was crystal clear on the news coverage, as he gave his final command to his counterpart: "CAIN, FIRE!"

The obedient ape pulled both of his semi-automatic pistol wielding arms around the sides of his master's head, accurately aimed them at the horrified woman, and unloaded at least twenty-something rounds into her skull. The man bent and picked up the bag of money, then turned and exited the building, cool as a cucumber!

The news anchor warned prior to showing the tape it was extremely graphic and viewer's discretion was advised. "Graphic" was an embarrassing understatement! Tune in to the ten o'clock news and see a man get blown to bits like it was nothing. This country and its media coverage...

I couldn't believe it though, that psychopath held up a bank in broad daylight, in a busy urban town, wearing gas masks like it was World War II. Not only did he have the audacity to do it on the day following his last armed robbery, but he killed two innocent people too?! Well, technically the chimp did, but under his orders. Just who

170

did this asshole think he was?!

Immediately, I grabbed the phone and called Russ, who was working and didn't answer. After the missed call, I texted him: "URGENT," and he called me back.

"Everything okay buddy?" he asked me over the clank of dinnerware loaded into an industrial-sized dishwasher.

"No, everything is NOT Okay. Have you heard or seen the news tonight?" I asked him.

"I've been in front of the stoves all night bud. No rest for the wicked, right?" he responded.

"Our monkey-man friend from last night struck again, a bank this time. Right in broad daylight with that atrocious ape hanging off his back!"

"No fucking shit! Was there another video?" Russell asked.

"Yes, but it gets worse. He shot and killed an off-duty police officer, who was in there and tried to stop him. Then they killed a woman. Actually the chimp shot them. They keep showing the poor guy's picture. He leaves behind a pretty, young wife and two little kids. And the woman was a survivor of the Boston Marathon Bombings. That piece of shit wasted them like he was swatting flies, not a care in the world."

"Holy hooligans... Could you see his face this time or was he wearing his Halloween costume?"

"Yes," I said, "they both wore gas masks and tear-gassed the place, but he lifted his mask up eventually, and you could see his face. He obviously is NOT concerned about being identified."

"Are you kidding me?! Talk about stepping up his game a couple notches, and just overnight. I'd hate to see what he has in store for tomorrow. Speaking of which, do you want me to come by around lunchtime, and we can discuss this in a little more detail?"

"Please, come over whenever you roll your lazy ass out of bed. I've recorded the news in case you miss it or just want to go home and crash. We can watch it tomorrow together."

"Oooh like a little date? I'm starting to like the sound of this. Are you getting sweet on me Dr. Karlin? What would Braddock Dix think if there was another rooster in his hen house?" Russ teased.

"Can you ever not be gay?" I wanted to know.

"Not when it comes to my little paddy cake, peanut-puffing princess I can't. Hahaha!" he bellowed out with his gruff laugh, only amusing himself. "Alright, I gotta get back to it. I'll be there tomorrow before twelve," he said, and we both hung up.

My head hurt, and thoughts ran rampant. What should be my next move? Should I sit around and see if the police can catch this sociopath before he hurts anyone else? What if he strikes again tomorrow? Or the next day? *ARRRGHHHH!* My head was really starting to pound. I took two Aspirin tablets and a mild sleep aid and laid in my king size bed alone.

If I wasn't thinking about a man with an ape robbing and murdering at random, I was missing my dear sweet Eve. I told myself after she passed, I was going to downsize my bed to a full to make it seem less vacant without her next to me, but I haven't gotten around to it yet. It's on my "To do" list, well one of them anyway. Finally, I fell asleep but not to much avail. I had nightmares all night of that monstrous madman, with his backpack beast throwing gas canisters and firing randomly into crowds of innocent people. It was terrible, and I slept like shit. When I finally woke, I was furious, but one thing had become clear: the "Butcher of Boston" was about to come out of retirement.

Chapter 21

Russ has a key and knows the security code to my house for emergency situations, and for the times he likes to come over while I am out of town and host his own guests. He sometimes uses my home, with its indoor swimming pool and movie theater, to impress a lady friend, but I don't mind.

The following day he tried to sneak in to startle me at about 9:00am, but he forgot I have security cameras covering every square inch of my home, even the six bathrooms. I was already up and had gone for a morning jog to blow off some steam long before he was out of bed. I stepped out of the shower and noticed a brief alert on my cell phone saying the front door had been opened, but then it disappeared, so I knew Russ was in the house.

It was a sort of sick but exciting game we played, seeing who broke into the others home undetected and scared the living shit out of them better! I usually win because, well because I am more agile and light-footed. I bet that time he thought he was going to get me. I threw on my shorts and t-shirt and hustled out of the master bathroom and back into my bedroom, where I stuffed some pillows together to make it look like a body under the blankets. Then I squeezed between my long dresser and the wardrobe, that are across from my bed. I hid and waited for my unsuspecting friend. After a few minutes, I listened but heard nothing, I pulled my cell phone out of my pocket and opened the home security app. I clicked on the zone monitoring button, and all the cameras were in view. I narrowed it down by selecting "upstairs," and there he was, creeping toward my bedroom door. Right before he turned the doorknob, he glanced upwards into the camera and paused for a moment, as if suddenly realizing I watched, but then a look of placidity came over his face, and he turned the knob and entered.

The room was dark; red satin curtains on the windows reached the floor and blocked the light out when they were closed, which they were. Only a sliver of light reached out and made it halfway across the room before fading into the shadows, where I remained motionless. Step-by-careful-step he tiptoed to the foot of my bed planning his strike. I saw the mischievous smirk on his face through his thick black goatee. He wore shorts and a black tank top, which made it a little harder to see him than I would have suspected, but my eyes adjusted and honed-in on him with relative ease. When he was right at my bedside, he leaped into the air and landed on the mound of pillows yelling, "Wake up, Jackoff!"

Russ quickly realized he was alone in the bed as I did my best to keep from bursting out with laughter at his botched scare tactic. A little baffled by the recent turn of events, he got up and walked over to the bathroom door, peeking in, but the lights were off, and I wasn't in there. I pulled my knees into my chest and prayed he didn't see me as he made his way to the exit. He walked out into the hallway and was just about to pull the door shut behind him while forward facing. I crept up from behind, threw my arms around him, and tackled him to the floor. "Got you, Dickhead!" I yelled.

I felt his whole body jump up in fright as I startled him tremendously! We wrestled for a few minutes on the floor of the hallway, like two dogs fighting in an alley. It got to the point where I was hanging on for dear life as my pissed off pal bucked like a bronco and tried to free himself from my death grip. I rolled him on to his stomach and managed to get him in a headlock. "Say, uncle! Uncle bitch!"

"Fuck... err.... you, pansy!" he groaned as I applied pressure to his shoulders. He made a few more failed attempts to escape and tried headbutting me too, before finally succumbing to my demands. "Uncle, asshole. Uncle!" he yelled going limp in my arms.

I released my hold on him and spun to a sitting position next to him on the carpeted floor. "You're going to have to wake up earlier than that to pull one over on this sly fox, yessiree," I proudly boasted.

"Whatever, I was more worried about interrupting you playing with your little dinky than I was actually scaring you," he pathetically replied.

"Ha! You nearly shit yourself, in fact, I think I smell your brand. Burnt popcorn and walrus balls... Yup, that's yours. Ugh!" I pretended to vomit on him, and we both laughed.

We headed downstairs where I offered him breakfast and coffee. He passed on the food but took me up on a pot of the fresh Colombian coffee I drank. As we sipped our first cups, I turned on the recorded news broadcast from the night before in the living room. "Wait until you see this," I said slowly for dramatic effect.

"In this here Enterprise Bank location at 488 Broadway in downtown Natick, the alleged same gunman, accompanied by a chimpanzee, that robbed a liquor store not more than eighteen hours ago, struck again, only this time claiming the lives of two of the hostages: a thirty-four-year-old, off-duty police officer, Richard Parmenter, a seven-year veteran of the Taunton Police who leaves behind a wife and two young children, and forty-six year old Jessica Reef, a former Miss America winner and survivor of the 2013 Boston Marathon Bombings."

"Reports from eyewitnesses at the neighboring "Pleasure In Pain" tattoo parlor claim that the thief walked in with the chimp on his back and, without saying a word, threw at least two exploding canisters of tear gas into the center of the bank. The smoke choked and blinded the terrified workers and customers as the manager was forced at gunpoint to open the bank's vault at gunpoint. The chimpanzee incredibly and accurately carried three different guns, while the man himself was unarmed throughout the whole ordeal. He used his free hands to make a withdrawal of one hundred and fourteen thousand dollars."

The report went on to show the videotape with a blurred spot over the undercover officer once the fatal shots were fired. Russ sipped his coffee and watched the coverage with his dark brown eyes bugging out of his head in disbelief. When it was over, I rewound it to a frame showing the madman standing in the center of the bank holding his hands up in the air. We both stared at the image for a few moments letting the insanity of the situation sink in.

I'm the kind of man who isn't intimidated or scared of any other man, with one exception. I know how to fight, and I had never lost one in my life, even when I was outnumbered and outsized. But there's a line I draw were certain precautions have to be taken to protect myself. There is nothing more dangerous than a man with nothing to lose, and the man behind the mask with the ape on his back showed all the signs of just that kind of person.

He either had nothing to lose or had already lost his all, and he was so far gone mentally he believed he could continue terrorizing innocent people unchecked and without repercussions. Someone like that had to be dealt with, with extreme caution because he could explode at any moment, taking all who are within his blast radius down with him. Very rarely have I seen that type of insanity, lacking any trace of guilt or remorse: the makings of a true sociopath. It was apparent that anything and everyone was expendable to him, there was no limit.

People like him typically worked alone and lived reclusive lives on the fringes of their community with little to no hope of getting better. The paths they chose in life usually wind up in prison, an institution, or the cemetery. It's sad to say, but it's too little too late by the time they reach adulthood to do anything to help. But the pity party stops abruptly once one of them decides to take up arms against his fellow citizens and commits acts of terror.

The masked monkey-man probably lived in a ghastly house somewhere moderately rural, living in complete and utter squalor the way a psychotic primate would live, I figured. What he thought he needed the money for was a great question. Perhaps he didn't even want the money, perhaps his motivation was simply the thrill of it. *That* is the kind of loose cannon I fear: the kind of person who wants to set the world on fire, so he can sit back and roast marshmallows as everyone else burns. I entertained available options to avoid such a delinquent, if possible. If all else failed, then I would approach with extreme caution and find a way to subdue my foe. Some kinds of crazy you just couldn't cure.

After staring at the television screen for those few moments, Russ finally spoke, "We've gotta do something to stop him. He's setting the bar very high, with his blatant displays of anarchy. Wackos like that are the kind that rapidly get worse and worse until they eventually self-destruct, taking everyone around them down with them. I don't want to have to watch in horror the devastation caused when that freak reaches his breaking point, do you?" he asked.

"No, of course not. And you're right, he's way out in left field. Not the kind of person you bring a negotiator in to try to talk some sense into. You really have to play their game, get just about as crazy as they are to level the playing field before taking them down."

"You up for taking a dip in that much craziness Doc?" Russ asked me with concern in his voice.

I paused for a few seconds, looked at him with a big smile and said, "I'm gonna hunt down Furious George and the Chump in the Yellow Hat and have them beg for death before I'm done having my way with them."

He punched my fist and replied, "Let's fucking do this Nero."

Chapter 22

Three days after making his first appearance on the evening news in the liquor store hold-up, the identity of the chimp burglar was released to the public. Dr. Silas Wilde was the suspected criminal and images of him were all over the news. A mugshot from his arrest in San Diego seemed to be the favorite.

He was a big man, a VERY big man, standing six feet six inches tall and weighing a reported three hundred and twenty-seven pounds! He looked like what you can imagine a sociopathic zoologist would, after spending most of his life living among primates. He sure seemed like an outdoorsman, with a rough appearance detailed by multiple scars on his face and bald head. Some of the scars had to have been claw marks that started toward the back and frantically traced the contour of his cranium, cutting deep into his flesh. They almost looked like the circling swirl of a Doppler radar hurricane, that went around and around, or like the results of wearing a crown of thorns or razor wire.

In the mugshot, he wasn't smiling but did have a sort of smug look on his face, as if he somehow knew the charges wouldn't stick, and he would soon be released due to a major police fuck up. He was originally from Spring Valley, Ca, but he disappeared immediately after his previous cases were dropped.

Once again, the press labeled him simply "The Wild." They flashed his pictures again and again as details ran across the bottom of the screen on the breaking news ticker. The press had a field day trying to make connections between the latest burglaries and the terrorist conspiracy charge he avoided back in California. The investigators didn't miss a thing. They went back through other news stories about the San Diego Zoo and uncovered the one about the chimpanzee who was almost beaten to death then eaten, who had to be eventually removed from the park. It was amazing how quickly they made that connection, and lo and behold they had their two prime suspects just in time for dinner and the evening coverage.

I watched in amazement as they pinpointed the major facts of the story. When the image of Dr. Wilde came up on the screen, I paused it and snapped a picture with my phone for my personal records. The police had done most of the heavy lifting by identifying their suspects, all that was left for me to do was to find them and bring them to justice. It was a matter of who was going to get to him first, me or the police. I had to find out where this psycho and his ape companion called home. It was time for Russ to spring into action.

The soup kitchens were social gathering spots for the city's less fortunate, as they gossiped about what was happening out on the streets while eating bowls of minestrone soup or pieces of yellow pound cake. They gathered in different cliques; blacks, whites, Hispanics, drug addicts, the crazies, and even a group of recovering addicts sat together and shared stories in the shelters. Russ knew people in each of the different circles, and that would prove to be an excellent starting point for our investigation.

The media passed on a few stories where low-life felons were butchered by an unknown attacker, but the homeless population sure took an interest in them. Rumors had spread about the vigilante headhunter, who was on the warpath and who was mercilessly taking out criminals at random. But not just any criminals, the real sleazy scumbag criminals who deserved it the most. Those who had a clear conscience were excited, those who worried did so for a reason. Were they going to be the next headless body to be found on the side of the road? That thought invoked a special kind of fear in the guilty that penetrated through them directly to their core, exactly as I intended.

"The Butcher of Beantown," as I am referred to, became somewhat of a local celebrity and everyone had their theories about who I really am. Russ eavesdropped and interjected comments of his own when he sat with them.

"I heard he's an ex-marine who was dishonorably discharged for butchering enemies after they had already been shot dead," one man said.

"No, he's actually a CIA agent on a special mission to clean up the city, you know black ops style," said another.

"Remember that crazy gypsy lady that was on the news years ago, who killed single fathers because she was a cold-hearted, half retarded, single mother who wanted revenge for some reason? What was her name? Nicole Furman or something? Well, I heard it's her son doing the killings for his mother, like some psycho shit." whispered a soup kitchen regular.

Russ tried not to laugh while conversing with the enthusiastic vagrants. A man named Clyde was one of his favorites to talk to since he was full of interesting and outrageous stories. He loved to talk and carried on, seemingly without taking a breath, to anyone who listened. Maybe not the smartest man around, but he didn't do drugs, and he had a heart of gold. He was just the man Russ was looking for.

At the Maple Street Inn was where he found him. Russ looked for the twenty-six-year-old drifter for a week, during which time there were no more robberies by the monkey man. Clyde came to the shelter that night looking for a bed and a hot meal courtesy of the best chef he knew, and the only one. As usual, once everyone had a tray, Russ went out into the mess hall and searched for his pal.

"Everybody, run and hide, it's Clyde!" Russ said with a laugh, as he patted his friend on the shoulder.

"This is the best pasta I've ever had, hands down. Mmm! Spot on Big Dog, spot on," he replied.

He was eating plain rotini with marinara meat sauce. Russ hadn't done much more than add some fresh, roasted garlic and ground beef to the cans of store-bought sauce, but it did not matter.

"Thanks, buddy. It's the secret ingredients; rat's ass and roach paste."

Clyde froze with his hand in mid-air, just as he was about to take another bite. His eyes widened, "You, clever son of a bitch! How did you know those were my favorites?!" he asked.

The two of them shared a laugh, and Russ sat across from him at the long banquet dining table. They sat at one end, with a half dozen others sitting on the opposite side. Russ leaned over the table and motioned with his head for Clyde to meet him halfway. When he did, Russ whispered to him, "What would you say if I told you I know who "The Butcher of Beantown" is?"

Clyde's eyes almost popped right out of his head into his plate of pasta. "You're shitting me?!" he responded a little louder than Russ had liked.

"Shhhhh! You have to give me your word that you will not tell a single other person before I say another word."

"Yes, of course, I promise," he said eagerly as if it was a well-known fact just how solid his promises were.

Russ knew he wouldn't last twenty minutes without telling someone though, actually he was counting on it.

"I just happen to be pals with the guy," Russ went on. "He and I go way back, we used to work together too."

"He's a chef?! I shoulda known by the way he carves people up..." the baffled vagabond said.

"That's right, he was a great chef who decided to dish out hot servings of justice to delinquents rather than feed the fat and rich over-priced meals at some gourmet restaurant. He trusted me enough to ask if I had any information on that crazy zookeeper who robbed the bank. It seems he's fixing to go after him. Dr. Wilde is his name, have you seen or heard about him?" Russ inquired.

"I don't know anything about that, but I'll try to get you something solid if you tell me the Butcher's real name. I promise I won't tell. I promise!" he begged like a child.

"You ask around and get me something, anything I can report back to him and I'll tell him it was you who helped out and provided the tip. And, yes, I'll tell you his name."

Clyde lit up like a Christmas tree. "Do you think he would want to meet me?" he asked oozing with excitement. "I can get all kinds of information as long as you don't let anyone else know it's me telling you. People don't take kindly to rats, especially around these parts," he said in a lowered voice, skimming his eyes around the dining hall.

"We'll see, he likes to keep a low profile. Just work on getting some good info and meet me back here around the same time in two days," Russ said as he stood up.

"Wait, where are you going? You didn't tell me his name," Clyde protested.

Russ pretended to look around to make sure nobody else was listening to what he was about to say, though nobody paid any attention. He leaned down and whispered into Clyde's ear, "He's a German fellow named Mr. Titsoff, first name Ader."

Russ has never been one to pass up on the opportunity to shell out a tongue-in-cheek joke, and his sarcasm tends to run wild at times.

Clyde looked him in the eyes and winked, assuring the secret was safe with him. Russ patted him on the back and walked away. Clyde couldn't believe it! He knew someone who knew the badass headsman who was causing criminals all around the Boston area to shit their pants! Not only that, but he might be able to assist him in taking down his next victim and even possibly meet him!

Suddenly, he felt very important like the local hero was relying on him to come through in the clutch, aiding him in his take-down of a dangerous bank robber. The excitement was almost too much for him to handle. He scarfed down the remaining pasta on his plate, barely chewing it, then zipped up his soiled sweatshirt and made his way back out into the night.

Russ gathered his belongings and exited the Inn from the rear kitchen door. He left his SUV parked by the dumpster since there was a camera recording the area. As he backed down the alley between buildings and entered Maple Street, he pulled out his cell phone and dialed Nero. "The squirrel has found his nuts," he said when I answered.

"What the hell are you talking about?" I asked. "I'm still waiting for the day when you can talk to me without using homoerotic profanities."

"I just left Maple Street Inn, and our good friend Clyde was there. I finally tracked that little bastard down and planted the seed in his head to get us a tip, or something that we can use to find "The Wild." He's a very resourceful guy, and I have faith in him."

"Don't call him that, please. You know, "The Wild," I don't want to feed this asshole's ego any more than it already has been. He's not some untouchable badass you read about in comic books. No, he's just a big goon, who likes playing with his monkey a little too much, who has a couple of screws loose, not balls of steel like I first thought. It doesn't take balls to do what he's doing it takes a lack of character that all sociopaths are missing. I wouldn't care if he was three times bigger than me instead of almost two, I'm going after this prick and taking his ass down." My face must have been red because I was feeling amped up.

"Whatever you say, Doctor," Russ replied sensing the frustration in my voice.

I hated when assholes like Dr. Wilde were thought of like a big shot, tough guys by others just because they had the nerve to do something out of the ordinary. He wasn't some battle-hardened adversary who was a force to be reckoned with. I saw the doctor for what he really was; a big oaf who was used to people being intimidated by his size, who thought he was clever by using a smarter-than-average chimp to aide him in sophomoric heists. He might physically be the biggest obstacle I faced, but not the smartest. He can take his knowledge of animal behaviors and shove it up his ignorant ass. I had the upper hand when it came to wits, I was the smarter of the two of us. Sure, I might sound a little bit presumptuous, but why shouldn't I be? What has he done that was so impressive besides train an ape how to point a gun and squeeze a trigger? What were all his impressive credentials?

Nothing the news reported struck me as anything remotely close to brilliant. I was the true mad scientist who was the force to be reckoned with! I cured addiction, I developed a safe way to assume others' identities and bring criminals to justice, I was the one with the balls and strength to quickly dismember useless pieces of shit right out in public without getting caught!

"The Butcher of Beantown" didn't take a backseat to this freak. I admit I was a little disappointed with the lack of coverage my killings earned, despite having to keep anonymous, but a little recognition for my efforts would have been nice. With the help of Russ and what his informant provided, I would gladly show this city who the true genius was as I delivered the good doctor to the local authorities in bits and pieces. "The Wild" huh? I'll show those oversized organ grinders how the WILD boys of Boston roll!

Chapter 23

No new incidents involving Dr. Wilde, or his fuzzy friend surfaced in the following days. I remained at my house in Franklin for the most part, except for when I headed out for my daily jog. Other than that, my home was where I stayed and monitored the news channels on the television, as well as online, for anything that was of possible help in my search for Dr. Wilde.

Russ checked in daily with little or no news that seemed relevant, until the night he returned to the Maple Street Inn and met up with Clyde once again. He called me after the two of them had a lengthy conversation outside and away from any nosy eavesdroppers. The homeless people who hung around there, loved gossip and Russ took no chances. I answered the phone anticipating bad news: Clyde hadn't appeared or had no useful information. I was pleasantly mistaken.

"Guess who pulled through with a tasty little nugget of information for us?" he asked me in a playful voice.

"Are you serious? I'm really not in the mood for any jokes if you will. It's been a long, unproductive week and I don't feel like getting my hopes up for nothing," I said sounding like a grump.

"I'll be over in thirty minutes to fill you in. You need anything? You want me to bring you a plate of grub? Shepherd's pie tonight, it was a big hit."

"I ate already, but thanks. I don't need anything other than some good news."

"Well sit tight, I'm on my way," he said before we said our goodbyes and hung up.

I wondered what Clyde found out. I didn't want to get too hopeful, so I tried to put the thought out of my head for the time being. I went to the front door where I taped a note on the outside that read, "Meet me inside at the pool." It was time for me to unwind a little with a quick swim.

My indoor pool was added to the original plans of our house as a surprise gift for Eve. We both loved swimming, and it was the perfect complement to our gorgeous new home. The ceiling overhead was glass, as were two of the parallel walls, giving a stunning panoramic view of the surrounding woods and backyard. Eve and I spent countless nights floating on our backs, staring up at the star-lit sky and chatting about silly things couples in love share. All those little meaningless conversations now seemed like the most important talks I've ever had, and I would trade all the other moments since her passing for just one more evening star gazing with my love.

I changed into my bathing suit and turned the thermometer to the pool's heater to 74 degrees. I laid the extra bathing trunks I grabbed for Russ, in case he felt like joining me, across the back of one of the Adirondack chairs that faced the pool. Next, I walked over to the opposite side, just past the deep end, to the bar and took two bottles of diet cola out for my friend and me. The remote to the televisions was on top of the bar, so I turned them on.

One was on the wall just above the entrance to the bar, the other television on the wall directly opposite by the shallow end of the pool. Channel Six News was what I chose although it aired a segment called "Inside Man," starring none other than my old pal Braddock Nix. That guy really gets around. ThePatriotPress.com was greatly successful, though not enough to satisfy that hot bag of wind. I turned the volume down, so I didn't have to hear his voice as much and turned the closed captioning on before diving into my wonderful pool.

For the next thirty minutes, I lazily floated around, mostly on my back, and I enjoyed the last of the sun's rays that painted the clouds and the sky with beautiful shades of magenta, pink, and purple before darkening as the evening drew near. I wondered if, wherever Eve was, she was able to enjoy the same radiant display I witnessed. Would we ever share another moment like that again?

I don't believe in heaven or hell, but during times like that, I sure wished I did. I wished I believed we would be reunited in some indescribably breathtaking paradise where we spent the rest of eternity together, but logic and my scientific way of thinking prevented me from doing so.

My parents used to say, "What you lack in faith you make up for with ingenuity."

Whenever I thought of Eve, I envied those who were believers and had faith because it seemed so simple and comforting. Oh well, I still had my best pal to keep me company, and his sense of humor and positive attitude always lifted my spirits.

Noting the time and realizing it was longer than thirty minutes since I got off the phone with my friend, I made my way over to the edge and pulled myself up and out of the water. Just as I reached for my towel, the door opened, and Russ walked in. He removed his coat and draped it over the back of another chair and then approached me. "How's King Karlin doing this fine evening?" he asked before slapping my lower back with a stinging whack.

"Ouch! You prick!" I shouted, as I dropped the towel and lunged toward my buddy. I quickly got him in a headlock and walked over to the edge of the pool.

"No don't! I have my phone in my pocket!" he pleaded, but I didn't care.

I leaned my weight back and pulled him in the water on top of me. I knew he was lying, he hated having stuff in his pant pockets and typically kept his keys, wallet, and cell phone in his jacket. We wrestled for a few minutes, each taking a turn drowning the other before coming up for air. He splashed a wave of water at me and howled, "You asshole! I could have really had my phone on me! You're lucky these boots are waterproof."

"You're lucky I'm glad to see you and went easy on you," I responded.

It was the truth, I already felt better, and my thoughts were no longer on my dearly departed Eve. What would I ever do without Russ? I probably would go insane or drink myself to death or both. I wonder if he knows just how valuable he is to me. From that signature mischievous grin on his face, I'd say so.

"Wait until you hear what I have to tell you. Do you want to hear it now or wait until we're done swimming?" he asked.

"Why don't you change into that suit right there I took out for you and tell me when you come back in?" I suggested.

He nodded and got out of the pool, his jeans and shirt sopping wet. He picked up the swimming trunks and walked behind the bar where he quickly changed.

"I'll throw your stuff in the dryer when we get out," I told him.

Again, he nodded.

I watched as he made his way on to the diving board and curled his toes over the edge. Diving was something he was terrible at, but he was a stubborn son of a bitch, and so I was lucky enough to bear witness to numerous botched attempts that usually ended in a loud slapping belly flop.

This attempt was no different. With a look of serious focus and determination, he bent his knees and sprang forward, hands pointed above his head. Just as he always did, he panicked halfway through the air and straightened his body out just before landing smack down on his stomach and face. The sound alone made me cringe, and I burst out into laughter. I was laughing so hard no sound was coming out, and tears soon streamed down my face. Russ surfaced with a pained look on his face, as he hugged his arms across his stomach. "What the fuck..." he moaned. "I think I shattered my sternum and ruptured all of my organs."

He slowly made his way to the shallow end, to where I was still laughing at him. I could see his skin was already bright red like he had a sunburn covering his front.

"My goodness, you suck!" I chuckled.

I don't usually laugh when my friend is in pain, but this was different. How could I not?!

"You ready to spill the beans or are you going to float around whining until your vagina feels better?"

"You wish I had a vagina you sicko. I'm sure you have a camera behind your bar that taped me getting undressed, and you're going to

188

watch later tonight when you're all curled up in your bed. I know your game."

He tilted his head back and brushed his shoulder length, long, black hair back as he ran his fingers through it. Pulling it tight and twisting it into a ponytail, he snapped an elastic around it to keep it in place. As he did, I looked over the tattoos that covered his chest and abdomen. It wasn't like I hadn't seen them countless times before, but I admired the excellent attention to detail the artist had achieved.

There was a cattle skull with demonic horns on his left pectoral muscle that melted down into droplets and formed little dancing demons with tridents and spears. On his other pectoral was a ghastly devil wearing a business suit and smiled wildly as he churned the handle of a meat grinder. Children fell into the top of the grinder and came out as ground beef, landing on a plate in front of a priest sitting at a table. There was a saying tattooed in a circle around his belly button that read, "Do not go gentle into that good night, rage, rage against the dying of the light." It is a quote from Dylan Thomas I believed. He was covered with tattoos and every time I looked, I swore I noticed one I hadn't seen before.

"You done checking me out? I'm not just some piece of meat for you to drool over you know. There is a person behind this perfectly chiseled physique," he said trying not to smile.

"Get over yourself. Make with the story, would you?" I insisted.

"Alright, but it's going to cost you. You might be surprised to learn that you've developed quite the fan club amongst the soup kitchen patrons. You're somewhat of a celebrity. Anyway, I met up with Clyde, and it appears he actually came through, and big. I'll tell you what he told me then you decide if you want to question him further before making a decision about the validity of his information."

"That sounds just fine. So, what did he hear?" I inquired.

"Okay so get this; he claims one of his buddies told him he was out at some strip club in the north end, The Dancing Spider or The Barking Spider, something like that. Anyways, this guy was shooting the shit with some other guy at the bar there, and the two began getting chummy as the drinks were downed. After a few rounds of shots, the guy really starts flapping his jaw about how he had been fired by his psychotic boss for not shooting a random stranger in the face. He said in a drunken stupor something about how he was replaced by an ape but then changed the subject once his drinking buddy showed interest and questioned him about that statement. He tried to brush it off and act like he meant something else, but Clyde insists his informant heard him say "ape" and was no doubt talking about the one and only Dr. Wilde from the news. He told Clyde the man mentioned how his feet were killing him because he had to walk all the way from Oxford to Douglas that morning. Clyde is positive the guy his friend was drinking with and talking to worked for Dr. Wilde and that he was somewhere in the town of Oxford. What do you think about that?"

I pondered what my dear friend had just revealed to me as I had doubts about the source of information. "Are you sure Clyde isn't making this up?" I asked him.

"Positive. He's a bit of a character, but he wouldn't make up a blatant lie, especially since all he has to gain is meeting you. I didn't give him any cash, I was leaving that decision up to you," he replied.

"Meeting me? What the hell are you talking about? Who said anything about meeting me?" I asked confusedly.

Russ looked down and rubbed the back of his neck. "Well, I didn't promise him anything, but he didn't ask for a payout, only that he can meet you. I figured if he thinks he's going to meet the infamous "Butcher of Beantown" he's not going to risk making up some lies, pissing off the man who is hacking people up with a machete. You could wear your ski mask and have a light in his face as you question him for yourself, the way the cops do in the movies. He's not lying, I'm sure of it. But that's up to you to ultimately decide."

I sighed and shook my head. "If you trust him, that's good enough for me. I'm not meeting him, not now anyway. Pay him off next time you see him and thank him for me. Tell him when shit settles down, and the zookeeper and his ape are in custody or dead, then I'll think about meeting him to personally thank him. But for now, everything is low key."

"You got it, Boss. What do you think about Oxford?" Russ asked.

"I think that's the perfect town to hide in. It's rural but close to the Mass Pike, so it's convenient to get to. There's a lot of land out there where someone could easily house a chimpanzee without any neighbors close enough to take notice. We will start there, check out the town and see what we can find. But first, tomorrow we will head up to that strip club in the north end and see if we bump into the guy your informant was talking to ourselves. It shouldn't be too hard to spot some poor chump who's down on his luck and sipping his worries away in a gentleman's club. Most men that go to places like that are in good spirits and enjoying the entertainment. If we don't find him, then we will head to Oxford and start by checking out the local bars there. Something is bound to surface."

Russ agreed to my plan, and we both were satisfied with the little nugget of information his buddy from the soup kitchen provided. We finished our swim, and I offered him dry sweatpants and a shirt to wear while I tossed his clothes in the dryer and made us dinner. I assumed he would sleep over, as he occasionally did, and I was correct.

We stayed up until midnight snacking on peanuts and beef jerky as we watched a low-budget horror movie. Those were our favorite kind of movies, and we had repeated the same routine countless times before. We were simply just two great friends sharing some good times and some good laughs like any other normal people, we just happen to hunt and murder dangerous criminals on the side.

Chapter 24

There were about a dozen patrons inside The Barking Spider, which I imagine was typical for a Thursday evening. Russ and I made our way past a row of tables toward the back of the club, near where the main stage was. That's where the majority of men were sitting, with creepy, perverted grins on their faces as they waved dollar bills at the dancers.

I was never a fan of strip clubs and found the customers who went there to be just as shady as the low-rent dancers. But that night we were in search of something other than watered-down rum and coke and glitter covered nude entertainment. We were looking for the man who spilled the beans to Clyde's associate. We sat and played along as if we were just two more typical horny guys drooling over a malnourished, twenty-something-year-old, who had two names tattooed on her upper arms, probably her kid's, and an obvious c-section scar just below her navel. She might have been a little bit cute if she didn't look like she was strung out, and maybe put on a couple of pounds. Russ tucked a five into her G-string as she stuck her ass in his face. He smiled from ear to ear.

"Now I know where they got the name The Barking Spider," he said with a grin.

Apparently, he didn't seem to mind the attention, and soon there were two more dancers standing beside us, asking if we wanted private dances in the back room.

"I'm all set for right now, come back later," I said, much to her dismay, her pout was anything but cute.

"What do I get for a hundred bucks?" Russ asked the prettier of the two blonde ladies.

"Two songs and you can touch me anywhere you want, but only with your hands and only after you clean them with the hand sanitizer on the wall," she informed him.

He stood and took her by the hand as she led him off in the direction of the booths. I cleared my throat loudly to catch his attention, and when he looked back at me, he smiled and shrugged his shoulders, like there was nothing he could do. Some wingman he was! We were supposed to be scoping out the customers, not getting our jollies from the working women!

I went to the front bar where there were two men sitting, both flirting with the busty brunette bartender whose breasts were spilling out of her skin-tight top. I pulled a seat in between the two men and ordered a diet cola. One of them looked at me for an instant and chuckled at my order like I was less of a man than he was because I wasn't drinking alcohol. If only he knew who I was, then we'd see who had the last laugh. I ignored him and turned toward the other man. "Boy is she something else or what?" I said referring to the bartender.

"Oh, you're not kidding. I've been coming here for the past three years regularly just to check her out. She never ceases to amaze me by how small of a top she can squeeze into. Her tits somehow defy the laws of gravity, boy oi oi," he said to me.

I wasn't sure I would brag about stalking a young woman bartending at a strip club to anyone, let alone a complete stranger. Perhaps this was the guy I was looking for though. I nodded in agreement and sipped my coke.

"You come here that much huh? You're obviously not married. My wife would kill me if she knew I came to a place like this," I lied to him.

"Yeah well, I work right down the road, so it's easy for me to pop in here from time to time. Plus, the beers aren't that over-priced, so I can't complain," he remarked.

Obviously, he wasn't the guy if he worked down the street. The man I was looking for had been working in Oxford supposedly. I turned to my left, toward the man who scoffed at my drink selection.

"Can you pass the peanuts?" I asked him, motioning to the bowl of bar nuts to his left.

He grabbed them and slid them toward me without taking his

eyes off the bartender, who leaned over chopping the ice with a plastic scooper in the cooler below her. His eyes were fixated on her jiggling chest and protruding nipples. "What a scumbag," I thought even though it was a tough sight to resist.

She was an attractive young lady, but seriously, show a little bit of class. I guess that was the last place I should have expected such behavior from my fellow man.

"It doesn't get any better than that," I whispered softly but loud enough for him to hear.

"Amen," he said in agreement. He shook his head from side to side. "Mmm mm mm," was all he could come up with.

"Does she ever get up on the stage and dance?" I asked, half making conversation and half a little curious.

"Boy, do I wish. The bartenders here only serve drinks and tease us with their tight little shirts and short shorts. I've asked and even offered a hundred bucks for a private dance, but she won't do it, says even if she wanted to, she's not allowed to."

Who was this guy kidding?! I wondered if he actually believed there was a chance in hell she might honestly consider giving him a private strip dance but couldn't because of the strict club rules. What a chump! There was no way, even for two hundred bucks, that a woman of her caliber would be interested in a sleaze ball like him, even if she tended bar at a strip club. I searched for the right words to say. "Do you work in the area?" I asked harmlessly enough.

"Nah, I work in Quincy. I live not too far from here though. And my wife doesn't say shit about me coming here. I don't give a fuck what she says. She knows who's in charge. Besides, coming here and seeing all this hot ass wandering around is the only thing that keeps our sex life alive. She should be happy I come here." he said, sounding every bit like the overbearing, pig-headed, douchebag he was.

He probably was physically abusive as well as verbally. I couldn't get thrown off track by this prick though or else I just might snap, take him outside, and lay him out on the pavement. This wasn't the guy I was looking for either.

I finished my soda, ordered another one, that time even louder than the first to see if he would make a comment, but he didn't. Taking my delicious, ice-cold cola back to the main stage, I sat on one of the empty stools, leaving empty seats to both my left and right. There were two men sitting in the front row there with me, and I was determined to talk to them both, if possible, without looking suspicious.

Three dancers took turns dancing to one song and then walked off to the side to let the next one perform. I waited until the man to my left caught me looking at him before I asked if he had change for a ten-dollar bill. He pulled out a wad of ones, counted out ten, and then handed them to me.

"They can give you all the change you need at the front ya know," he said to me sounding slightly annoyed.

"I'm sorry. I just didn't want to miss any of the action," I said, motioning my head to the bare ass that was bobbing up and down just a couple of feet in front of us.

"Oh, heh heh heh... I hear ya loud and clear bro," he said with a devilish smile. He sounded like he had a bit of an accent, but I couldn't place what kind. Was it a southern Californian accent?

"How are the private dances? Do they let anything go or are they strict about you not touching them?" I asked though I pretty much knew the answer.

"Well that all depends," he replied. There was a long pause as his attention was focused entirely on the dancer, and I could even see his eyeballs moving, following her every dip, twirl, and split.

"It all depends on what?" I asked impatiently.

"It all depends on which gal you're talking about and how much you're willing to part with. What's the matter Bucko, haven't you ever been to a titty bar before?" he asked me with a bit of frustration in his own voice.

"Sure, I have, but they're all different. I just moved to the state, bought a place out in Oxford, but I'm working out around here. This is the first one I've been to in Massachusetts. The ones I used to go to in Atlanta you could touch all you wanted. They would even finish you off after a private dance for fifty bucks. I was just curious if it was the same here." I tried to sound as casual as possible.

Atlanta popped into my head because I visited plenty of times for business and knew enough of the area to bullshit if I got called out on something. He didn't seem too interested.

When the song ended, the petite-figured dancer with the enormous fake breasts picked her bikini top off the floor and left the stage. As the next song came on followed by the next dancer, the man sitting a few seats over to my right leaned over and whistled softly to get my attention. "Pssst. Hey buddy, come here," he called.

I looked to my left and to my right to act as if I wasn't sure he was talking to me and then pointed to myself, mouthing the words, "Who me?"

"Yeah you, come here for a second." He patted the empty seat next to him.

I rose to my feet and moved over and sat where he had motioned to.

"Can I help you?" I asked cautiously.

"Where did you say you were from?" he wanted to know.

"Atlanta," I responded.

He shook his head quickly with his eyes shut. Placing his index fingers on the top of his nose in between his eyes, he rubbed his face and said, "Not Atlanta, where are you from in Massachusetts?"

"Oh, I just moved to Oxford. Is that what you mean?" I questioned the seemingly stressed individual.

He pulled his head back and opened his eyes quickly, frowning for a second as he tried to focus them in on me. He was clearly intoxicated. "Yeaaaa, yea, yea, that's it! Oxford IS what you said, I thought so. Good ol' ox country. Say, how long have you been living there exactly?"

"I moved there right after the hurricane passed through here," I lied once again.

"Yeah, that sure was one fucker of a storm, wasn't it? My unlucky ass was stuck out in the middle of the Atlantic on a smelly cargo ship for most of it, imagine that. You haven't felt shit like the sea sickness I had, sailing through that goddamn hurricane."

He was animated as he talked, with his arms flailing and head gesturing as he struggled to get each word out. The man had obviously been over-served, but he kept on going. Taking a big swig from his beer bottle, he slammed it down on the table in between the stools and the stage. "Aaand another thing. Who the fuck goes to Africa, let alone wants to live there?" he slurred.

"I couldn't tell you. Not me, that's for certain." I humored him.

"You're goddamn right not you! Not you, not me, not Titties McGee dancing around up there... not nobody! But no, wait... I do go there, er, rather I did go there. Like a chump, I agreed to go there and risk my life and my ass and all for what? To get shit-canned a couple months later for not offing some meathead gym rat? You've gotta be kidding me. What kind of butt-fucking chump do I look like? Do I look like a butt-fucking chump to you pal?" he asked me as his head bobbed from side to side and his eyes widened. What a mess he was. But was he the man Russ and I were looking for?

"Well, why on Earth did you go to Africa, my friend?" I asked.

"Don't you patronize me, Bucko. And don't think I went there on some save-the-world peace corps mission or some yuppie safari shit. I went there for work and work I did. I trudged through sweltering jungles with bugs that will suck you dry in minutes and more poisonous snakes than you could count. What a shitty time that was. Luckily, I had a good friend of mine with me to help me keep my sanity. Otherwise, I woulda said fuck the damn chimp and took a flight back home. What do I know though? One day I think I'm in good with my boss and making good money, the next I'm run out of town like some fucking leper. All because of "loyalty," loyalty my ass. Where was the loyalty to me? Who have I ever fucked over that deserves firing me? No one, that's fucking who."

He grabbed his beer bottle aggressively and pounded the remaining half that was left, slammed it back on the table again, and belched, wiping his mouth with his sleeve. "Ahh fuck it, I've said

197

too much. For all, I know you probably work for him and came here to take me out. Is that what you're planning behind that stupid look on your face? Are you thinking about taking me out Bucko?" he turned to face me squarely and leaned toward my face.

I was in no mood to be hassled by this drunken oaf even if he was the man I was searching for.

I cleared my throat and said very sternly, "Buddy, I have no idea what the fuck you're talking about. I came here to see some skin and enjoy myself with my friend. I don't know you from a glory hole in the wall nor do I care."

He seemed satisfied with my answer but then he looked around as if searching for someone. "Who the hell is your buddy? Do I know him? He's not here to start trouble with me, is he?"

"He is in the back getting a private dance, something I'm about to do as well. How about you, do you have any recommendations as to which girl I should pick?" I asked.

"The hell if I know! They all got two tits, and three holes, don't they? What's the difference, you're asking me? I don't waste my money on the whores unless they're the real kind, you know the ones you can fuck. You won't be getting any of that here. Maybe a hand-job if you're lucky and one thinks you're cute. No, if you want some real action, I know just the place. Not far from here, I'll take ya if you're serious about going. I could use a good lay after the past few days I've had." He sounded physically drained. He must be the man Clyde's contact talked about.

It seemed crazy he was out in public, belligerently intoxicated and talking to complete strangers about his work with Dr. Wilde. He had to be in real bad shape to be conducting himself in such a careless manner.

"Yeah, I'll go check it out with you. Can we just wait for my friend to return and then go? I'll buy the next round," I offered, assuming the drunker he was, the more information he'd spill.

"Sure, if you're buying, I'm drinking," was his response. "Make it a pale ale my good man."

"No problem. I'm Robert by the way," I said as I extended my hand to shake his.

"Jacob Stills at your service. A pleasure to meet you. Now let's make with the drinks and get a move on. I want to get over to the "who-a house" and get my smash on. I've had a chub for the past three hours from hanging out in this joint," he said as he adjusted himself by shuffling his hand around in his front pocket.

It was at that moment I understood why they called places like that one "gentleman clubs."

A strong hand suddenly squeezed my shoulder almost causing me to spill my drink as I was just about to take a sip. "What's up, ladies? Did you make a friend? I take you to a strip club filled with loose women, and you pick up a guy? So typical," Russ said shaking his head.

It never ceased to amaze me just how much he liked to bust balls, even with complete strangers. He had no idea who this guy was I was talking to was, nor did he care. Nobody was off limits to his mischievous ridicule and wisecracks. Russ wasn't intimidated by anyone, and with good reason, he sure knew how to handle himself in a scrap. He sized up the man I had just met and introduced himself, "I'm just fucking with you. I'm Shaquille, and you are?"

What an asshole! What kind of nonsense alias did he use?!

"Uhh, yeah. I mean I'm Jacob. Nice to meet you too, Shaquille. How was your dance?" Jacob asked Russ.

"Oh, it was great. That chick had no "off limits" if you know what I mean! And her downstairs smelled like peach cobbler. No lie, who wants a whiff?" he asked holding out his three fingers.

"Jesus Christ, Robert what's wrong with your friend?!" Jacob asked with a laugh. Russ looked at me and winked.

"Yeah Robert, what is wrong with me? I should be asking what's wrong with you for passing up on such a professionally exotic dance. All I did was place my hand facing upward on my knee, and she bumped and slimed all over me. She was digging her crotch into my hand like she was trying to engrave her initials into it. It felt

199

like I was hand-feeding a manatee, spectacular!" Russ was like a kid on Christmas morning. He couldn't control himself or his immaturity. And he even looked like he belonged there, as he wore his black sunglasses inside an already darkened club. Jacob and I stared at him.

"We were talking about heading over to a different type of club where there really are no limits on what happens in the back rooms. A place where you get more than just a few fingers wet," Jacob told Russ. He perked right up at this revelation.

"You don't say? Robert, you're interested in going to this new place?" Russ asked me.

"Well yeah, it beats just sitting here as our pants get tighter and our wallets get lighter," I answered him.

"Well put, well put. Jacob, would you mind if I had a quick word with Robert before we go? It's a small business matter I want to tell him about before I forget. Then we can go."

"Sure, do what you gotta do. I want to finish my beer then take a leak anyway, so I'll just meet you in the front by the door in ten minutes, okay?"

Jacob got up and headed for the men's room.

"Sure," we both said at the same time.

I nudged Russ' shoulder to move on forward toward the door and then followed him out. We stood outside the entrance, underneath the awning, and faced each other. There was nobody else around, and the security camera that was covering the front door was the kind that recorded video only, not audio.

Feeling it was safe enough for us to talk openly, I started off the conversation, "I think he's our guy. He's the guy Clyde's informant spoke with. I told him I just moved to Oxford from Atlanta two months ago after the hurricane hit. He asked me how long I had been there and then went on rambling about a trip he took to Africa to find a chimp and then how he got fired for not killing someone. He sounded all upset about it and slightly confused. It had to be him. How many other people go to Africa to retrieve a chimp? That was no coincidence, he must know Wilde and be his former employee."

"So, what do you want to do with him? What do you have in mind?" Russ asked me.

"I say we hang out with him, keep feeding him drinks, and act like we are taking him to this whore house he keeps babbling about. But instead, we'll take him to the Boneyard." Russ liked my idea, and his eyes lit up.

"You, vicious bastard. Getting all Guantanamo Bay on his ass huh? I like your style," he replied.

The Boneyard was an abandoned boxing gym in a rough area of the city where gang members used to torture their enemies. There once was a highlighted segment on Channel Six News that Braddox Nix did, that detailed the different types of torture devices found inside during a police raid. Up until the raid, law enforcement mostly stayed out and left the building alone since most of the crimes that happened there were gang-on-gang, and nobody really cared. That was until a twelve-year-old girl was reported missing and a tip from a police informant led them to the Boneyard, where the girl was recovered with bodily harm.

There were evil contraptions of all sorts scattered about the four-story crumbling brick building, that was brought to the public's attention in Nix's report but never removed or destroyed after the girl was safely recovered. The only measure that was taken to keep people from trespassing on the condemned property was a chain link fence was erected around the lot. Not the kind with razor wire at the top or anything, just a plain seven-foot chain link fence with the occasional "No trespassing" signs attached every few sections. Anybody with a desire could hop the fence and enter the "fear factory" as the locals call it.

When Jacob emerged from the building, he staggered a bit as he tried to walk and zip up his jacket at the same time. Russ and I looked at each other and smiled. He was getting good and hammered. I told him I would drive since I didn't drink alcohol and he went along without argument. He climbed into the back of my truck and reclined his seat as far back as it would go.

Was he ready to pass out already?! Things were going along much easier than earlier anticipated. I started my truck and pulled out of the parking lot, turning west toward our secret destination. Jacob had his head back and his eyes shut. For a moment I thought he had passed out, but then he suddenly perked up and came to life. "We're going to Somerville, head like you're going to the Museum of Science. When we get there let me know, I'll ride you the guest of the way," he slurred in a drunken stupor.

With that, he closed his eyes and dropped his head back again with his mouth open facing the ceiling. Man, was he cocked! Again, Russ and I exchanged silent grins as we headed in the opposite direction and got onto the expressway. It only took twenty minutes to reach the "fear factory," and I pulled to a stop along the side street, out of view from any other surrounding buildings. The only other structures in the area that might have watchful eyes peering out were two other abandoned buildings the homeless sometimes took shelter in. No matter though, even if someone saw the three of us enter the building, there would be no call to the police since their presence in the area would be called into question as well. Nobody who was around these parts wanted those pesky policemen poking their noses around.

When I finally put the truck into park and shut off the ignition, I pointed to the glove box in front of Russ. He opened it, revealing a bunch of plastic zip ties, which he picked up and stuffed into his coat pocket. We both quietly exited the vehicle, and I walked over to the passenger's side to the rear door. I gently lifted the latch and swung the door ajar. There before us was one very intoxicated, very unconscious man who was the key to finding out the whereabouts of the infamous Dr. Wilde. Russ opened the toolbox in the bed of my truck and pulled out a heavy-duty pair of bolt cutters and tucked them into the back of his jeans. We both took hold of one of Jacob's arms and pulled him forward until his feet dangled outside of the truck.

"On three. Ready, one, two, three!" I counted, and we pulled the rest of him out and propped him up between the two of us.

"Ughhhh..." he moaned as we kicked his feet and lifted his slouching body upwards.

"Jacob, we're here. The whores are just inside the building, but we need you to help by walking inside. We'll keep you steady, but you've got to stand on your own," I instructed him.

"Yeah, you don't even have to look. Keep napping if you want but keep moving your feet until we get inside. Then we will lay you in a nice warm bed with a nice warm woman," Russ added.

"You guys are fucking killing me with this bullshit," moaned Jacob, but suddenly his feet began to work.

One by one, he took baby steps, and we walked him to the chain link fence. He and I leaned against the fence while Russ took out the bolt cutters and snipped away at the section next to us. "Instant door," he said as he booted out the section.

He stepped through, and I handed Jacob to him, holding his head down, so he didn't poke out an eye as he passed through. From there we made our way to the entrance of the crumbling building, and again Russ booted in the door. "Honey, we're home!" he shouted.

"You're getting pretty good at that," I remarked.

"Why thank you, my good man," he replied with a bow.

"Come on, let's get him seated and strapped in. There's a chair over there, I can see the outline." I motioned with my head across the vast, dark, dreary void that made up the large room we stood in.

There were scattered old blankets and tarps that someone probably had once used on one side of the wall. Broken beer bottles made the ground crunch occasionally as Russ, and I made our way across the room. On the far end was a boxing ring, with the four corner posts leaning inward and standing out in the shadows, like four hunched over witches holding on to one another by the sagging ropes. Next to it was the judge's table that still had the round bell on it. We made our way over to the table and sat Jacob down on one of the steel folding chairs. Russ held him steady as I secured his feet to the legs of the chair with the zip ties, then I put one around both of his wrists and zipped them together behind his back.

Like a good hostage, he made no fuss or put up any resistance until that point. I told Russ to stay with him, and I went back outside and retrieved a smaller toolbox and a flashlight from the back of my truck. Returning once again, I used the flashlight to guide me through the large room back over to where Russ and Jacob were. On the edges of the beam of light, I saw roaches and a few mice scurry out of sight.

"How's he doing?" I asked as I shined the light on Jacob's face.

"Out like a baby. Seeing someone in this state does my sobriety wonders. I don't envy him at all," Russ declared.

I agreed with him one hundred percent.

I lifted the toolbox and placed it on the judge's table and stood across from Jacob. Russ had pushed him in so that he was sitting directly in front of me. The metal latches popped as I slowly opened the lid of the box. Russ positioned the flashlight on the table so that it was shining directly on Jacob. From the top compartment, I removed a smelling salt packet and handed it to Russ. Then I took out a pair of needle-nose pliers and a blow torch.

"Are you going to give him a chance to come clean or just jump right in feet first?" Russ asked me.

"Wake him up, and we'll see how belligerent he's going to be. I'll make the call based on that," I instructed him.

"You got it, boss. One wake up call's coming right up, courtesy of the "real deal" Shaquille," he answered with a smile.

He truly was in a world of his own, but he was my friend, and I trusted him with my life. I knew no matter what, he would never sell me out or let me down. That was why he was currently my partner in a kidnapping and about to help me torture information out of our hostage. I used to joke with him and tell him, "We'll always be best friends, you know too much."

Russ gave a quick pop, and the smelling salts worked their magic. Jacob abruptly lifted his groggy head and shook it from side to side. It took another minute or two for his eyes to open up but once they were, he surveyed his surroundings in a bewildered, discombobulated state of confusion. Then he tried to move and realized his hands and feet were bound. Looking down at his feet then back up at the table in front of him, the reality of the situation seemed to sink in. "What the fuck?" was all that he managed to say at first.

Russ sprang into action before I was able to say anything. Grabbing Jacob by the back of the head, he slammed his face forward smashing it into the metal bell causing it to ring loudly, *DING!* "Wake up asshole! Welcome to your worst nightmare! Ha ha ha!" he shouted in his ear, but it mattered very little since our hostage was once again unconscious.

"What the fuck Russ?! Are you trying to kill the guy before we even get him talking?! You can't start off with a devastating blow to the head like that!" I exclaimed frantically.

He stepped back quickly and held his head down.

"Sorry boss, I guess I got carried away. I'm really over-excited right now, sorry if I took it too far," he said sounding like a scolded child.

"Yeah, just take it, easy man."

I got out another smelling salt and popped it open myself. Our hostage slowly lifted his head. His lip was busted from eating the bell.

"Give him a chance to come to his senses so we can get some answers out of him, jeez," I wasn't angry, just concerned for our captive man.

Alcohol and head injuries do not mix well, and I wanted to make sure we got every bit of information that we could out of him before the night ended. Jacob moaned and held his head back, looking up toward the ceiling. "Ugh... what the fuck you, assholes," he mumbled just before spitting a mouthful of blood on the floor.

His glossy eyes opened, surveying his surroundings. I pulled my handkerchief out of my back pocket and wiped small pieces of his busted lip and nose from his face. He winced and pulled his head away as I did.

"Wake up Jacob. We have some important matters to talk about," I said in a cool but serious voice.

"What the hell is going on? Where the fuck are we? Why am I tied up and why are you hitting a man while he's bound at the hands and feet? Pussies. Cut me free, and we'll have a talk all right. We'll talk about how only cowards hit a man when he can't fight back."

He spat again, this time at Russ' feet. Immediately, Russ grabbed the bell off the table and belted Jacob across the face before I could intervene, *DING!*

"ARE YOU FUCKING KIDDING ME?!" I exclaimed.

"Look what he did to my boot!" Russ responded, pointing to some bloody phlegm barely spattered on the tip of his boot.

Jacob was back asleep as Russ, and I argued and swore back and forth with each other for about twenty minutes. I was yelling in his face, and he was barking in mine. We shoved each other a few times and eventually exchanged blows. That wasn't the first time we've scrapped, and it's probably not going to be the last. Sometimes that's our best way to communicate, but we get over it quickly. When he again woke up, Jacob was the one who broke up our fight.

"What the hell is going on?! Where are the whores? And why is my bloody all bloody?" Jacob questioned in a drunkenly damaged way.

Russ and I stared at each other, huffing and puffing for a moment. Then we turned our gaze to our hostage and got back to business. I turned the gas nozzle and clicked the flint button of the blowtorch, which fired right up on the first try. That got Jacob's attention, and he quieted down immediately. I saw how he was quickly sobering up from the adrenaline rush the seriousness of the situation had given him. Suddenly, he realized he wasn't dreaming or having a terrible nightmare as Russ put it. No, the whooshing flame I held in my hand was very real, and he understood completely.

"What, the big, scary, chimp whisperer can't take me out himself? He's gotta send you two pussies to do his dirty work for him? And they call him "The Wild," there's nothing wild about this. He's too chicken shit to face me man to man. What's so wild about that, huh? Please tell me before you do whatever it is, he paid you to do to me," he said with a final surge of courage flowing through his words.

"So, it is Dr. Wilde that you work for. Or should I say worked for? I thought so from your drunken ramblings earlier in the evening. You really should watch what you say when talking to strangers, you never know who might be listening. I heard you had been at that shitty strip club, bitching about getting fired because you pussied out of an ordered hit. You talk a big game for someone who doesn't even have it in him to shoot another man. Tell me, was it Dr. Wilde who bailed your ass out and popped the guy you were supposed to shoot?"

"Fuck you, Robert! I ain't no psycho who just blows dude's heads off for shits and giggles. I have no problem killing a man who deserves it, like you two pricks."

"Listen punk, it's time now for you to take orders from someone who's much smarter than the previous doctor you were just working for. That man in front of you wants you to do as you were doing before and sing like a little birdie. Tell us all about Dr. Silas Wilde and his operation. We want names, address, dates, everything," Russ barked in Jacob's face, pulling his hair and holding his head up. He doesn't stand for disrespect, especially when I am the one being disrespected.

Jacob looked at me as I walked around to his side of the table and brought the flame from the torch within inches of his face and neck. I wasn't aiming it at him but rather holding the flame, so it ran parallel to his skin, still giving off plenty of heat to get my point across. His eyes glowed with the reflection of the blue and orange blaze.

"Whaaah... what do you want exactly? Put down the torch and let's talk," he said, quickly changing his tune.

"Before I do anything of the sort, I want you to tell me where Dr. Wilde sleeps at night. I want to know where he houses that disgusting beast, he totes around with him. Tell me that and then I'll think about saving your face from becoming a charred piece of leather."

"You've gotta promise you won't tell anyone I told you. I'm no rat, I'm not a snitch. I've seen what he does to people who just argue with him, he's completely nuts! If he finds out I ratted him out, he'll cut me up and feed me to that fucking ape!" Jacob said with sincere terror in his voice.

I was losing my patience. I nodded at Russ, who pulled Jacob's head to the side, exposing the entire right side of his neck. Quickly I waved the torch from side to side aiming it at his bare flesh. His scream was probably heard three blocks away. The color of his skin turned from a whitish pink to crimson red and black. I stopped and took a step back. Russ released his head, and it slumped forward silently.

"Shit, he passed out again. This guy is going for a new record," I said to Russ.

He made a nervous smile and looked at me for instructions. Shutting off the torch, I placed it back in the toolbox and removed three more smelling salts. I turned and tossed them to Russ and said, "better safe than sorry." I made it clear I meant business.

The third salt packet worked just as well as the first two and soon Jacob re-joined us. He moaned continuously, rolling his head in the opposite direction from which he got burnt. I held the pliers in my hand and approached his right side once again. "Are we ready to start talking like a good little rat?" I asked him mockingly.

"Whatever you say, man. Just leave my head alone. I've got a wife and kids at home, and I don't want to terrify them." he uttered pathetically.

"Jacob, Jacob, Jacob... we're really not off to a good start here. How can we work together when I can't trust you? I know you don't have a wife or kids, you were bragging to some other schmuck at the club about how many strippers around the city you've slept with. I heard you make fun of the guy for being married when you asked him if his wife ever lets him take his balls out of her jar to play with. Why are you playing me for a fool? Oh Jakey, Jakey, Jake, this isn't good. Not good at all."

I circled around his back with the pliers in my right hand and grabbed hold of his left hand with mine. He pleaded and squirmed but I was able to slip one side of the nose under his thumbnail, and then I clamped down and yanked. His entire nail tore right off as his thumb began to run with blood.

"How many lies did you just tell me? Let's see... we'll just call it two."

Grabbing his index finger, I repeated the same process despite his best efforts to clinch his fist shut. The index nail came off with less effort than the thumb.

"We've got all day, jerkoff. Tell us what you know and be done with it. Or don't, this is actually a lot of fun. Makes no difference to me," Russ interjected.

"I'll tell you! I'll tell you! Please stop..." Jacob said weakly.

"Where does he live? Where is he now? How many men are in his crew?" I asked clenching my teeth.

"Oxford. He lives in Oxford in a farmhouse. There's a big barn next to it where he has a lab and keeps the chimp. There were five of us living there but now that I'm gone that number is down to four unless he's found a replacement for me. I don't know nothing else, honest," our weakened prisoner said.

"Why's he robbing businesses and where is he planning on striking next?" I pressed on.

"I don't know what he plans on doing with the money or where he wants to hit next, honest I don't. He keeps everything a secret until the day of the job. We never knew what to expect. Some days we were remodeling his barn, the next we were running and hiding in the woods and were human targets for him and his fagot chimp to practice shooting at."

I looked at Russ somewhat disbelieving what I heard. Did he have a master plan all figured out or was he flying by the seat of his pants?

"Tell me about the guy he wanted you to kill. Who was he and what happened?"

"He was nobody I have ever met or seen before. We drove out to his house in the middle of the woods, and they made a drug deal.

Everything was fine until he got back in the van with me and ordered me to go up to the house and kill the guy, for no fucking reason! He got his stuff and paid the man. There was a brief conversation that seemed a little heated, but in the end, they made the deal. I had no idea why he wanted him dead, let alone why I had to be the one to kill him. When I drew my gun on him, I froze. We wrestled in the doorway for a moment, and then a shot rang out from behind me. Silas wasted him and left him right on his doorstep. The next morning one of the other guys told me I had failed his test and that he would kill me. So, I split. That's everything, I swear."

He looked exhausted, like a man who had endured a bit of torture. I studied his face for a moment and decided he was telling the truth. I stepped away from him and returned my pliers to the toolbox.

"Are we done? Please..." he pleaded.

I hate begging, it's pathetic. I looked him in the eyes again and then shifted my stare over to Russ. We exchanged a look in silence for a moment. It must have seemed like an eternity to Jacob.

Finally, I nodded and said, "We're through here, you're free to go."

Jacob let out a big sigh of relief and smiled. "Please don't tell anyone I talked. I'll be out of town tomorrow, I just need a day to get my affairs in order, but if he learns I squealed, I'm a dead man."

I looked at Russ and gave him a nod. Jacob saw this and suddenly grew nervous again. He watched as Russ bent and removed a six-inch, razor-sharp bowie knife from his boot.

"No, no wait...You said I could go! I'm sorry, I shouldn't have said anything. I'll stop. Please, please just let me go..." he rambled on.

Russ reached behind him and with a quick upward swipe, cut the zip ties off of his hands. Then before Jacob realized that he was being set free, Russ whispered into his ear, "Boy, you really need to learn to shut the fuck up," and with that, he grabbed Jacob by the back of his head again and smashed his face forward on the bell, making another *DING!* noise. Jacob's body went limp as he was knocked out once again.

I shook my head and laughed at my crazy counterpart.

"What?" he said with a shrug.

I packed up my toolbox, picked up the flashlight, and put my arm around Russ's shoulder. "Come on buddy, our job's done here. You did great work gathering all this information, you did just great Shaquille. I don't know what I'd do without you."

"Thanks, boss. But if you try to hold my hand, I'll ring YOUR bell," he said, in typical Russ fashion.

Chapter 25

Three days after our interrogation of Jacob the unthinkable happened. Dr. Wilde robbed another bank, this time it was the Colonial Bank of America located right downtown Boston, one of the largest banks in the state. I couldn't believe the audacity he had. And how did he manage to pull off another successful heist without getting caught?! Could he possibly be that good?

The news was right there alongside all the drama, catching every minute and every witness' version of what happened, and it was all consolidated nice and neat as always for the evening report.

According to Channel Six News, Dr. Wilde, with his chimpanzee in tow, waltzed into the bank just after 3:00pm wearing their gas masks and wielding semi-automatic machine guns. Well, the chimp was at least. The video footage depicted Dr. Wilde quite clearly, from his outfit to his facial features behind his mask.

He wore a pair of beige overalls he tucked into a pair of black combat boots. His chimp carrier was black and strapped across his chest and up and under his armpits. The deformed primate sat safely and comfortably in the harness where he had a full range of motion of both arms and legs. In his hands were two submachine guns and in his feet were two 9mm pistols. Just as he had the last time, Dr. Wilde tossed two canisters of tear gas into the main room of the bank. He also threw another two behind the counter since this bank was much larger than the last one he robbed.

All at once the customers and employees hit the floor. Wilde called for the bank manager to open the door leading behind the counter and she obliged. She was clearly shaken by the incident and had a hard time with the set of keys at first. Coughing from the gas, she fumbled with the key ring and dropped them not once, but twice as she tried to unlock the door as quickly as possible. Wilde grabbed her hands with one of his and lifted up his mask with his other hand. His face was seen quite clearly despite the fog of smoke clouding the room. He leaned over to her and with his face almost touching hers, mouthed the word, "relax." This only caused her to burst into tears, but somehow, she managed to unlock the door.

Once he gained access to the inside, he walked, pushing the manager in front of him, over to the first door leading into the vault. It was a combination lock only the bank manager and president knew. This time, she performed much better and quickly unlocked the three-and-a-half-foot thick steel door. Just beyond that was one final bulletproof glass door that required a retinal scan from either of the same two bank employees.

Wilde shoved her head down on to the scanner and smiled as he heard the unlocking noise of their granted access. He then threw the poor woman to the floor behind him and proceeded over to the racks of shelves that held countless stacks of bills. He stuffed the large hockey bag he had with him full until he could barely zip it closed. He was in and out of the vault in less than two minutes. The entire time his chimp kept aiming in all directions providing perfect cover.

Just as he was about to exit the front door, he turned facing the security camera above the main entrance, lifted up his mask and winked into it. He had officially gone off the deep end. Maybe he didn't care anymore now that the authorities knew his identity. Still, wasting a few precious moments when he should be making his getaway to taunt the camera was a bit over the top. His ego had clearly gotten the best of him. Did he believe he was unstoppable? He must if he was setting his sights on such a large bank in a very congested section of the city. How the hell was he getting away? How has no one identified his getaway vehicle? There were too many unanswered questions.

Russ called me as soon as he caught wind of the story. "Can you believe the set on this guy? Where does he buy pants that support balls that big?" he asked me just as shocked as I was.

"I hate giving that whack-job any credit, but damn... I really don't know what to make of this guy. It's almost as if he knows he's going to get away and is just having fun at this point."

It really bothered me to acknowledge his success, but he sure seemed like he was in control at all times and he certainly knew he was the man in charge.

"We have to get a move on and find this loser before he causes any more chaos. What's the plan? When are we going out to Oxford?" Russ inquired.

"You said it, we need to move quickly. I'll pick you up tomorrow right around noon, and we'll head up there and do some reconnaissance. Bring your spy gear and anything else you think we could use. I still have your night-vision goggles, they'll come in handy. Also, pack that super telescopic camera lens in case we can't get too close. And make sure you eat, we could be out for most of the day."

"I'll be ready and waiting boss. See you then," he said and then hung up.

I could barely eat anything my nerves had my stomach in knots. I decided to do a few laps in my pool while I stared up at the stars again. This time, I left the televisions off. Too much news had given me anxiety. I needed to unwind and clear my head.

As I floated on my back and stared at the evening sky, I recalled one special vacation Eve, and I took to Lake Tahoe for our tenth anniversary. I had planned it out for months, every detail, sparing no expense. I rented a beautiful log cabin that overlooked the lake, a fourteen-foot Cape Cruiser boat with an outboard motor, two kayaks, and a 4x4 Jeep Wrangler to go off-roading in. I loved those memories because we were so healthy, so happy, so in love with each other. I mean we always were in love with each other, but for those ten days, something magical happened between us. We were so closely connected we could sense each other's feelings and presence. We were connected spiritually and emotionally like nothing I've ever experienced before or since. It was the happiest time of my life, celebrating ten marvelous years with the most incredible woman on the face of the Earth.

How could I have been so lucky? I knew I had the most precious possession a man could ask for. She was my goddess, the kind wars are waged over, like Helen of Troy. I would spend every waking day worshiping the ground she walked on, and I still pray to her like the magnificent angel she must be. She was truly one of a kind.

214

I recalled that vacation clearly and especially how Eve literally seemed to radiate with life. She walked around with a certain glow about her others besides me picked up on and fed off of.

One night, when we were out for dinner, an elderly couple sitting across from us came over to our table when they had finished their meals and complimented us on what a beautiful couple we were. The man stood holding his wife's frail hand in his as they spoke. They told us they enjoyed watching us over the course of their meal because they could tell how madly in love we were with each other and it reminded them of their youth. They ended up paying for our meal and told us thanks for making their evening. The whole night I gazed deep into her eyes and lost myself in a sea of harmonious tranquility. There were times when her eyes resembled electrified emeralds, demanding my attention as they cast their enchanting spell on me.

We spent almost every night either on the water on the boat or overlooking it from the deck, where we lay on a blanket and made love under the shimmering stars. Everything was just right that week. There was never a dull or negative moment. We couldn't have asked for more perfect weather or a more perfect cabin. I couldn't ask for a more perfect life with my more than perfect wife. I thought we would re-visit that place again when we were a little old couple ourselves, but life had other plans for us. It was funny how fate seemed to pick and choose whose lives it was going to turn upside down at random. It didn't matter how much good we've done or how priceless and perfect our life was, at any given moment we could have everything ripped right out from underneath us without warning or sympathy.

Lying on my back, I got up and dusted myself off so I could begin to sort out the pieces of my shattered existence. Some never recover, many didn't believe in fact. I didn't think I could, but Russ refused to accept that. I was fortunate enough to have a second guardian angel live and in person, and in the disguise of a rowdy, tattooed, master chef. Who knew?

Floating and reminiscing about happier times apparently made me a bit sleepy because before I knew it, I had passed out on my inflatable pool chair. When I woke, the sun's rays peaked over the horizon but were partially blocked by the trees at the edge of my backyard. I paddled over to the shallow end and got out. The clock told me it was time to make something healthy for breakfast before heading out for my morning run.

Two veggie sausage patties and an egg white omelet did the trick just fine. I avoided the television because I tried not to stress about the latest burglary until it was absolutely necessary. I also avoided listening to any live radio while out jogging around the neighborhood. Instead, I opted to listen to good old-fashioned American heavy metal to give my heart rate a jump start, Lamb of God to be exact. By the time I returned from my run, I had burned off my breakfast and then some, as well as received a momentum boost in the form of an endorphin rush. A quick shower later and I was, at last, getting dressed for the day's upcoming events. It was now less than an hour before I had to leave to pick up Russ. I selected my recon wear: black sweatpants I'd tuck into my black combat boots, a sleeveless undershirt underneath a black pullover hooded sweatshirt. I packed a small gym bag with the remaining articles I would put on once we arrived on location: two black ski masks, two pairs of leather gloves, one with the fingertips cut off, Russ' night-vision goggles, and two, two-way radios. Russ would bring the camera and flashlights.

With everything packed up, I took my bag and drove to Russ' house in my favorite black pickup truck. I owned two other vehicles, an over-priced sports car, and an SUV but my favorite was my truck. When I arrived, Russ was sitting on the outside step of his apartment building waiting for me. He knows how prompt I always am, and so when I said I would pick him up around noon, he knew to be ready at 12:00pm on the dot.

He placed his backpack in the back seat before climbing in the seat next to me. "You ready to do this brother?!" he yelled like a professional wrestling announcer.

"You know I'm always down for a little seek and destroy action!" I shouted back, trying to match his enthusiasm.

He gave me a fist bump as I pulled the truck out and headed for Oxford, the hometown of our unsuspecting new targets.

"I was up most of the night going over satellite images of the town of Oxford looking for houses with barns and let me tell you, there are quite a few. I marked ninety-eight properties with detached barns or garages and highlighted them in yellow on the map. Dr. Wilde only moved to the area recently after he fled San Diego, and that happened just about eight months ago. So, I went through the public records of properties sold around that time period and cross-referenced them with the homes that had barns on the map and narrowed it down to fourteen. Upon further examination, I was able to eliminate ten of those since they don't have electricity. And so here you have it, a list of four possible farmhouses, complete with suspicious barns," he said as he held up a folded portion of a map with four addresses handwritten in the corner.

"You are amazing, seriously Russ, thank you so much," I said as sincerely as possible.

"You don't have to thank me, but you're welcome anyway. I want to see this bastard brought to justice just as bad as you do. Have you decided if you're going to let him live or not? Are you going to dismantle him piece by piece or subdue him and leave him out for the police to pick up?"

"I have thought about it, but I can't make up my mind. I think it's just going to have to be a spur of the moment decision. I'll know for certain once I come face to face with that piece of garbage and look him in the eyes. Either way, he's on borrowed time," I said confidently.

Feeling the adrenaline rise at the mere thought of the inevitable confrontation, I pressed play on the mp3 player attached to my truck's stereo, and once again, it was Lamb of God that got me in the mood to kick some ass.

"Yeah!" Russ exclaimed, pumping his fist to the rhythm of the drums. "Let's go! Address numero uno, I hope you have a good plumber because you're going to be shitting bricks when you see us heading your way, whooo!" he howled like a madman and head-banged to the intense metal guitar riffs.

I turned the GPS on, and Russ plugged the first address in and within seconds our destination was routed before us. Twenty-two

217

minutes eta it read. We both played air drums and guitar while speeding down the Mass Pike.

Russ and I have been to several concerts together, and music is something we have almost identical taste in. There is nothing like some pure American metal to get the blood pumping!

Once we turned off the highway, the GPS indicated we were less than three miles from the first address. As the numbers on the mailboxes got closer and closer to the one we were looking for, Russ began to attach the extended lens to his camera. The road we were on was a rural one with most homes sitting on decent sized pieces of land. Just as we neared the address on the GPS, Russ told me to stop so he could jump in the seat behind me to get a good view of the house. I had barely stopped the truck, and he jumped out and ran around the front then entered the door behind me. With his window down just enough to squeeze the camera lens out, we slowly rolled past the driveway going about ten miles per hour.

There was nobody outside that we could see but the house looked quite busy. Four different style vehicles parked along the length of the driveway that led up to a small ranch house. Just as we anticipated, there was a barn at the end of the driveway. The front lawn had more junk on it than grass. All sorts of decorations were scattered about in no particular order, and it made the place look like a dump. Russ snapped multiple pictures as we rolled past. Once we were out of sight, I turned the truck around. We rolled by slowly and snapped pictures of the residence. When we were again out of sight, Russ said, "I don't think that's our lucky number. Whoever lives there has been there for longer than eight months according to the garbage on the lawn."

I agreed. It was too sloppy for a doctor to want to set up a home-based operation and lab. Russ read the next address, and I entered it into the GPS, which showed we were six and a half miles away from our new destination. We found the street and liked the looks of it. A narrow, windy, wooded road snaked through the outskirts of the town with very few houses on it. We only passed three mailboxes before coming to the one we were aimed for. It was on my side of the road, and Russ had taken his position behind me once again. There was nothing to photograph, however. All we saw was a wooden mailbox modeled after a quaint colonial house, complete with shutters and window panes. The front door looked like it might pull down revealing the mail slot. But the actual house wasn't seen from where we were, slowly rolling past the end of the driveway. Russ and I looked at each other.

"Jackpot!" I said with a smile.

He nodded and said, "Let's find somewhere safe to park and check it out."

I drove farther down the windy road in search of a pullout where we could stop. I finally found one about a half a mile past the house, a tiny dirt parking lot and a sign indicating there were state forest trails up ahead. That worked fine. If anyone saw us, we could claim to be hikers or birdwatchers.

I got out and grabbed my bag from behind my seat. I wore my ski mask on top of my head until we got closer where we might be spotted. It was only just after 1:30pm, so we didn't need the night-vision goggles yet, but I made sure I had them in my pack before zipping it shut. I had no idea how long this was going to take. We needed to gather as much information as possible, and that meant even if it took us all day and night.

Russ pulled a camouflaged ski mask on the top of his head and hung his camera around his neck. We pulled on our backpacks and headed down the road in the direction of our target.

No cars passed us as we walked for about fifteen minutes. We kept looking around in all directions to make sure nobody spotted us. At last, we saw the mailbox up ahead. Stopping about twenty yards away I suggested we split up and each crept down the driveway on opposite sides to expand our visual range. Russ nodded and took the right side as I headed through the woods on the left. Luckily, the ground was a little bit damp, so our footsteps were muffled by the sogginess of the earth rather than crunching over dry sticks and leaves.

I made my way from one tree up to the next, stopping briefly behind each to survey the area. Finally, I could make out the shape of a farmhouse through the pine tree branches up ahead. It was more on Russ' side of the driveway, which was good because he could get close-up shots of the house.

I continued pressing onward through the thick forest until I eventually saw a clearing. Standing behind one of the last trees wide enough to cover me, I peeked out from around the corner to take in as much of the scenery as possible. The lawn was about ten yards wide on both sides of the driveway as it led from the edge of the wooded area where I was hiding, right up to the front porch. About halfway in the middle of the lawn on my side was a massive weeping willow tree with branches so long they swept the ground as they swayed in the gentle afternoon breeze. That was the only other cover between me and the end of the driveway. I would have to make a run for it. Before I did, I looked over to where Russ was holding up, behind a cluster of pine trees, and waited for him to look over in my direction. He was trying to get a look at the house through the thick, bushy needles of the pines with little luck. When he finally gave up on the idea, he turned to see where I was. I waved and pointed to the willow tree, gesturing I was going to head in that direction. He looked back and forth between me and the massive tree and nodded in approval.

Keeping as low as I possibly could, I stepped out from my cover and dashed for the safety of the weeping giant. I made it in about eight seconds and burrowed my way through the thin hanging branches. To my surprise, there was a large granite bench beneath the cover of the tree totally hidden from the outside. There also seemed to be some sort of grave marker off to the side of the trunk. Perhaps from a family who lived here before Silas Wilde bought the place, a beloved pet I would guess.

I sat for a moment on the stone bench to regroup. As I ran toward the tree, I caught a pretty good glimpse of the farmhouse and then the barn that was adjacent to it. I took my cell phone out of my pocket and slowly parted the hanging branches in front of me. From a crouching position, I peeked out and took in a full view of the house. It was a white colonial house with black shutters and a farmer's porch that wrapped around the front and side facing the driveway.

There was a blue pickup truck parked in the driveway and in

front of the truck was the entrance to a large barn. The two front doors were about ten feet tall by six feet across. There were no windows that revealed what was kept inside. I saw a tractor on the far side of the barn but no signs of livestock or crops. Then I noticed the cameras. Black cameras were mounted on both the front and side of the barn as well as at least one I saw on the house. This had to the house. Why would an average citizen need security cameras watching over an average, run of the mill farmhouse? Shit, I hope Russ spotted them too.

I snapped a few more pictures and then texted Russ. *"CAMERAS ON HOUSE AND BARN!"* my message read.

A few moments later, I received his response, "10-4."

I estimated the range of sight for the camera on the barn was no more than twenty feet from the side entrance, where they were most likely focused. That meant I could creep up and take cover behind the truck. The camera on the house probably aimed down the driveway more, at least that's the way I would have positioned it. As long as I kept close to the truck, I could get up close without being caught on camera. I texted Russ once more and informed him I was making a move for the truck. He responded and told me he would meet up with me there shortly after I arrived.

Once again, keeping as low to the ground as possible, I darted out and made my way to the rear of the big, blue, diesel pickup truck. Suddenly, I realized just how close I stood to the crazy doctor's home. Was this where he conspired to rob the businesses he had hit and where he trained that chimp to use semi-automatic weapons?!

The thought made me paranoid. I took out my phone and snapped pictures of the house, barn, cameras, and even the truck. Then I turned to take pictures of the front yard just as Russ came running up on me.

"Jesus!" I shouted but in a whisper.

"Sorry, I saw movement in the bottom floor window, the living room from the looks of it. I had to make a run for it when I got an opening," he explained to me.

"Was it Dr. Wilde?" I asked hopefully.

"Couldn't tell. He looked like a big guy though, so it very well could be him. I don't see any other areas that aren't covered by the cameras that we can access. This might be as close as we're going to get for now. I'll go around the truck and take as many pictures as we'll need. You see if you can get a visual on a circuit breaker. The electric panel has to be outside somewhere, both on the house and another one on the barn. If you spot them snap a few pictures." Russ barked orders like a colonel leading his troops into battle! He certainly proved himself irreplaceable. I realized how glad I was to have him by my side in such a dangerous situation.

I waited for Russ to make his move first, as he crawled on his belly underneath the front of the truck and snapped pictures of the porch, the door leading into the kitchen, the different windows, and the cameras. Then I ran sideways over to the tree line that lay just beyond the far side of the barn, the front left side if I looked at it from the front. There was no camera on that side since there was no openings or entrances to be tampered with.

The tractor sat in the overgrown grass next to the barn, and that's just where I dashed to. I made it there quickly and squatted down behind the large rear tire. I neither saw nor heard anyone, and I knew I wasn't being watched by an electronic eye, so I stepped out and walked over to the side of the barn. There, all the way at the far corner was an electrical panel. It was exactly what Russ told me to look for. I removed my phone and snapped pictures from different angles. As I repositioned myself, something behind the barn caught my attention. Two long-range shooting alleys had been built and practiced on from the looks of it. This had to have been where he trained the chimp. It still seemed unbelievable despite seeing the video evidence of the gun-toting ape.

The thought provided a sudden reality check of how dangerous the man we hunted really was.

I retraced my steps until I was back behind the truck with Russ.

"I think we're ready to wrap this up," he said making a circular motion in the air with his finger. "We need to regroup, make a plan, and return when we're good and ready."

His words made sense, though a big part of me wanted to walk up to the door and do the deed while we were already there.

"You got it, boss," I said, making my best impression of Russ.

He didn't smile, he was all about business right then. He was right, it was time to leave. One at a time we took turns scurrying across the lawn to the safety of the willow tree and then back again through the thick woods until we reached the road.

"Did you get everything we need?" I asked referring to the necessary pictures.

"You know I did. Where do you want to set up shop? I figure if we're going to try to return here tonight, then driving all the way back to either of our homes would be an unnecessary waste of time. We passed a Round Roof Inn when we got off the exit, and there's a Home Headquarters Warehouse in the town over. It's 3:40pm now, we can set up shop, devise a plan, head over to the store to stock up on supplies, and return here later tonight when they're asleep. Say 1:00am. What do you think?" he asked me.

"I think I don't pay you enough for your services," I replied.

"You don't pay me at all for my services!" he shot back.

"Let's do it, we can make this happen tonight and rid the world of this psycho once and for all."

We walked back to the truck and drove to the Round Roof Inn. We sat in the parking lot for a moment and quietly went over possible outcomes of the evening and different variations of a plan. Russ seemed to be in a trance. "Are you sure you're up for this?" I asked him.

The most he had ever participated with me before was when we tortured Jacob. He hadn't been with me any of the times I killed someone. I think the reality of that possibility was sinking in. The night could very well end in a bloody butchering. I thought perhaps, Russ was asking himself whether or not he was ready to witness and/or partake in such events. Was he thinking about bailing? Should I offer him an out before things got serious?

Before I could say anything to him, he looked at me and said, "Let's take these despicable terrorists down, all the way. No mercy, both the doctor and the ape. Let's fucking kill them both."

Chapter 26

The room Russ and I booked at The Round Roof Inn had two queen- sized beds, a nightstand between them, a dresser with a shitty television on it, and a desk in the corner. That was all we pretty much rented the room for: to use the desk as we figured out a course of action. I stuck the sim card from Russ' camera into my laptop and uploaded the pictures. Then I sent all the ones from my phone to the laptop as well.

We laid a map upside down and drew our own of the entire layout of the property on the blank side. We marked with highlighters the fields of view for each camera. I also added the electrical panel on the shed and Russ provided the one on the house, which he obviously had located. Despite a very detailed blueprint of the property, two big problems remained; we didn't know the exact number of men inside, and we didn't know what type of firepower they were packing.

It was apparent they had access to tear gas, sawed-off shotguns, submachine guns, and semi-automatic pistols. Jacob claimed there were three other hired goons besides him, the doctor, and of course the chimp. That meant there could possibly be a total of four men and an ape all capable of carrying some type of firearm. Russ and I had a total of zero firearms. We had to out-think our opponents, a challenge I greatly anticipated and looked forward to.

I made a list of items we needed for the night's festivities:

spray paint

spray gun

gasoline cans

road flares

tool belts

So far, our plan was pretty basic. We would sabotage any and all vehicles first. Next, we would block out the cameras on the barn and porch using spray paint. As we ran around the outside of the house and barn, we would leave a trail of gasoline as we went. Then we would take out the rest of the cameras by cutting the power. If the men woke up and tried to exit the house to investigate, we would take them down one at a time. If we could sneak around and get everything done without waking them, we simply would torch the whole place and let them burn to death.

The fact that we were going in there without a single firearm was stressing Russ out, though. He didn't think we stood a chance if they managed to escape the house with their weapons. We were sitting ducks waiting to get popped. I assured him we wouldn't go in there empty-handed. Besides machetes and gasoline, I planned on picking up a couple more weapons that should level the playing field.

As Russ sketched additional details out on the map, I put my jacket on and reviewed the list of supplies one last time, adding a few more crucial items.

"I'm going to head out and get this shopping over with. I'll grab some grub on the way back. Is there anything else you can think of?" I asked.

"No, not at the moment. If I do, I'll send you a text. I should be done with the plan when you come back. And don't worry about food, I'll order us a pizza, and have it delivered."

"Alright, I'll be back within an hour," I said glancing at the clock on the nightstand. It was 5:42pm, there was plenty of time. We planned on returning to the farmhouse around 1:00am when all should hopefully be asleep. Once I had all the supplies, the rest was a waiting game.

At the Home Headquarters Warehouse, I managed to find all the items on my list. The added tools I wrote down just before I left the motel were two hose-less framing nail guns. The gentleman working in the power tool section was more than happy to assist me in selecting just the right ones. I explained to him I wanted the most powerful nail gun with the largest clip capacity, the cost was not an issue. He perked right up when I added that last bit of information.

Eventually, he sold me two of the latest models, most expensive, air compressed guns, each with a 30-nail-clip capacity. He assured me they were powerful enough to drive a spike through even the hardest wood. I was tempted to ask him if a human skull would be a problem, but I bit my tongue. I was sure there would be no problem penetrating flesh and bone. After he demonstrated how they worked, I realized there was one small problem. The gun needed to be pressed down on the nozzle in order for a nail to be fired. There was a little plastic lever that had to be pushed in for a nail to shoot out. I found the answer to that problem a few aisles over in the adhesives section. The wonders of some Flex Tape would do the trick. I checked out and headed back to the motel.

Russ was amazing with his hands, besides being a great chef, he could fix just about anything. I laid out the items from my shopping trip on one of the beds. He laughed when he saw the nail guns, but it was a laugh of relief. We wouldn't be going anywhere that evening without a little firepower of our own.

I explained to him the situation with the safety mechanism and how I bought the Flex Tape to fix the problem. He took the guns and the tape and went to work. After I got everything organized and squared away, I sat on one of the beds and helped myself to a slice of pepperoni pizza. It was almost 8:00pm, and we still had four and a half hours until showtime. I tried to nap but failed. My mind kept going back to Dr. Wilde's house and what we might find inside that barn. What kind of unethical laboratory he built beneath that roof? I wanted to take a tour of the inside before we set it up in flames.

Another two hours passed, and I still couldn't sleep. Frustrated, I decided to go out and fill the gas cans at the 24-hour gas station at the end of the road. It was a perfect little business, straight out of the stone age. The pumps had rolling dials instead of digital displays, and they dinged as they spun. More importantly, there were no cameras on the premises. I wasn't taking any chances.

After I filled the two five-gallon cans, I put them in the back of my truck, secured them with a bungee cord, and returned to the motel room. Russ was sound asleep. How I envied him. I couldn't sleep until I completed my task and put an end to Dr. Wilde's brief but brutal reign of terror.

One hour to go. I loaded some of our gear into the back seat of my truck. I made sure nobody watched as I removed my machete from the toolbox and brought it in the motel room to sharpen it. Russ wasn't bothered or awakened by the slow scraping of the blade dragging across the sharpening stone.

I had it razor sharp in less than five minutes. I took a piece of paper listing the local restaurants and sliced it in half like nothing. Man, I loved that blade. There were seven small notches on the handle marking the number of kills. There was a good chance I would add at least two more to that number by the next morning.

Russ had succeeded in taping down the safety guards on both guns so they would fire as soon as we pulled the triggers weather it was pressed down on a flat surface or not. I filled the clips and attached one as I headed outside.

There were only three other cars in the parking lot, and one belonged to the man working at the front desk. I walked across to the far end where no cars were parked and looked for a target. There was nothing but one street sign and a whole bunch of trees lining the lot. I aimed at the trunk of a birch tree from about fifteen feet away and squeezed the trigger. A loud poof rang through the still night air as I hit my target with surprisingly decent accuracy. Next, I aimed at the metal street sign that stood about twenty feet away from me. *POOF! PANGGGG!*... The sound of the nail striking the metal street sign rang loud enough to wake the dead. I was satisfied, the aim was accurate enough and returned to the room.

Just as I was about to turn the doorknob and enter the room, Russ flung the door open and gazed at me squinting his eyes. "What the hell is going on out here?!"

He obviously heard my target practice. Like I said, it was loud enough to wake the dead!

"Sorry, I just wanted to make sure these things worked properly. We're all set, let's start getting ready."

I pushed past him and checked the clock on the nightstand for the thousandth time. It was 12:13am, time to finally get moving! "Hurry up and finish getting dressed. I'm going to load the rest of our stuff in the truck and then return our keys and checkout. Meet me in the truck in ten." I ordered.

I heard him moan as he rubbed the sleep out of his eyes and stretched. It only took me about five minutes to pack up the truck and check out of our room. The man at the desk was kind and charged me a discounted rate since we didn't spend the night. He probably thought we were using the room for drugs or to fulfill some deviant sexual fantasies. I couldn't care less because I was too excited about the upcoming events.

Russ was already in the passenger seat when I returned from the office. I hopped in and started the engine. We did a quick check of our clothing, making sure everything was tied and tucked in to avoid any accidents like tripping or catching a piece of loose clothing on a nail. Every little detail mattered. Once we were both satisfied with our clothes check, I pulled onto the street and headed towards the long and windy back road that Dr. Wilde lived on. It only took twelve minutes to arrive at the dirt parking lot for the state forest trails.

Stepping out into the cool air, I got a chill down my spine. Russ noticed and asked, "You're not getting cold feet, are you?"

"Hell no! Just a chilly night, nothing a little home invasion can't cure," I said trying to sound as confident as possible.

We attached the tool belts I purchased and clipped the loaded nail guns to them. I handed Russ three extra clips of nails and took three for myself. Next, I pulled my backpack on fastened the machete to my side. Russ put his backpack on too and then adjusted his night-vision goggles to his liking. Lastly, I put my ski mask on the top of my head and picked up the spray paint gun. I was in charge of disabling the first few cameras, and Russ was handling the evening's pyrotechnics, as he grabbed a gas can in each hand. We were finally all set. Exchanging nods, we started the half mile walk down the dark street toward the sleeping, unsuspecting household.

Once we reached the end of the driveway, we split up to opposite sides exactly as we had hours earlier. Russ would get into position behind the group of pine trees and wait for me to take out the cameras. As I once again darted from tree to tree, I listened for any sounds of life coming from the farmhouse up ahead. When I reached the willow tree, I saw a couple of dim lights in the house. Peeking out from the cover of the willow branches, I could make out what seemed to be a light on in the kitchen, perhaps over the stove, and another from one of the upstairs windows.

This time there were two trucks in the driveway. The blue one seemed to be in the same position and parked to the left of it was a black two-door pickup. I watched for a few minutes and saw no movement or signs of life. Deciding it was safe, I bolted out in my crouched run until I reached the back of the big, blue truck. Again, I paused, listened, and watched for anything that suggested someone was awake and moving about. But I heard and saw nothing.

I looked in the window of the blue truck and, ever so gently, lifted the handle and opened the driver's door. Next, I popped the hood latch and then closed the door as quietly as I had opened it. Moving over to the front of the truck, I lifted the hood and propped it open. From my pocket, I pulled out a pair of wire cutters and snipped the two battery terminal cables. I lowered the hood and left it unlatched since shutting it tight could make too much noise.

One down, one to go. I tried opening the passenger door, but it was locked. I saw through the window that the driver's side was locked too. Time for plan B. I pulled a buck knife from my pocket and opened the blade. Doing one more check of the area, I still saw no signs of life. I stabbed the front tire with my knife, and it let out a hissing noise. Pausing to see if I drew any attention, the house remained silent. So, I went over to the rear tire and did the same thing. And then again to the other two tires until they were all flat. Objective 1 completed.

I put the knife away and picked up the paint gun. With a click, I twisted the spray paint can and locked it into the nozzle. There was a long handle on the spray gun that extended up to four feet and provided the reach I needed to block out the camera on the barn. Making sure the coast was clear one final time, I scurried out from behind the truck and ran up to the front of the barn, stopping directly below the black camera lens. I quickly reached up and pulled the trigger, spraying in back and forth sweeping motion until the lens was completely covered in primer gray paint. I then quietly tip-toed up the porch steps and stood flat against the wall beside the door which led to the kitchen.

I listened for movement, but the sound of my heart beating out of my chest made it difficult. I saw the camera at the end of the porch facing directly at me. I couldn't linger. I peeked through the kitchen door not seeing a soul, so I proceeded to tip-toe across the porch and, just like the first time, stopped underneath the camera. I raised my arm and pulled the trigger, blocking out the second camera. As quickly as I could, without making any noise, I hurried back down off the porch and ducked between the two trucks. Objective 2 completed.

It was Russ' turn. In the dark, I couldn't see him behind the group of pine trees where he hid. I took out my phone and texted him, "YOU'RE UP."

After a moment, I saw a shadowy figure running hunched over both to avoid being seen and from the weight of the two gas cans. He came up quickly and joined me behind the truck. I took one of the cans from him and untwisted the cap. There was a long spout sticking down into the can that I flipped around and screwed on to the opening. Russ did the same with his can.

"You do the barn, I'll get the house," he said.

I nodded and broke off to the left side of the barn where the tractor was sitting. I sprayed the outside walls of the barn with gasoline, moving down the length of its side as I did so. I circled the entire structure running out of fuel just as I came back around to where I started. I waited between the trucks for Russ to come around and meet me. I saw him circle around the front and then he walked up the porch steps backward, spilling a trail of gasoline as he went. He made a pass up and down both the front and side of the porch really giving it a dousing. I noticed how he made an effort to pour out more in front of the side and front doors, very clever. When he finished, he scurried back between the trucks and joined me. Still, there was no movement or sounds coming from the house.

"It's showtime kid. Are you ready to do this?" he asked me with both fear and excitement in his voice.

"Let's roast these bastards," I said.

He nodded as he pulled the map out of his pocket and unfolded it in front of me. He pointed to a spot on the opposite side of the house.

"This is where the main breaker is. I'm going to go around and throw the switch after you hit the one on the barn. Go back there, kill the power, and hurry back to your next position, right beside the kitchen door. I'll wait for you to text me when you're in position and then I'll shut down the power in the house. As soon as I do, I'm going to haul ass to my position, next to the front door. You and I will wait there for someone to come out and when they do, we take them out."

"What are you going to use?" I asked not thinking about it until now. He leaned down and patted the six-inch bowie knife that was tucked into his boot and smiled up at me.

"That will work," I said giving my approval.

"Okay, let's do this Nero. Fuck those maggots! We don't stop until the doctor, AND the chimp are eliminated. Remember, if shit gets out of control quick, we light the whole place up and take them out as best we can. Be smart and be safe. See you soon Buddy," he said as he patted me on the back and darted off around to the back side of the house.

I made my way around the side of the barn again and stopped in front of the dark gray metal box that was on the wall. Prying it open there were three small breakers and then the main one. I took a deep breath and threw the switch, shutting down all electricity going into the barn. That was the easy part, now for the tricky one. Reaching back, I drew my machete from its sheath and stared at it for a moment with envy. Then I circled back around to the porch steps and made my way up and next to the side door. All I smelled was gasoline. With the machete in my left hand, I removed my cell phone from my pocket and texted Russ, "*IN POSITION.*"

I waited for about a minute and then I heard the power turning off inside. My heart was beating fast as I stood to the side of the door with the machete cocked back in my hands like a batter holding a baseball bat. If anyone came out that door, I was swinging first and asking questions later.

Russ came around the corner and up the steps in front of me. He had his bowie knife in his hand as he turned around to the front of the porch and stood beside the front door, his arm cocked up above his head ready to strike down in a hacking motion like a sculptor chipping away at a block of ice.

Five minutes passed before we heard noise from within. Footsteps from the upstairs were getting louder as they made their way downstairs and moved across the wooden floor. They sounded heavy, and Russ felt the house shake a little as whoever had woken up walked around investigating. I remained completely still and out of sight if anyone happened to enter the kitchen and peek outside.

The footsteps grew louder, coming in my direction. Someone was moving around in the kitchen, but what they were doing I did not know. The person stopped walking and started causing a commotion. Whoever it was rummaged through drawers. I wondered what they were searching for. A gun perhaps? Do people keep guns in their kitchen drawers? This guy committed crimes with a mutilated pet chimp, so anything was possible.

Just then, a beam of light shone through the door and then disappeared. He was looking for and found a flashlight. I heard the sound of a door opening slowly with a moaning, creaking noise followed by footsteps going down a wooden staircase. I peeked around the corner and inside to see the door to the basement ajar and nobody in sight.

Five long minutes passed before I heard footsteps return from the basement. The door slammed shut, and the man in the kitchen mumbled something I couldn't hear, probably cursing under his breath. The sound of sneakers squeaking on the floor was followed by a chair being dragged. I peeked around one more time and saw a very large man sitting with his back to me, putting his sneakers on as he continued to utter profanities out of frustration, this time he was loud enough for me to hear him.

I pulled my head back as he stood up, and I returned to my batter's stance. The light from the flashlight suddenly beamed through the door again as it got bigger and bigger. Then the doorknob turned as the kitchen door swung open. Out stepped the enormous man who came outside to investigate. As soon as he stepped both feet on to the deck, I swung with all my might at his big, thick neck. The smell of gasoline had caught his attention immediately though, and when he stepped out, he looked down at the puddle of flammable liquid.

The awkward position I ended up in caused me to stumble as he jumped up suddenly when he realized he was under attack. I made an effort to draw back the blade again and strike him properly, but a massive fist clenched my wrist and pushed my arm down. He was so much bigger than I and clearly, more powerful. I began to lose feeling in my right hand from his tight squeeze, so I finally loosened my grip, dropping the machete at his feet.

I tried to act quickly by catching him with a left hook to the jaw, but he caught my fist in mid-air and countered with a left hook of his own. He hit me right on my temple, and I immediately saw stars and felt my legs go out from under me. I couldn't believe it! One punch and I was down. Everything seemed to be spinning, but I managed to open one eye as I saw my assailant bend down and pick up my machete. I managed to roll over and pull myself into a sitting position as he closed in on me. There was nothing I could do, nothing but let out a moan when he raised his arms above his head, held the handle of the blade with two hands, and prepared to cleave me in two, right down the middle.

POOF, POOF, POOF, POOF, POOF, POOF!

Those familiar sounds suddenly filled the air followed by a gruesome shriek. I opened my eyes to see Russ standing behind my attacker, aiming his nail gun at his face. There was another shriek, and the massive man dropped the machete and held his hands up to his neck. That's when I saw the tiny streams of blood squirting out from multiple holes in his neck. Russ had shot the nails in through the back and then out the front of his big, thick neck. He touched the holes and then held his hands up to observe the blood. Again, he let out a cry, but this time it sounded angry. He suddenly charged Russ and tackled him to the ground. I couldn't believe my blurry eyes! The two wrestled for a bit, but the big, bloody brute was positioning himself to pin Russ down by pressing his knees on Russ' shoulders. If he got into that position and hammered punches on Russ' face, he wouldn't last long. The guy was too strong. I had to do something.

I shook my head violently a few times trying to wake up. I brought myself to my knees and crawled over to the machete. Just then, I heard Russ let out a groan. He was really taking a beating! I brought myself up to a wobbly stance and stopped just a foot behind Russ' attacker. I knew I had only one shot, so I had to make sure I landed it right.

Through two dizzy, blurry eyes I squinted and aimed for what I hoped was the center of his head. Arching back like a lumberjack, I thrust forward with all my might, embedding my machete halfway down his skull. It stuck there, and when I finally let it go, he fell on top of Russ completely covering his whole body.

"Get this nasty fucker off me! Ugh... Nero, please! His blood just got in my mouth!"

Russ kicked and squirmed until finally, he could slip out from underneath the enormous corpse. I held out my hand and helped him to his feet.

"Thanks, buddy, I owe you one," he said sincerely.

"Don't mention it. You saved my ass from getting halved. You don't owe me shit."

I bent down and frisked the man. In his back pocket was his wallet. I took it out and opened it up. "Brutus Boone," I announced.

"What a goofy name. It's perfect," Russ said shaking his head.

I put his license back and dropped his wallet next to him.

"I have an idea," I said. "Let's nail the doors and windows shut before we set it on fire."

"Sure, good thinking," Russ said with approval. "I'll cover the front and the two windows over there. You get the side door to the kitchen and the barn door. Stay there until I come back around to meet you."

"Alright, be careful," I warned him.

He smiled to reassure me he would be fine and turned the corner to the front of the house. I took my nail gun out and pressed it on the top right corner of the kitchen door at an angle, so the nail would shoot into the wooden door frame. Six nails went across the top of the door followed by eight going down the side. When I tested it, the door wouldn't budge. I pushed with all my might, slammed my body into it to make sure I had secured it well enough, and still no movement. I heard the faint popping noise of Russ' gun doing the same thing to the front door and windows. It didn't seem loud enough to wake anybody, but I wasn't sure there wasn't already someone else awake, also investigating the power outage. From my view into the kitchen, I didn't see anyone else.

Russ finished and met me as we planned. "Turn around" he ordered me.

I did, as instructed, and he unzipped my backpack. Reaching in, he removed four road flares and then closed up my pack. "Here, take these two," he said handing the two red sticks to me. "Light the barn, and I'll do the house."

He didn't wait for a reply as he ran to the front of the house and went down the front steps. There he stood facing the front door as he lit one of his flares. I hadn't moved yet, so he waved his arm and pointed to the barn. I snapped out of it and hustled down away from the house and out to the rear of the barn. There, the siding was still wet from the gasoline I doused it with. The first flare popped as it lit, and I touched it to the overhang of the siding, just above the foundation. A whoosh of flame shot up and to the sides as it quickly ignited. Next, I circled around to the side door of the barn facing the house. Since it appeared the large front doors were not used, I made it a point to soak the side door and the ground in front of it, just in case someone was inside.

I used the nail gun once again to secure the door shut and then lit the second torch. I barely had to hold it a foot in front of it, and the sparks shooting out ignited the entrance with a burst of heat and energy. My face got hit with a surge of warmth that made me squint my eyes and then look away.

The front barn doors were also saturated with gasoline, and I did the same thing, wetting the bottom and ground below. That was all I did, throw the flare in front of it from a safe distance and watch as it caught fire. Retreating back between the two trucks, I stood and waited for Russ as the barn quickly went up in flames. From behind the blue super-duty pickup, I saw the light of the fire coming from the front of the house. Russ was now standing at the bottom of the side porch steps where he lit his second flare and tossed it. The door to the kitchen quickly became walled off by a growing inferno that ran down the side and around to the front, following the trail Russ had left.

"Let's go take cover underneath that willow tree where we can see both the front and side of the house. The two second-floor windows are the only way out now, and we'll need to have a view of the front in case someone tries to escape through either of them."

He was right. I gave him a thumbs up, and he led the way, as we made it down the driveway and over to the side yard in the direction of the tree. It was about forty yards away from the front of the house, but we both made it there quickly, as we sprinted in full stride.

Under cover of a veil of branches, we regrouped and caught our breath. Russ stood watching out as I removed my backpack and tool belt. I decided to carry the machete in one hand and the nail gun in the other from then on out. I rolled the tool belt up and stuffed it into the backpack along with the wire cutters. I put my cell phone in the front pocket of the pack and zipped it shut. Suddenly Russ gasped, "There's someone!" he reported, as I spun around to see.

I had to move closer to him to see through the branches where he had them pulled open a bit before I caught sight of what he was talking about. There was a man upstairs looking out of one of the windows!

Russ and I watched as the shadow of a man ran from one window over to the other. There were two bedrooms on the second floor, and the man had opened the windows to both. He looked out and put his hands on the back of his head showing signs of distress. He then disappeared for a moment, but we saw him moving across the room downstairs. It was definitely the same guy and not someone else because he continued holding his hands up in a panicked state. I imagined he checked the doors on the first floor, discovering they were not an option for escape.

Five minutes passed, but the man was nowhere to be seen. Both the barn and farmhouse were almost completely engulfed in flames. On the porch, the fire had spread all the way up and began rolling around the top, starting to move across the roof and toward the second-floor windows. The panic-stricken man re-appeared back upstairs in the bedroom on the left. We watched as he tossed a comforter out of one of the windows. From the way it moved, it appeared to be extra heavy. He must have wet it somehow, perhaps in the shower. Pretty smart. Next, he stepped out on to the roof of the porch, one leg at a time, and picked up his wet bedspread. Slowly he walked down toward the edge where the flames were shot up and draped the comforter over the edge, dousing the flames. Directly below was safety, all he had to do was jump.

Russ turned to look at me and said, "As soon as he's airborne, we run over to him and take him out. Get ready..." He turned back to watch the man on the ledge. I took a deep breath and squeezed the handles to the machete and nail gun tightly. Russ took a deep breath too.

"Ready... and... GO!" he shouted.

I followed him as we both came bursting out from under the tree, sprinting as fast as we could back across the forty-yard dash, across the side yard and over to the front of the house. The man had jumped and landed hard, his legs not bending at the knee as much as they should have. It looked like a bad landing as he immediately fell on his side and clenched his left knee. The fall was about twelve feet, high enough to cause exactly the kind of injury we needed. The man was a little on the heavy side, and perhaps if he was a bit slimmer, he would have landed better and not blown out his knee.

I ran faster than Russ, so I reached the man first. As I approached him, I noticed something laying in the grass by his side. It was an Uzi submachine gun! He must have been holding it under the blanket because neither of us had noticed it from where we were watching.

He caught sight of the two of us charging him and reached out to grab his weapon. I held my machete above my head like a tomahawk and dove at his arm. With one powerful hack, I hit him squarely on his wrist, and it separated from his arm. I rolled to the side in one fluid motion and hopped back up to my feet. An ear-piercing scream echoed through my head as the man grabbed the bloody stump with the only hand, he had intact. Taking a deep breath, he started to let out another cry, but I quickly silenced him. I bent over and chopped with tremendous force at his neck once, twice, then a third time until it was disconnected from his body.

Russ was next to me then, watching on with an impressed look on his face. He surveyed the scene and nodded his head. "Let's see who we have here," he said as he bent down and reached for the man's back pocket.

Just then the man's leg moved a little, probably from the nerves releasing one last bit of energy. Russ jumped back and shouted, "Holy shit!" and he fired his nail gun a dozen times into the headless corpse.

I laughed at his expense, but he didn't seem to find it funny. "Fuck you man! You get his wallet then!"

I tried not to laugh so much because I knew my friend's ego was hurt, but it was hard not to. The body looked like a pin cushion thanks to my timid partner.

Once I finally got a grip and stopped, I bent down next to the face-down body and went to reach for the dead man's wallet. Suddenly, something bumped into my leg. It was his head! I fell backward on my ass as I heard Russ break out into laughter. That bastard kicked the decapitated head at me! "Oh, look who's chicken shit now!" he roared as I got up from the ground.

"You're fucked up," I told him.

"This is coming from the guy who just severed the head and hand of another guy," he rebutted

I did my best to ignore him because my ego had been bruised. Again, I knelt down and reached into the man's back pocket. I removed his wallet and stood up.

"Mack Chestercove," I read out loud as I viewed his Massachusetts driver's license. "Never heard of the guy. He's an organ donor though. Should we cut them out and put them on ice until the EMTs get here?"

"You wouldn't..." Russ said with a look of disgust on his face.

I laughed and wiped my machete off on the back of my victim's clothes. Just then I noticed the lights on the back of the pickup trucks light up. It wasn't like they had been turned on, it was more like they were reflecting light. I turned around toward the end of the driveway, and sure enough, there were two headlights coming slowly down. Russ and I froze, standing right in front of the house in plain sight. As the vehicle drew closer, I could tell it was a van. The fear that it was the police escaped me, and I was suddenly able to move again. I dropped to my stomach and Russ did the same. The light from the burning house behind us made us more visible than I preferred. I crawled on my belly around the back side of the house, away from the driveway. When I turned the corner, I brought myself up to a squatting position, and Russ followed suit.

"Who the hell is that?" I asked as if he would know.

"I would guess the doctor. That's a pretty good vehicle for transporting a live chimp in, don't you think?"

He was right. Quickly I gave the orders, "You stay here, and I'll circle around to the other side of the house. If he gets out, wait for him to get as close as possible, and we charge him. If he tries to take off again, we get as close as we can and shoot for his tires."

Russ agreed, and I left him, heading off to get into my position.

When I reached the other side, I peeked around the corner, standing about ten feet from the house. The flames made it so that was as close as I could safely get. The van stopped, and the driver was still inside. I could see his shape, but it wasn't clear, the reflection of the house burning was bright and made it difficult to see. I squinted trying to figure out what he was doing. It looked as if he leaned down toward the passenger seat and disappeared for a moment. When he did, I took off running and took cover in front of the blue truck. I was within ten yards from him at that point. I held my nail gun in my right hand since I could aim better with that one. I peeked around the front of the truck. The figure inside faced forward-looking right in my direction. Had he seen me? I didn't know for certain. It stayed like that for a few minutes.

The door to the van finally opened. Out stepped the man I had watched countless times on numerous news reports. It was no doubt, Dr. Silas Wilde and boy, was he HUGE! I prepared myself to rush the asshole when all of a sudden, I noticed something in his hand. He was carrying an assault rifle! It looked like AK-47 judging from the stock and clip. Moving in my direction, he raised it and sprayed rounds ferociously! That answered my question, he knew exactly where I was. I hid with my back pressed against the grill of the truck as bullets bombarded the side sounding like pebbles being poured into a tin can.

I waited until finally there was a pause in the gunfire. As soon as the bullets stopped, I ran in the opposite direction, around the back of the house to where I left Russ. When I came around the corner, he ran up and met me halfway.

"Who's firing?! It sounded like a war zone!" he asked. He was panicking almost as much as I was.

"It's Wilde, and he's got an AK! He saw me and opened fire. Last I saw, he was standing between his van and the back of the truck," I reported.

"What the hell are we going to do? We can't take him if he's packing an AK!" he said stating the obvious.

"Let's see where he is. He could be walking up behind us as we speak. If he is, we see if he left the van running and we take off in it. If we can't jack the van, we head back to my truck, using the trees as cover." It was the best I could think of that kept our asses from getting riddles full of holes.

We both peeked around the corner of the burning house, again standing about ten feet away to avoid the heat. The fire had made it up to the second floor and was lighting the house up like a giant beacon glowing in the dark of the night. Wilde was nowhere to be seen. Taking the lead, I crept along the front, moving parallel to the porch, past Mack Chestercove's body, until I was almost at the corner by the driveway.

I was close to the van, which was not running, and the doctor was not around. He had to be creeping around the back, trying to sneak up on us. Laying on my belly again, I crawled so I could see around the side of the house. There was still no sign of him. I motioned for Russ to follow as I jumped to my feet and made a dash for the van.

I reached the passenger's side door and pulled the handle. No luck, it was locked. Russ came up behind me, and when he saw I was unsuccessful in my attempt to open the door, he ran around to the driver's side and tried his luck. Again, nothing. I met up with him and looked inside. The keys were dangling from the ignition. Wilde must have used the keypad under the handle to lock it up.

"Stand back, I'm going to bust the window," I instructed him.

Russ stood behind me, with all my might, I punched the window with my gloved hand. It didn't break. I tried three more times without any luck.

"Here, allow me," Russ said politely.

He stepped in and pounded the glass with his nail gun. The window exploded. Immediately following the sound of glass shattering, we heard a muffled screech coming from the back of the van. We both hesitated and stared at each other.

"The chimp..." Russ said.

I nodded. It was in the back and must have been startled by the sound of the window breaking.

I jumped in the driver's seat, and Russ ran around to the passenger's side. I pushed the button to unlock his door and reached for the keys to start the engine. As I did, so something caught my eye. Up ahead, the shadowy figure of a man came walking around the corner. In between the house and the barn, the flames provided plenty of light to make out the doctor's face. He looked crazed, smiling widely as he lifted his gun and aimed.

"GET DOWN RUSS!!!" I shouted. Bullets pelted the front of

the van relentlessly. Russ and I lay facing the center of the cab, our heads almost touching. He reached behind me and turned the key, starting the van.

"Get us the fuck out of here!" he said to me.

I positioned my body, so I was sort of slouching upwards while keeping my head below the dashboard.

"I can't reach the pedals like this," I told him, trying my best to maneuver into some kind of drivable position without getting my head blown off. The bullets continued to ping pang the hood and windshield.

"I'll do the pedals, you steer," he said as he reached below me, pushing in the brake.

Once Russ applied the brake, I shifted out of park, and Russ hit the gas. I held tightly to the wheel as we backed down the bumpy dirt driveway. The chimp in the back made grunting and chirping noises, not sounding very happy.

"Can you see where we're going?" Russ shouted up to me.

The bullets were still hitting us but began to get lighter and lighter.

"Not really, I can see a little from the door mirror but not too much," I replied.

I sat up a little, so I could see more of the mirror. It was enough for me to keep us on the driveway and prevent us from going off and into the woods on either side. We passed the willow tree and came to a bend, which would have put us out of our assailant's sight when suddenly there was a loud blast.

The front right tire had been shot out. Immediately the van pulled to that side, and I lost control. Before I regained control, we rolled down an embankment and smashed into a tree. The two of us banged our heads and got tossed about. From the back came a loud thud and then a cry from the chimp. He must have hit the back doors pretty hard.

"Are you okay?" Russ asked.

"Yeah, you?"

"I'm good. Put it in drive and let's see if we can get ourselves unstuck" he told me.

I did as he said but we only spun the back tires. I tried turning the wheel back and forth, but we didn't go anywhere, we were good and stuck. I noticed the bullets had stopped. Were we out of his sights now? I slowly sat up to have a look.

The van sat adjacent to the house, facing the opposite side of the driveway. Russ sat up and held his face. His nose was bleeding.

"You're bleeding. Move your hand and let me see."

He listened, and I checked out his injury. "It's not broken, you'll live."

Just as he was about to say something, I saw movement from behind his head. I looked out his door window and could see Dr. Wilde walking down the driveway coming toward us. He was about fifty yards away when he raised his weapon and aimed it at us again.

"GET DOWN!" I said, grabbing the back of Russ' head and pulling it down next to mine. Once again, we were getting hammered with bullets. It was like heavy rain on a tin roof.

"We need to get out of here. Keep down and follow me." I said as I opened the door behind me.

I slithered out of my door and stood back up against the van. Russ crawled over and slid out too, head-first. Once we were both out, we ran through the trees down the length of the driveway. Behind us, we heard the van still getting lit up by the gunfire.

It was difficult maneuvering through the woods in the dark. We didn't have time to stop and dig our flashlights out of our backpacks. My backpack! Shit, I forgot it on the granite bench under the willow tree! But there was nothing I could do about it at that moment. We finally made it out to the road and were making our way back to my truck. "I left my backpack under the willow tree," I confessed to Russ embarrassed.

"You did not! Oh, shit, that sucks. I'm sorry," he said in a nasal voice, he had his nose pinched with his index finger and thumb.

"It gets worse, my phone is in it."

The more I talked about it, the more ashamed of myself I became.

"Damn. Maybe he won't find it," Russ offered, trying to comfort me.

"Well, if he doesn't, the police or fire investigators will," I said.

"What do you want to do?" he asked.

"There's nothing I can do but wait. Wait to see who comes looking for me first, the doctor or the police."

We were finally in my car when that realization sank in. Whoever finds my backpack could tie me to the fire and the murders of Brutus Boone and Mack Chestercove. If it was the police, they would arrest me and put me in prison. If it was Dr. Wilde, he would want revenge for his dead buddies and for the burnt house. At least the police wouldn't find any fingerprints to connect me to the evidence. Could I come up with a believable lie about someone stealing my cell phone? It would be a stretch but just maybe... It was a mistake that would no doubt come back to haunt me.

We got in my truck and drove on the dark side road. When we reached the end and were about to turn onto the highway, two fire engines roared past us, lights flashing and sirens screaming. I wondered if Dr. Wilde escaped before the authorities got there. He would certainly hear the sirens momentarily. Would he try to set free the chimp and risk getting caught or would he leave it in order to make his getaway?

The answer would show just how insane and/or ballsy he truly was. I hoped the police would capture him, that way our efforts weren't for nothing. We would have successfully taken the evil doctor and two of his henchmen off the streets where they could no longer harm the innocent. But something told me it was not going to be that easy.

Chapter 27

It was now Monday, the third day after our raid at Dr. Wilde's farmhouse. The news covered the fire, stating simply that the house had burnt to the ground due to what was believed as faulty wiring in an old home. Bullshit. The police must have figured out who was living there and were keeping it a secret while they continued to investigate. They hadn't issued a warrant or arrested me, so I assumed Dr. Wilde found my backpack and made off with it.

The news reports didn't mention a thing about the two dead bodies, the discovery of any stolen money found, or any traces of the chimp. As far as the general public was concerned, it was just an accidental fire that didn't harm a soul. A story that would be forgotten in no time. That was, by everybody except me.

I still hadn't slept. My paranoia was at its max. I kept my tablet with me at all times so I could monitor my security cameras. I even installed four new ones, two on each side of the road approaching my driveway. I had a gate with a keypad at the entrance to my driveway, but I also stored most of my passwords on my phone, which I foolishly didn't keep locked.

I used to have it locked with my fingerprint but removed the security feature after I burnt mine off. What was the point of having a fingerprint password when I didn't have any fingerprints? Anyone who had my phone could access my notes saved on it detailing my passwords to my email, social media page, the keypad on my truck, the keypad to my gated driveway, and the code to disarm the alarm to my home.

I called to change my home security code but didn't know the answer to the security question; "What street did you grow up on?"

Eve had originally set it up, and I didn't know what she put. She lived in several foster homes as a child, so she could have picked any one of them. A technician was scheduled to come the following Tuesday to manually change and update it for me. Until then, I was on high alert.

Russ came over and let himself in. He was the only person who knew the codes to my gate and front door.

"Did you arm the alarm after you came in?" I asked him.

"I did. Don't worry, I'm here now. I'm all the security you need," he said trying to reassure me.

"Thanks, I appreciate you coming here. Tomorrow they're coming to change the codes, so I'll be all set after that." I informed him.

I knew he didn't mind staying here, in fact, he loved hanging out and using the pool.

"I'm making steaks for dinner. If you want, you can go for a swim while I go out back and grill them up."

"How about I grill them, and you relax for a bit in the pool?" he offered.

I was pretty stressed out and could use a dip to help unwind. "Alright, if you're sure you don't mind."

"I insist," he said with a warm smile.

He washed his hands in the kitchen sink and dove into the fridge. He was at home in the kitchen, so I left him to do what he loved, cooking. I went up to my bedroom and changed into my bathing suit. When I came downstairs, I grabbed two towels out of the laundry room and went into the pool room. It was nice and warm in there. I kept the climate control on 72 degrees, but it felt a little bit warmer. Outside was much cooler causing the windows to cloud up with condensation, the ones that faced the back of the house and overlooked the patio and backyard. Russ was out there starting up the grill, but it was hard to see him clearly through the foggy windows. I planned on having a door installed so I could go out back rather than go down the hall and exit through the sliding door in the kitchen, but I procrastinated. One of these days...

I put my towel on a chair and stretched my arms above my head. My lack of sleep was catching up with me. I heard a tapping on the glass behind me. When I turned around, I saw Russ pointing at me, flexing his arms and making fun of me. I laughed and flipped him off before diving into the deep end of the pool.

I swam a few laps lengthwise to get my heart rate up. Once I got my blood pumping, I rolled over and floated on my back, staring up at the evening sky. It was about 7:00pm and starting to get dark. I closed my eyes and let my mind wander. I almost dozed off as I reminisced of better times spent with my dear sweet Eve.

There was a meteor shower one summer and Eve, and I camped out to watch it. My backyard was over a row of waist-high hedges that separated the patio from the lawn. The back was about five acres, and it came to an end at a little beach on the edge of the lake. When we moved in, I had fifty yards of sandbox sand spread along the edge to create our own little private beach. There it was, perfectly hidden from any neighbors.

That was one of the biggest selling points for me, total privacy. Nobody could see my backyard beach or dock from the surrounding shore. We were set back in a cove that only someone in a boat could see. I kept my fishing boat tied up to the dock, and two jet skis sat covered up in the sand just off to the side. We loved to play on the water.

I dreamed of the night we set up a tent in the grass just beyond the edge of the sand and lit a bonfire in a makeshift pit I dug out by the water's edge. We made S'mores and snuggled as mother nature put on a dazzling interstellar display. I could almost hear her playful laughter over a chorus of cricket chirps and bullfrog croaks. She loved the outdoors as much as I did. It was a beautiful, romantic evening when we ended by making love beside the fire. We didn't make it into the tent but rather fell asleep snuggling in the sand as the glow from the fire kept us warm.

The next morning, I awakened to a scream as Eve ran her hands up and down my bare torso. She had warned me to put mosquito spray on, but I told her I would wait until after we were done being romantic so that she could kiss me all over. Typical of me to let my libido interfere with logic. I certainly paid the price as I was covered from head to toe in bites the next morning. It wasn't enough to ruin the precious time we had spent together, and I would gladly let a whole swarm of them bleed me dry if I could make one more enchanting memory with my beautiful Eve.

When I opened my eyes, I half expected to be itchy. I waded to the edge and looked at the clock on the wall behind the bar. It was 8:10pm and dark out. Where the hell was Russ? I walked to the shallow end and got out of the pool. After I wiped my head down and tied the towel around my waist, I walked over to the windows. The grill was still smoking, but Russ wasn't out there. Had he eaten already by himself? Why didn't he wake me up?

I left the pool room and walked down the hall heading for the kitchen. When I got there, I looked out the sliding door to the patio. No sign of him. He was probably messing with me and going to jump out and try to scare me, I thought. "We'll see about that."

I retrieved my tablet from the kitchen table, opened the security app, and played back recorded footage.

I watched clips from 7:00pm on. There he was in the kitchen washing his hands and talking to me. After I left, he cut the vegetables and put them on skewers. He seasoned the steaks next and then carried the two plates of food outside. I continued speeding through the footage of the empty kitchen waiting to see him come back inside but he didn't.

Suddenly, a figure appeared in the lower corner of the screen. It was a man that was NOT Russ! Right there before my very eyes entered Dr. Silas Wilde holding hands with his chimp! They were in MY house! I watched, trembling in fear and anger as they walked slowly over to the slider and opened it. I saw Wilde carrying a pistol in his left hand. As they exited the house, he lifted his arm and pointed the gun in the direction of the grill. He kept it aimed, let go of the chimp and with his other hand, he closed the slider behind him. After that, they went out of view.

I quickly went through the other camera angles to see if either one of them appeared. The one camera that covered that part of the backyard didn't give a good view of the sliding door, it was positioned directly above the door and showed the area with the patio furniture such as the table, umbrella, and chairs. Russ and Wilde were nowhere in sight. I slowly walked back to the slider and opened it as quietly as possible.

As I walked outside, I kept glancing from the tablet to the outside area around me. I walked around the patio looking for clues but found none. Then as I walked in front of the grill, something moved in one of the cameras. I clutched the tablet and enlarged the window where I saw movement. It was the camera above the sliding door. As I entered the picture, it had gone partially black. I zoomed out and tried to focus it before realizing that I was standing right in front of it.

Turning around seemed to take a lifetime in my state of anxiety. I looked up, there was an atrocious looking, mangled, mangy chimpanzee hanging on to the roof, snarling with his big pointy yellow teeth! Before I had time to think, it lunged at me, knocking me back and to the ground. I hit the cold patio hard and got the wind knocked out of me. The disgusting animal grabbed at me, scratching and clawing at my bare chest and neck. He also jumped up and down on me, pounding his fists with fury.

I did my best to fend off his blows, but he moved quickly. He felt as big and strong as Russ! Finally, he landed a little farther back, with his feet straddling my knees, and I made my move. I pulled my leg up, bending my knee, and kicked him in his stomach with all my might. This sent the ape tumbling backward, and he rolled to a stop just in front of the sliding door. With a new surge of adrenaline, I pulled myself up, holding onto the side of the grill.

As I got my balance, I pulled my towel off from around my waist. The chimp was back on his feet charging at me. I threw the wet towel at his face, and it wrapped around the sides of his head, temporally blinding him. He screamed underneath it as he reached to pull it off.

Out of the corner of my eye, a flame from the grill caught my attention. The skewers were still on, and the veggies were burnt to a crisp. I grabbed two of the skewers just as the chimp removed the towel from his face. Again, he screeched as he came flying through the air. I held out both of my hands, and the skewers entered each of his eye sockets and disappeared halfway into his head. He fell before me and twitched for a moment, frantically pulling at the handles but not budging them. A low, eerie moan escaped him as he finally stopped living.

Standing quietly, I took in the scene and went over what had just occurred. I heard a faint but familiar sound. It was the sound of an outboard motor starting up. I turned and looked down toward the lake and spotted Dr. Wilde leaning over and untying my boat from the dock. He went back to the wheel and leaned heavy on the throttle. I took a deep breath and sprinted across the yard toward the dock. I ran to the jet skis and quickly yanked the cover off one. I grabbed the rope tied to the front of it and dragged it down the sand and eventually to the water's edge. Once it was close enough, I got behind it and pushed it completely in the lake and then jumped up on the seat. It started right up, and I took off after the fleeing boat.

Wilde made it just about out of the cove when he stopped steering and turned toward the stern of the boat. I watched as he reached into his jacket, removed a pistol, and fired. Lowering my body with my head down enough to see and still steer, I swerved left and right trying to avoid his fire. I heard the bullets whiz by me as he unloaded his revolver. After the sixth shot, he removed the shells, reached into his pocket and pulled out more bullets, and began to reload.

I accelerated almost to top speed and aimed directly for the boat. Just as I came within about ten feet, I jumped off the watercraft and let it smash into the boat. It hit with such force that Wilde toppled backward over the side with a loud *SPLASH!* I swam to the side and pulled myself up and over the edge of the boat. There, lying on the floor hands and feet bound with zip ties was Russ.

"Nero! You, crazy son of a bitch! Help me, please cut these binds off me."

I looked in a side compartment where I kept random tools and extra fishing gear, but there wasn't anything sharp. Suddenly there was a splashing noise as Dr. Wilde threw both of his arms up over the side, right above where Russ was laying. He pulled himself up, and his head appeared over the starboard edge.

"NERO!" Russ called me, wiggling his leg to get my attention.

Then I saw what he was getting at. I dove for Russ' feet and pulled the bowie knife out from his boot. As soon as I had it firmly in my hand, I swung my arm upwards, gouging Dr. Wilde in the throat. He released a loud, gurgling breath before falling back into the water. I leaned over the side to make sure he was down for good. He remained face down with his arms clenching his throat until they released their grip and went sideways.

There he was: a massive, maniacal, monster floating like a piece of driftwood in me and Eve's precious lake. He was finally dead! All the horror and chaos he and his pathetic primate caused had finally come to an end. The thought of him intoxicating the wonderful water Eve and I swam and fished in was making me furious. Hopefully his last sights were images of the brown, murky, fish, turtle, frog, and beaver waste that blanketed the bottom of Echo Lake because that's where he was heading. If I had a whaling harpoon, I would have plunged it right through the despicable Wild's back.

"Are you alright?" I asked my friend, noticing he had a lump under his right eye.

"I'll be just fine when you cut these damn ties off me!" he said, his voice shaking a little.

I used his knife to cut him free, and he sat up straight, rubbing his wrists. "Thanks again. This time I definitely owe you."

"I know just how you can repay me. Help me get rid of a dead doctor and his disgusting chimp," I said, smiling.

"Fish food?" he asked.

I nodded.

"You did great Nero! You really saved my ass this time."

"It's nothing you wouldn't have done for me. You're the most important person to me, the only family I've got. We have to stick together. As long as we do we'll be just fine. I love you, Russ," I said to him as I patted him on the shoulder.

"Yeah, I agree. But if you try to kiss me, I'm gonna ring your bell," he said in typical Russ fashion.

Thank you for reading, I hope you've enjoyed. To my Eve: I love you, you know who you are ;)

A sequel is being written, and Nero will face a new nemesis:

Pariah

<u>Birth Name:</u> Randall Rodriguez

<u>Backstory:</u> The Satanic Temple in Salem, Ma was performing a ritual, offering a lamb as a sacrifice. When Satan arrived, he was angry and disappointed that a human life was not being offered.

A few blocks down the street, a speeding car driven by Randall Rodriguez, a member of the Satanic church who was running late to the dark sacrifice, crashed into a telephone pole and caught Satan's attention. As Rodriguez lay dying in the wreck, The Dark Lord made a deal to save his life in return for doing his bidding. The newly reborn "Pariah" travels the world seeking out desperate individuals willing to trade their souls for one wish.

To stay updated, please visit www.evinall.com

Table of Contents

Evinall

(ee-vuh n awl)

"There will forever be some Eve in all of us."

By Adam Witkowski